**ALSO BY KEITH LEE MORRIS**

*The Greyhound God*

*The Best Seats in the House and Other Stories*

*The Dart League King*

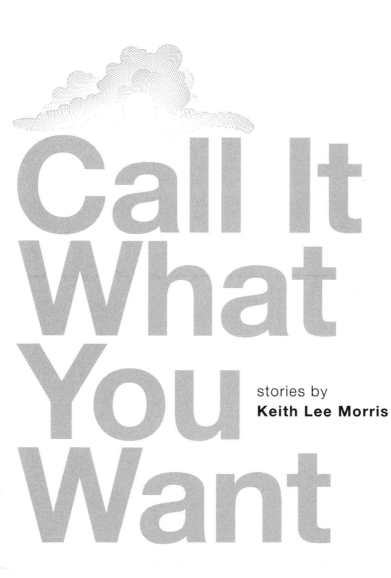

# Call It What You Want

stories by
**Keith Lee Morris**

Tin House Books

Copyright © 2010 Keith Lee Morris

Published by Tin House Books, Portland, Oregon, and New York, New York.
Distributed to the trade by Publishers Group West, 1700 Fourth St., Berkeley, CA 94710,
www.pgw.com.

Library of Congress Cataloging-in-Publication Data

Morris, Keith Lee, 1963-
 Call it what you want / Keith Lee Morris. -- 1st U.S. ed.
    p. cm.
 ISBN 978-0-9825030-8-9
 I. Title.
 PS3613.O7735C36 2010
 813'.6--dc22                                    2009041312

First U.S. edition 2010
Interior design by Laura Shaw Design, Inc.
www.tinhouse.com

These stories were published previously, sometimes in slightly different form, in the
following publications: "Testimony" in *A Public Space*; "Camel Light," in *Ninth Letter*;
"What I Want from You" in *Tin House*; "Guests" (published as "The Presidential Suite"),
"Tired Heart," "The Cyclist" (published as "Notes for an Aborted Story Called 'The
Cyclist' That Turned Out to Be Too Much Like 'The Swimmer'") in *New England Review*;
"*Ayudame*" in *Third Coast*; "Visitation" in *Cincinnati Review*; "Desert Island Romance"
in *Manoa*; "My Roommate Kevin Is Awesome" in www.fivechapters.com; "The Culvert"
in *Southern Review*.

"Tired Heart" was reprinted in *New Stories from the South 2006*;
"Testimony" was an honorable mention selection for the Pushcart Prize 2008;
"The Culvert" won the *Southern Review*'s Eudora Welty Prize in Fiction for 2005.

Printed in the United States of America

Then the dark began to go in smooth bright shapes, like it always does, even when Caddy says that I have been asleep.

—William Faulkner, *The Sound and the Fury*

*For Jay, Bryan, Chase, Doug, Pat, and Bob—*
*great friends who've been there with me the whole way*

# Contents

# Testimony

I'd been sitting there in the courtroom all day, looking at the backs of people's heads, mostly Andy Munson's. In that situation you couldn't help but sit and wonder what went on inside there, in Andy's head. I'd known him as long as I could remember. There were a lot of people in town I'd known as long as I could remember, and some of them I knew better than Andy, but I suppose I knew Andy better than most. But there was always something about Andy you couldn't know. Maybe it was hard to figure out Andy because Andy didn't spend a lot of time trying to figure out himself.

The courtroom was cold, it was a fucking icebox, I would have rather been outside in the snow almost, even in just my long-sleeved shirt. I didn't dress up to testify, only a collared shirt and a newer pair of jeans, because I didn't have any nice clothes. It was snowing like crazy in the morning when I got to the courthouse, and I was wondering whether I'd be able to get home without my snow tires, which I'd taken off the week before. It was practically April. So I knew the snow was piling up, but the thing kept dragging on, and I couldn't leave to go check the

weather because they wouldn't tell me when I'd be called to testify. Every once in a while the judge would send the jury back
to the jury room so he could settle some point of law with the
attorneys, but he never said the court was recessed or told us we
could go outside for a smoke, and I could have used one.

Honestly, I was getting a little nervous. They'd told me what
to say, the prosecutors, or not *what* to say specifically, but how
to say it, like, OK, that's good, that's fine, Robert, just tell it like
that, just tell the truth like you'd naturally tell it, or if they didn't
like how I was saying something they'd wrinkle up their faces,
the two of them, the county prosecutor and the deputy prosecutor, both women, the second one good-looking enough for
me to have kind of fallen in love with and the first one not, and
they'd say, Is it possible that you're leaving something out? Is
it possible that you might remember that in more detail? And
then they'd say stuff like be confident because you're telling the
truth and speak loud and clear and so on. But I was beginning
to think that was easier said than done.

They had Andy's girlfriend, Jessica, up on the stand, and
between the two sides, the prosecution and the defense, they'd
worked her over pretty good. The county prosecutor was a little woman, barely five foot I'd guess, with a stringy body that
didn't even feature any breasts beneath her jacket and shirt as
far as I could tell, and she walked just like an edgy little man,
someone who was on edge all the time, and she talked hard
and fast and she was tough as a fucking badger, even though
she talked nice enough to me. Why shouldn't she talk nice to
me? I'd turned state's witness in order to avoid an accessory to
murder charge. I was on the side of the State of Idaho.

So was Jessica, though, and that hadn't helped her much.
She'd been crying ever since the prosecutor made her describe

how Andy had hit her on occasion, how he'd cracked her front teeth with a beer glass, etc., and I knew Jessica was crying because of the things she wouldn't get the chance to tell, how Andy could be really sweet when he wanted to be, how he'd bought her a necklace and they were going to get married when he came into the rest of his inheritance, the shit she would always say whenever you told her she should just get the fuck away from him, or at least when she wasn't saying he was the biggest asshole on earth. And now the defense attorney was taking his shot at her and she was crying because, unlike the prosecutor, he was insisting Andy *wasn't* the biggest asshole on earth, and suggesting that none of that stuff had ever happened or it had mostly been her fault, which might have been kind of true, in a way. She was a piece of work, no doubt, always. I wouldn't have gone out with her, and my standards are pretty low. And by that time she was basically a meth whore, skinny as shit and all bedraggled, so whatever attraction there might have been at one time was long gone.

I figured I could handle myself better than Jessica, but none of it looked like too much fun. I kept telling myself I wasn't in any danger, there was only one thing I intended to lie about, really, and it was something mostly inside me, and because Nolan wasn't testifying the only one who could tell what I wasn't going to was Andy, and it wasn't in his best interest.

I was looking at the back of Andy's head again and drifting in my thoughts, nervous, like I say, when the prosecutor declined the chance to follow up and the judge called next witness and the prosecutor said the State called Robert Jerome Scott to the stand. That was me.

I went up and they made me state my name and they made me put my hand on the Bible and swear the oath and then they told me to sit down and I did, and a funny thing happened—I felt completely relaxed. Sitting up there on the witness stand, higher up than anyone but the judge, it felt like my courtroom. Dark green carpet, varnished wood, stark overhead lighting— mine. I hadn't felt that feeling in a while. I turned and looked right at the jury. They didn't bother me. The room didn't even feel all that cold anymore.

Could I tell the court my relationship to the defendant?

Yes, I could. I was his friend.

How long had I been friends with the defendant?

I didn't know. Fifteen years, give or take a few. I thought I remembered playing with him on the playground as far back as first grade.

State my age for the court?

Twenty-two.

Did I remember the events that occurred on the afternoon of August 8 of last year?

Yes, I did. If that was the day Jeremy died.

Where was I on August 8?

I was at Andy Munson's house.

For the record, the house owned by Andrew Munson at 314 Lake Street?

Yes.

Were there other people there?

Yes.

Their names.

Jeremy and Nolan.

Jeremy Schiff and Nolan Saylor?

Yes.

And on that afternoon Jeremy Schiff was killed?

Objection. Legal explanation regarding objection, so on and so forth.

Sustained. Rephrase the question.

And on that afternoon Jeremy Schiff died?

Yes.

For the first time since I took the stand I looked at Andy. It wasn't that I'd been avoiding looking at him. It just hadn't occurred to me up to that point. It felt good that he had so little hold on me. It was surprising, though, how he looked, and it threw me off for a minute. I'd never seen him look like that. He looked half dead. He looked shit at and hit. He looked like he might have been crying when Jessica was on the stand, which I was kind of shocked to see, because I hadn't imagined, of all things, Andy Munson crying about anything, ever, and he was kind of slumped down in his chair and even his expensive charcoal-gray suit couldn't help defeat the overall impression of someone who'd lost whatever there was to lose in this world. I was embarrassed for him. It wasn't how you wanted to look. I wished Nolan could see him like that. He would have turned state's evidence like I did. Fuck Andy. Nolan was afraid to say that, was still afraid of Andy, would rather face serious jail time than screw him over. Me? I was ready to let Andy end up where the legal system said he should end up. If they set him loose, I was probably in for some shit, but what was he going to do, kill me? He'd already gone that route once, and look where it got him.

What was I doing at Andrew Munson's house that afternoon?

Hanging out. Getting high.

What did I mean by getting high?

Doing drugs. I shrugged at her.

What kind of drugs?

Meth. Pot.

Methamphetamine? Marijuana?

Yes.

What else was I doing?

Hanging out, like I said.

That was the first time I noticed the look in her eye, this look that meant maybe she'd gone too far with the confidence deal, that I'd turned a corner from confident to cocky, and she could sense it, and she wasn't too happy.

What was Jeremy Schiff doing during that time?

Same thing.

Drugs?

Yes.

Methamphetamine and marijuana?

Meth. He didn't smoke any pot that day that I knew of, at least not when I was with him.

What time was I with him?

From, like, maybe three o'clock or so until, like, maybe seven.

According to the coroner's report, Jeremy Schiff died at approximately 6:00 p.m.

That sounded about right.

What time did we arrive at the residence at 314 Lake Street?

I'd say a little after four.

Where were we before then?

At the arcade.

She walked back to her table, and the deputy prosecutor flipped through some pages of notes and handed them to her.

At Buzzy's Amusements at 203 First Street?

Yes.

She put down the notes and walked like an excited little man back over to me.

What were we doing there?

Playing video games. I worked there. Andy and Jeremy and Nolan hung out there all the time when I was working.

She stopped for a second and looked at me like to say silently don't say too much, don't answer more than I'm asking. I wasn't worried about her, though, the badger, the prosecutor. By that point I'd already decided I could give a shit what she thought. I looked at the deputy prosecutor. Her name was Chris. She wore the same kind of shirt-and-jacket outfit but she filled it out a lot better. I'd had my eye on her since about September, pretty soon after they'd first arrested me. She had straight blond hair and water-blue eyes and a little pouty mouth with just a tiny bit of lipstick and she always looked exactly the same and spoke in exactly the same voice, kind of soft and moderately high. She also wore glasses with thin black frames, for no other reason than to make her look serious, I'd decided. During all the questioning before the trial she'd been extremely nice to me and I knew she'd been to law school and whatever but she wasn't much older than I was, really, I could tell that much, and the prosecutor had let her make the opening statement that morning at the start of the trial, and you could tell she was scared to death, that she didn't have much more experience in a courtroom than I did. And I didn't have any. I felt like I was looking at her to calm her down, tell her it was all right, we were on the same team, I liked her, she was OK by me.

So we had been at the video arcade until around four o'clock, at which time we left for the residence on Lake Street?

Yes.

And we were having fun at the arcade? No arguments, nothing of that sort?

Yes. I meant no, no arguments.

Nothing that would have made Andrew Munson angry at Jeremy Schiff?

No, not that I had seen.

Could I tell her about the relationship between Andrew and Jeremy?

Objection. Blah blah blah. Overruled.

They were friends.

Didn't Andrew Munson bully Jeremy? Was that what I called being friends?

Objection. Sustained.

Had I ever seen Andrew Munson injure Jeremy?

Yes. I meant, I guessed we'd all picked on him a little.

Had I seen Andrew Munson run over Jeremy with a car when Jeremy was walking down the street?

Objection. Immaterial, etc. Overruled.

Not exactly.

I hadn't seen Andrew run over Jeremy?

He didn't *run over* him.

What would I call it, then?

More like *struck*.

Andrew Munson *struck* Jeremy Schiff with a vehicle.

Yes.

What else? What other kinds of things did Andrew do to Jeremy?

Usual stuff. Twist his arm behind his back, rub his face into the carpet, things like that.

All just good clean fun?

More or less.

She crossed her arms and shook her head toward the jury.

You'd have had to know Jeremy. It wasn't like he asked for it, but you just couldn't help it in a way, although I was always nicer to him than his other friends, maybe because I knew him better. It wasn't that he was fat or weak or stupid or ugly. He wasn't. He was just different in a way that wasn't cool, like his hobbies and stuff. He had this huge collection of model airplanes, for instance. And he was nervous all the time. The guy worried about everything. If he had a perfectly good day with maybe one small thing that went wrong, he'd go to sleep at night thinking the whole day had been a disaster and his whole life was ruined. I know this because I lived with him. I lived with him when we were in junior high and I was living with him again, in this room above his parents' garage, at the time when he died. I first got to know him because his mother and father were my foster parents after my own mom and dad got divorced when I was in seventh grade. Neither one of them wanted me and neither one of them was "fit," so I got sent to live with Jeremy. And even back then Jeremy would go to bed at night talking about all the shit that was wrong with him, at least when he wasn't talking about planes. I've never known a guy who could see the glass half empty so consistently. He always thought he had a life-threatening disease. He always thought nobody liked him. At the rare times when he had a girlfriend, he would immediately be convinced that she didn't really like him, and he would drive her crazy with his questions and his insecurities, and then pretty soon she wouldn't like him anymore, and that would just make him more convinced he'd been right all along. He was incredibly paranoid about the cops. Every time we went to Andy's house he'd start worrying that the cops were going to raid the place. If you went out the side door to smoke a joint, just because it was a nice day outside for instance and you wanted to smoke a joint in the sunshine, he'd keep nagging you to go down to the basement. In fact, that might have been how the whole thing started that afternoon—him nagging Andy about making us come inside.

Could I tell the court about my own relationship to Jeremy Schiff?

We were friends.

In the same way that Andrew Munson and Jeremy were friends?

More or less.

She stood there for a second with her arms crossed, staring at me, then she walked back over to her table and sorted through some papers. I wasn't playing by the script was the problem. I knew what she was doing—trying to contrast my friendship with Jeremy to Andy's, so she could make Andy look bad—but for some reason I didn't want to make it easy on her. I wanted her to have to root it out, prove it to me, sort of. I guess the truth was I'd been waiting for the trial all this time to understand myself what it was that really happened that day and why and who was to blame and how much. I thought the State of Idaho should be able to decide that, and I didn't want to make it easier on anyone, including myself, by helping people jump to conclusions. I looked over at the jury to see how they were taking it all in—thirteen people staring at me, no big deal, none of them standing out for any particular reason, the anonymous faces of justice. I hoped they were keeping every-thing straight, and I was glad to see at least a couple of them were taking notes.

Wasn't it true that Jeremy and I were more like brothers?

She'd gotten that from something I'd told her once dur-ing questioning, but at that point it had basically been a way to cover my ass. I was still thinking defensively then. Andy's attorney got ready to object, sitting up straight in his seat, but then he decided to let it go. This was an important question, one I wasn't sure I knew the answer to. It made me look for a second at Jeremy's mother and father on their side of the court-room, and I wished right away I hadn't done that. The look on their faces didn't make me feel good. It was like I could see on their faces every misgiving they'd had about me for the past ten years.

I didn't know. If there was such a thing, we were foster broth-ers for a year in junior high, and we stayed friends after that. We were roommates in the apartment above his parents' garage before he died. I didn't have any brothers or sisters and Jeremy only had two sisters who were quite a bit older so I guessed maybe we were like brothers to each other in that way.

Hadn't Jeremy told me on at least one occasion that I was like his brother, like an older brother?

Yes, he had.

Why did I suppose he'd said that?

I wasn't sure. It didn't make any sense, for one thing, since we were the same age. But I supposed he'd kind of looked up to me.

Wasn't it true that Jeremy essentially followed my lead?

Maybe. I didn't know. He didn't have to.

But wasn't it true that when he didn't follow my lead, when he didn't act the way I thought he was supposed to, the cool way, the way Andrew Munson acted, he was made to suffer consequences?

Objection, objection. Leading the witness, etc. Sustained.

Why had I been removed from the Schiffs' home in eighth grade after living with them for a year?

Mr. and Mrs. Schiff thought I was a bad influence.

Why was that?

Me and Jeremy had started smoking pot.

And whose idea had that been?

Mine.

Could I tell the court about the occasion when Andrew Munson struck Jeremy Schiff with the car?

Objection. Immaterial. Overruled.

She was definitely pretty shrewd. It wasn't going the way I'd expected. I could see what she was getting at—Jeremy was easily manipulated, and when he didn't play along we took it out on him, and it was mostly my fault. It was an interesting way to look at things, and I wasn't totally unprepared to accept it.

Me and Andy and Nolan and Jeremy were at the movies. We'd snuck two bottles of vodka in and we were mixing it with 7Up. After the movie, Jeremy thought we shouldn't drive because the cops would pick us up for underage drinking and DUI, and—

How old were we at that time?

Seventeen, eighteen.

Go on.

So Jeremy wouldn't get in Andy's car. Andy told me to tell him to get in, but he wouldn't. He started walking across the parking lot like he was going to leave by himself. Andy let the windows down and started driving along beside him. He kept saying, Does Jeremy need a ride? And Jeremy would tell him to . . . he would cuss at him. And Andy kept saying, Does Jeremy need a ride, and Jeremy kept saying the same thing back, and pretty soon it got funny and Nolan and I started laughing. Then Andy stopped the car and let Jeremy get a little ways in front of him, then he said, Jeremy needs a ride, and he hit the gas and ran into Jeremy from behind, and Jeremy flipped up on the hood.

Had Jeremy been injured?

Yes.

What were his injuries?

Sprained ankle and some bad bruises.

How bad were the bruises?

Well, they were up and down his backside, so I hadn't exactly looked at them except the ones on his lower back. But he said they went all the way down to his thighs.

And what happened after that? After Andrew Munson ran into Jeremy?

Jeremy got in the car.

I checked out Andy again right at that point but he was looking down at his hands in his lap. The prosecutor went back over to the table and she and the deputy prosecutor put some papers in order. I was watching the deputy. I could see her calves under the table. She wasn't looking at me. The prosecutor marched back over to me and put her head down like she was concentrating really hard, then started talking in a little softer voice than she'd been using.

Could I tell the court what happened at Andrew Munson's after we arrived there from the arcade?

We turned on the TV and started doing crystal.

Describe how we did it.

We snorted it. We never smoked it or injected it, except I thought Andy maybe smoked it when none of us were around.

Objection. Approach the bench, your honor.

The attorneys approached the bench and they talked for a minute and the defense attorney waved his arms around a couple of times. I didn't really look at anybody or focus on anything. I was remembering us doing crystal that day at Andy's house, and it was starting to make me feel nervous again and a little sick. I could see it all pretty clear.

Sustained. Witness's last statement, beginning from "except I thought," etc., to be stricken from the record. Jury instructed to ignore. Witness please restrict his statements blah blah.

How long before that day had I been using methamphetamine?

Since sometime in the spring. Three months or so.

And when had Jeremy Schiff started?

Same time I had.

How often did we use it?

Pretty much every day.

How did we get it?

Andy got it from someone he knew.

Who paid for it?

Andy.

That was one of the things about Andy. He could be a real asshole, but he could also be very generous. He had a buttload of money he inherited from his grandfather, who was a famous doctor around town because he'd invented some device that was used in the treatment of paralysis victims. Andy had gotten part of his inheritance when he turned eighteen, and then he was supposed to get the rest of it when he graduated from college, which he never did. At the time when Jeremy died, he was going through legal proceedings that were supposed to get him the rest of his money through some loophole. He talked about it all the time, and it seemed like it would have been easier just to finish fucking college. But he never worried about money or made anyone else pay for anything or ever made you feel like you had to pay him back. He could be a good guy that way, and he could also be very funny at times, like just the way he would say things, and he was good-looking and women liked him, all of which made him worthwhile to hang around with, despite the fact that he very obviously used all those things to control you.

Please continue describing the events of August 8.

We were watching TV, some tennis match with Maria Sharapova. We'd just finished with the crystal. Nolan wanted to get high, so Andy went and got a baggie of dope and handed it to him. Andy and Jeremy didn't want to smoke, so Nolan and I went outside by ourselves.

Nolan and I went outside to smoke a joint?

Nolan had a pipe.

And the two of us left Andy and Jeremy alone together?

Well, yes.

Was that unusual?

No.

But then right away I started thinking how it was unusual. It was always all four of us or at least three of us going outside to smoke a bowl, or we just stayed in the house. It just happened that day that it was me and Nolan, and that we wanted to go outside because it was a nice day. But I couldn't see why the prosecutor would want to infer anything from that. What? That Andy was bound to kill Jeremy if they were left alone for ten minutes? That it was like leaving the house cat inside with a Doberman? She was trying to cut corners again, so I stuck with the answer I gave.

Then what happened?

Nothing. Nolan and I smoked a couple of bowls.

What sort of state were we in at that point?

I didn't object to a question like that. Here I was in front of all these people—the jury, Mr. and Mrs. Schiff, Andy's parents, who were back there holding hands, the deputy prosecutor—being asked to say what a fuckup I was. One reason I guess I didn't care was I'd been pretty much clean since then. First I was in jail, then with Andy in jail I didn't know where to get meth if I wanted to, because it was always Andy, and then I suppose I was just disinclined. It felt good being straight after a while. Part of the attraction of meth is that no matter how fucked up it makes you, it always gives you something to look forward to, and what you look forward to is that feeling it gives you that there's something going on, something meaningful and exciting, even if you're just sitting in a room with other fucked-up people thinking the same thing you are while everything goes downhill. But after I got released there was always something going on too, that took the place of the meth high, which was the fact that I was involved in a murder trial. And I can't pretend I was aware of it at the time, but I did feel even during the middle of my testimony that kind of deflation that comes when a high gets near the end. What would I be doing tomorrow? And then I also didn't care what I told people because I didn't really have any family and my friends were either dead or in jail. Who gave a shit?

Well, we were high, but that was kind of usual.

We were usually high?

Sure. Back then.

Would I say that I was able to think clearly, make rational decisions?

It seemed that way at the time. I couldn't really be sure.

But I felt at the time that I was in control of my actions?

Yes.

This was an important point for her, one we'd gone over fairly extensively, and I'd given her the answer she wanted with a minimum of fuss, and I could almost see her smiling at me, sort of caressing me with her eyes and patting me on the head. But I was only saying it because it happened to be the truth. I did *feel* like I was in control of my actions. All four of us acted like we were in control of our actions all the time. It was only the results that called the feeling into question.

Even after I smoked marijuana?

Yes.

And only me and Nolan smoked marijuana that day?

Yes.

Andrew Munson hadn't smoked marijuana?

No. Not that I knew of.

So, in my opinion, it would be safe to say then that Andrew Munson had been in control of his actions?

Objection. Sustained. Witness will refrain from answering the question. Would the prosecution please restrict its line of questioning to blah blah blah. It didn't matter. She'd scored her point anyway. Apologies, your honor, etc.

What happened when we were outside that caused us to go back in?

We heard the gun go off.

And when we went back inside, what did we find?

Andy was sitting in a chair and Jeremy was sitting on the couch, same as how we'd left them.

How would I describe Jeremy at that point?

He looked like he was hurt. I thought maybe he'd got shot.

I thought Andrew Munson shot him?

Maybe.

Why would I think that?

Because there was a gunshot.

And did anyone say anything?

I asked Jeremy what happened.

And what did Jeremy say?

Nothing. Andy said Jeremy hit his head.

She pointed her finger at me for a second and her mouth hung open. Then before I could even figure out what she was up to she'd gone back to her table and pulled out some papers.

Andrew Munson said that Jeremy hit his head?

Yes. I thought so.

She held up a paper.

In a statement given to police on the morning of August 9, I reported that Andrew Munson said, "He got busted upside the head."

I didn't know what to say. She looked angry. I just sat there.

Did I deny making that statement?

I couldn't remember the statement and I couldn't remember anyone ever asking me about it. I was in the room that day and then Jeremy was dead and then we'd had the police and the EMTs and everybody and then I had to answer a lot of questions and then they'd told me I was free to go for now but

I didn't have anywhere to go to, because I sure as hell wasn't going to go to my room at Jeremy's house, and so I slept in the grass down by the lake and the next morning the cops picked me up while I was walking downtown and arrested me and took me in for questioning. I couldn't remember what I'd said then and I couldn't remember exactly what Andy said, either, but right then, sitting on the witness stand, what I thought I heard him saying was, "He hit his head."

No. But that's not how I remember it now.

Approach the bench, etc. The judge sent the jury to the jury room. There was a discussion about, as near as I could tell, introducing my statement to the police as evidence. The defense won the argument, whatever it was, and the judge called the jury back in. The prosecutor got back to work, looking a little pissed.

Andrew Munson said that Jeremy hit his head.

She kind of stood there and frowned and tapped her foot on the floor, to show the jury she didn't believe my statement for one second, but unfortunately there was nothing she could do about it. She was very resourceful when it came to that sort of thing.

What was Jeremy doing?

He was just sitting on the couch kind of cradling his head.

What about the gunshot?

Andy said he and Jeremy were goofing around wrestling with the gun and it went off.

Where was the gun?

It was lying on the floor.

Did anyone touch the gun before the police arrived?

No. Not that I saw.

It was still there on the floor in the same position when the police arrived?

Yes.

She went over to her table and picked up the gun from a big box underneath and brought it over to show me. She'd shown it to me before. It had a little numbered tag on it.

Did I recognize this gun as that same 20-gauge shotgun belonging to Andrew Munson, the one that was lying on the floor?

Yes.

How was I sure it was the same gun?

It had the same gouges and scuff marks on the stock I'd seen before.

Where did Andrew Munson keep the gun?

On a gun rack on the wall in his bedroom.

Had I ever seen him take the gun down off the rack before?

Yes.

When?

He used to do it all the time as a joke.

Do what as a joke?

Take it off the rack and bring it out and threaten people. It was kind of a running joke.

It didn't sound very funny.

I guessed you had to be there.

What kinds of things would he threaten people for?

Disagreeing with him. Not listening when he was talking. Disrespecting his property. It was always just a joke. We laughed at him and gave him shit, I meant gave him a hard time.

Had the gun ever gone off before?

No.

Could we see that day where the gun had discharged?

Yes. It went into the ceiling. Andy was looking at it and complaining he'd have to get new ceiling tiles.

Andrew Munson was concerned about his ceiling tiles.

Yes.

She stopped for a second to let that one sink in.

And where did Andrew Munson say that Jeremy Schiff hit his head?

He didn't.

He didn't?

Well, not at first.

When had Andrew Munson mentioned how Jeremy Schiff hit his head?

After Jeremy was dead.

And he said Jeremy hit his head where, then, when he finally got around to mentioning it?

Objection. Prejudicial something something. Overruled.

On the coffee table.

How did he say that it happened?

They were wrestling with the gun, just goofing around, and Jeremy accidentally pulled the trigger and the gun went off and it scared Jeremy and he fell over backward and hit his head.

Jeremy accidentally pulled the trigger?

Yes.

Andrew Munson said that Jeremy accidentally pulled the trigger?

Yes. That's what he said.

And how would I explain the fact that when the gun was recovered the safety was still on?

Objection! Witness had not been submitted to the court as an expert on firearms.

Sustained.

I was surprised that she'd never brought this up to me before, but I wasn't surprised by what she was telling me. I knew Andy had killed Jeremy. I knew it. I knew it as a kind of fact that settled in over the course of time, but had been there from the very start. And the information she'd just given me helped to explain how it happened. If the gun went off when the safety was on, it wasn't because Jeremy pulled the trigger. It was because the gun had been struck against something, and hard.

Nolan and I had gone outside. Jeremy had probably started to complain—why didn't Andy make us come back in the house, what about the neighbors? And Andy went and grabbed the shotgun and came back out with it and told Jeremy to shut the fuck up. But it wasn't funny because Nolan and I weren't there. And so Andy started to get seriously pissed and told Jeremy he was like an eight-year-old girl or whatever. You know what the fuck your problem is, Jeremy? Your problem is you _____. Fill in the blank. And Jeremy said the same thing he always said when Andy pissed him off enough to make him stand up for himself, even if he knew it meant he'd get his arm twisted behind his back, or his face rubbed into the carpet, or he'd get punched hard in the chest. Fuck off. And since Nolan and I weren't there to tell them to cool it, Andy took it to the next level, and he pointed the gun at Jeremy and said, What the fuck did you just say to me, asshole? And Jeremy said, not looking up at Andy from where he sat on the couch, Fuck off. And so Andy walked around the coffee table to Jeremy and pointed the gun in his face. What did you say, asshole? Fuck off. And Jeremy shoved the gun barrel away. And Andy put it back again. And Jeremy stood up and grabbed the gun and tried to take it from Andy and they fought over it for a few seconds before

Andy pulled it away, because he was bigger and stronger, and then, because Andy was angry and because Andy didn't think much about the things he did or why he did them, he raised the shotgun and used the butt to hit Jeremy hard on the side of the head, and the gun discharged due to the impact and blew a hole in Andy's ceiling, and Jeremy suffered an epidural hematoma that led him to sit there on the couch for a while holding his head and then go into the bedroom to lie down, because he said he wasn't feeling so hot, and slowly bleed to death. I knew it like I knew my name.

Tell the court what happened after that.

Things pretty much went back to normal.

Things went back to *normal?*

Pretty much. Jeremy sat there on the couch holding his head and the rest of us talked and watched the tennis match.

We talked and watched the tennis match? What had we talked about?

Maria Sharapova. How Andy and Jeremy had blown a hole in the ceiling. About whether we should hide the drugs because some neighbor might have called the cops.

We didn't talk about Jeremy's injury?

No.

No? When had the subject finally come up?

After he was dead, I guessed.

She was standing there with her arms crossed and she hung her head and looked at the floor and stayed quiet for a few seconds. I looked at the deputy prosecutor. She was looking down at some notes. I glanced over at the jury and they were all looking at me, a woman in a dark blue dress, an old man with glasses, a younger guy wearing a collared shirt.

Tell the court about Jeremy's death.

I shifted in the chair. It was kind of an abrupt question, and for a second I actually drew a blank, couldn't quite remember it. It was a strange feeling, because it was something I thought about all the time.

He said he wanted to lie down for a while because he wasn't feeling good. He sounded kind of tired and groggy. He went in and lay down on Andy's bed. Me and Nolan and Andy just sat there talking. Then Andy went to the bedroom to put the drugs away, but he didn't come back for a minute. Then he came out and said Jeremy was dead.

How would I describe Andrew Munson's reaction at that point?

Objection, blah blah. Overruled.

I didn't know. He wasn't, like, panicked or anything. Sad, I guessed I'd say, right at first. He looked sad.

It was so hard to say with Andy. You just couldn't tell anything by looking at his face, looking in his eyes, never. The book was closed when it came to Andy. But I was drawn to look at him right then, right at that point in my testimony, and what I saw, I think, scared me more than anything else that had happened, scared me more than Jeremy dying even, more than getting arrested, more than going to jail. Andy was leaned forward in his seat, rocking a little back and forth, and he was sobbing. You could hear him. I didn't know how I hadn't heard him before. It was the loudest thing in the courtroom. And it was like, for me, everything had broken open, the world had come unglued. If Andrew Munson could sit there crying that way, then everything I'd ever known was wrong, a form of imposture, and we were all, all of us there in that courtroom, hanging on by a thin, thin thread. We didn't even know the kind of danger we were in.

And what happened when Andrew Munson told us Jeremy was dead?

We called the police.

Right away?

No, I guessed not, not right away.

What had we done first?

Andy told us about Jeremy hitting his head on the coffee table. We hid the drugs in the basement.

We hadn't gone in to look at the body?

We had gone in to look at the body. We had gone in to look at Jeremy. It was the first thing we'd done, actually. I had been hoping she would forget to mention it. Andy and Nolan stood at the foot of the bed, and I stood at the side, next to Jeremy. You couldn't see anything wrong with him except a little blood coming from his nose. I reached down and put my hand over his heart and I didn't feel anything. It was odd. You don't realize how used you are to feeling a heartbeat there until you don't feel one. I shook Jeremy's shoulder and said his name a couple of times. I thought he would lurch awake like he always did. His eyes stayed shut. He didn't move. There was something fucked up and strange going on, and I thought it had to do with the drugs. If I could just get my brain clear of the drugs, something different would be happening. Several months before that I had started snorting meth every day and when I was snorting meth I had come to feel that I wasn't doing any drugs at all and when I wasn't doing drugs I felt like I was on them, but not in a good way. Things had gotten twisted around somehow, what was real wasn't real and vice versa, and if I could clear my brain I wouldn't be standing there next to Jeremy Schiff's dead body. I would be doing something else, which would be the real thing. I would be doing what I was doing a couple of hours before, which was playing *Pac-Man* with Jeremy at the arcade. Jeremy and I liked the retro games. You didn't have to wait to get on the machines because nobody else played them, and there was something about the flatness of them, their innocence, the way they didn't try to thrust you in the middle of some scene of blood and gore. They made us feel like kids again. We would laugh the way we did in junior high and not care about anything. We didn't have to pay any attention to Andy and Nolan. I was the king of *Pac-Man*, and I was teaching Jeremy. I knew the patterns all the way up to the thirteenth key, but Jeremy could never make it to the keys, he always got stuck on the dragons. That day he had finally made it past the dragons but he had been so excited that he lost his last Pac-Man almost immediately when he got to the first key. I was proud of him, though. Not many people ever make it to the keys, and he would do even better next time. But he was still lying on the bed and not moving. The thing was to get him up off the bed and back down to the arcade. I pumped my hands against his chest a couple of times. I closed his nostrils and pulled down his chin and tried to blow air into his lungs. The same thing kept happening. He kept lying there.

After a minute I noticed that Andy and Nolan were gone. I could hear them out in the other room. I kept looking at Jeremy. He looked peaceful. Usually Jeremy looked agitated, his face tight and his eyes nervous, always moving his hands. He was quieter than I had ever seen him, quieter even than when he was asleep, when he used to toss and turn and sometimes grind his teeth. He looked like he was sleeping soundly for the first time in his life. I left him there that way.

Yes, we'd looked at the body.

All three of us together?

Yes.

Had Andrew Munson said anything then?

No. He just stood there.

When had he said how Jeremy hit his head?

When I got back out in the living room with him and Nolan.

I was in the bedroom alone for some time?

Yes.

For how long?

Just a minute.

And what was I doing?

Just standing there. Then I tried to give him CPR. Then I tried mouth-to-mouth.

Did I have any training in either of those procedures?

No.

She paced back and forth for a few seconds.

Who decided to call 9-1-1?

Andy.

How long had it taken him to decide?

A few minutes.

First he had taken a few minutes to tell us how it happened?

Yes.

How Jeremy hit his head on the coffee table?

Yes.

Had I heard the forensic pathologist's testimony that morning?

Yes.

Had I heard his testimony regarding depressed skull fractures of the type Jeremy suffered?

Yes.

Had I heard him say that a fracture of that sort was the result of significant force?

Yes.

Did I know what Andrew Munson's coffee table was constructed of?

I thought it was some kind of cheap composite.

And did it have sharp corners?

I couldn't remember.

She walked off for a second and I looked at Andy. He was still crying, but quieter now. I was glad he'd quieted down some. He didn't seem to want to look at me or anyone. I felt bad for him to have to be in front of all those people like that. It was like he'd been gutted and turned inside out, and it made me uncomfortable and scared.

Was this Andrew Munson's living room?

She was showing me a photograph. I remembered it then from witness preparation.

Yes.

His coffee table?

Yes.

How would I describe the corners and edges?

Blunt. Kind of rounded.

She went and put the picture back.

Who told the police about the gun?

Andy.

And had he told them the same thing he told me and Nolan? That Jeremy had fired the gun accidentally?

Yes.

When had he told the police?

As soon as they got there.

As soon as they got there? Would I say that Andrew Munson was in a bigger hurry to tell his story to the police than he was to call 9-1-1 in the first place?

Objection! Prosecution continues to something something, your honor. Sustained.

She crossed her arms and held one hand to her chin and closed her eyes like she was thinking really hard.

Had I heard the forensic pathologist say that only roughly 20 percent of epidural hematomas resulted in fatalities?

Yes.

And had I heard him say what the single most important factor in the treatment of epidural hematomas was?

Yes.

And what was that factor?

Prompt medical attention.

She nodded her head up and down to the jury and said the words over again—*prompt medical attention*—nodding her head up and down with each word.

During the time between when Nolan and I heard the gun go off and the time that Andrew Munson told us Jeremy Schiff was dead, had any of us suggested that we take Jeremy to the hospital?

No.

Had Andrew Munson suggested it?

No.

Had I suggested it?

No.

Had it *occurred* to me that it might be a good idea to take Jeremy Schiff to the hospital?

No, I guessed it hadn't.

Not when Andrew Munson said that Jeremy had hit his head, not when Jeremy said that his head hurt, not when he said he needed to go lie down because he didn't feel so hot?

No.

She was through being nice to me, the prosecutor, that much was obvious, and she was asking me questions she hadn't asked me before, and we were getting close to the area I didn't want to get close to, and I didn't know how to explain my reaction that day. The only thing that occurred to me at the time, really, was that we shouldn't have gone over to Andy's. I can remember thinking that much. I knew Jeremy wasn't happy with me for bringing him there.

About a week before, the two of us had borrowed Jeremy's uncle's boat to go water-skiing. It was something we used to do in high school, and Jeremy wanted to go out one day because he said we needed exercise and fresh air. We drove the boat out of the lake and up into the river, where the water was smooth like glass. But when we got all the way out there we realized we'd left the ski in Jeremy's uncle's garage. The sun was really bright, tossing yellow shafts on the water that burst up into my eyes and gave me a headache. We didn't have any drugs or alcohol. Jeremy cut the motor and we floated near an inlet where there were a lot of cattails and a turtle on a log and an osprey nest on the top of an old piling. I started thinking about how soon I could suggest we take the boat back in, and then once we were hitched up and back to town how soon we could go over to Andy's. I was thinking about how I could talk Andy into letting us smoke some. I knew he was smoking it when we weren't there, but he always pretended not, kept saying that we shouldn't smoke it because it was smoking it that made you addicted. I was already addicted anyway so the logic didn't hold for me. It was just another way for Andy to be the boss.

Jeremy was determined to get some exercise, so he stripped off his T-shirt and dove in for a swim. I watched him paddle around in the clear water and fiddled with a life jacket, adjusting the straps for no reason, just something to do. Pretty soon Jeremy swam back to the boat and held on to the ladder. "We going over to Andy's again today?" he asked.

"Sure," I said. "Why not?"

He laid his palm flat on the water and spread his fingers out and moved his arm in little waves, feeling the surface. "I could think of reasons," he said.

"Such as?"

"Such as he's an asshole. Such as why do we hang around with him anyway. Such as what exactly do we think we're accomplishing."

"Do we need to accomplish anything?" I said. "I didn't know we needed to accomplish anything today."

He started slapping the water with his palm, tiny slaps that made a kind of plinking sound, the only thing you could hear out there other than the cars humming down the highway on the other side of the river. "We need to accomplish something sometime, don't we?" he said. "Shit, you're the only one out of the four of us that even has a fucking job."

"Andy's got money. He's buying."

"Yeah," he said, and he lowered his mouth into the water and came up spitting water between his teeth. "Big fucking deal."

"You're still just pissed at him for yesterday," I said.

The day before, we'd been at Andy's sitting around the kitchen table. Jeremy had a beer and it was kind of behind his elbow on the table. Andy told him he was going to knock the bottle off the table with his elbow. Jeremy told him no, he wasn't, and he didn't. He kept putting the bottle in the same place whenever he drank from it and Andy kept watching him do it. When the beer was about half gone, Andy reached across real quick and shoved Jeremy's arm and Jeremy's elbow went back and knocked the beer off. The bottle didn't break but the beer went all over the floor. "Told you so," Andy said, and he made Jeremy clean it up.

Jeremy climbed up the ladder and got in the boat. He looked skinnier than shit. I looked skinny too, I knew. I didn't like to look at myself, which might have been why I didn't take my shirt off and go in swimming. I worried about that quite a bit, the not eating and not sleeping, and I used to check my teeth in the mirror to see if they were going bad, but they weren't, not yet.

"It's just why do I have to put up with that shit?" Jeremy said.

"You *don't* have to," I said. "Kick his ass." Which was a way of teasing him, really. Jeremy couldn't kick Andy's ass.

He put his hand on his chest for a second, to test out his heartbeat after he'd gone swimming. He always thought he had cardiac arrhythmia. For a while after he died I even thought maybe he was right, that that had been the reason. But then they got the coroner's report.

"How fucking old is Andy?" Jeremy said. "I mean, is he fucking twelve?"

Andy did act like he was about twelve sometimes. People tended to find it appealing, but I could see how it would start to wear off before too long. He didn't have too many years left of acting that way before he would just start to seem like an idiot.

"You know what, Robbie? I feel like I've outgrown all this shit." He was shivering, using his T-shirt to dry himself off, because we'd forgotten to bring towels, too. He tossed the T-shirt on the seat opposite him and kept shivering. "Enough's fucking enough. Maybe you and I should move to Spokane. We could find an apartment and get jobs and save up money for community college."

"Yeah, we could do that," I said. "That sounds like a plan." He looked up at me with a sort of hopeful expression. It wasn't a bad idea, I knew. We could both have used a change. But I wasn't ready to change just then, and if I wasn't ready to change, then Jeremy wasn't going to change, even though I never really understood why that was.

"You know, you're like an older brother to me, Robbie," he said, as if he was answering the question I had in my mind. That was when he said it, right then, what I told the prosecutors about later on. "We need to get each other out of this," he said.

I nodded, pulling the strap on the life jacket. It was yellow and black, and the foam rubber felt warm in my hands. "You're right," I said. "And we'll do that."

He was still looking at me with that hopeful expression, and I don't know what I looked like or what he saw in my face, but pretty soon he frowned and rolled his eyes and looked over where the cattails were, where the turtle was still just sitting there in the sun, never moving an inch. "Right," he said. "But today we're going to Andy's." Then he didn't say anything else and he went up front and hit the ignition switch and I went and sat across from him and we took the boat back to town and went over to Andy's house. And we kept going over there till the day Jeremy died.

Hadn't there been any indication that Jeremy Schiff was seriously injured?

I didn't think so. I wasn't sure. He seemed all right.

He seemed all right to me?

Sort of. I meant, I guessed.

Hadn't I said that he seemed hurt? Hadn't I said that he was cradling his head? Hadn't I said that he seemed "tired and groggy"?

Yes.

Was that the way he normally acted after using methamphetamine?

No.

Did he normally want to go lie down because he wasn't feeling well?

No.

In my judgment, didn't that seem like sufficient cause for alarm?

No. I meant, I guessed not. I meant, I wasn't alarmed at the time.

How had we responded when Jeremy Schiff said he wasn't feeling well and he needed to go lie down?

I looked at Andy. He had stopped crying for a minute but he was breathing very hard, like he couldn't get air in, like someone had punched him. He was looking at me, though, and I tried one more time to see if I could get his eyes to tell me something about him, but the only thing I thought I could see in them was that he was very tired, and that he wanted everything to be over with. He even looked maybe like he was feeling the way I'd felt at first, that he just wanted someone to get at the truth of the whole thing, so that everybody could let it rest, let Jeremy rest. He didn't look like he was afraid of what I was about to say. But I was afraid of what I was about to say. I could feel everyone looking at me. I felt like I was being chased, like I needed to escape into a corner somewhere. If I could get into a corner somehow, some place where no one could reach me, I could tell the truth. I had intended to lie, but now I knew I wouldn't. Everything seemed to be calling for the truth. It wasn't just everyone's eyes, it wasn't even just Andy's eyes, it was like even the air in the courtroom was calling for the truth, like the picture I had in my head of Jeremy was calling for the truth, like the truth was something inevitable. I just had to get in that hidden corner to say it. So I closed my eyes, and it worked. I was there.

We laughed.

My eyes were closed and it was quiet. Then I heard Andy start to cry again. I kept my eyes closed. The prosecutor's voice came from the air around my head.

We *laughed*?

Yes.

What on earth had there been to laugh at?

My eyes were closed and I was remembering and talking at the same time and I couldn't tell which was which.

Jeremy said he wasn't feeling well and he wanted to go lie down. He asked Andy if he could lie down on his bed. His voice was kind of slurred like a drunk's. Andy said sure, which surprised me. He said it in a soft voice, even. He didn't give Jeremy any shit. Jeremy stood up from the couch with his hand held to the side of his head and he took a step and he bumped into the table and then he kind of staggered to the bedroom. It was like the ground was shifting on him, he kept lurching to the side at each step as if he were trying to go around something, like he was a kid who'd just gotten off a spinning carnival ride. It looked funny. We laughed, all three of us, although I remembered now that Andy hadn't laughed like me and Nolan. His was more halfhearted, like he was just laughing because me and Nolan were. And maybe Nolan wasn't really laughing all that much, either. Maybe I was the only one who was really laughing. Maybe I was the only one who really thought it was funny. I don't know why. It was like the time with the car, it just looked funny. The sun was coming through the curtains and crossing the floor and the gun was lying there and I was laughing at Jeremy while the blood pooled under his crushed skull and put pressure on his brain, disturbing his equilibrium so that he couldn't walk straight.

I opened my eyes. I couldn't tell the difference between what I'd been saying and what I'd been remembering. I looked to see the look in the eyes of the eyes that were looking at me, and they were all the same, the jury, the prosecutor, the deputy prosecutor, Andy's parents, Jeremy's parents, Andy's even. All the eyes in the place were the same—flat, stony, dead, even the ones that had tears flowing from them like Andy's. All the eyes said it was over, done, the book had been closed on something. The eyes were through with me.

No more questions, your honor.

Would the defense like to cross-examine?

The defense lawyers lowered their heads and whispered and Andy sat there with tears coming from his eyes not looking at me anymore and no one was looking at me anymore and the defense attorney stood.

No, your honor.

Witness may step down.

They'd gotten what they wanted from me, and I suppose I'd gotten what I wanted from them. But I didn't want to step down yet. I didn't feel like I was finished. But they didn't give me a choice.

I walked out of the courtroom and down the hallway and out of the courthouse. It was dusk, and it was snowing still. I made my way to my car and cleaned off my windshield and my windows and got inside, but when I turned the key the engine wouldn't start. There was no one in the parking lot to give me a jump, and I didn't feel like waiting. I walked up the street to a bar and ordered a beer and gave the bartender some money and looked in my wallet to see how much was left. It was a dark, dingy bar and no one was there but a few serious drinkers who sat at the bar and didn't talk much and kept their eyes on the TV. But there was a fireplace with a slow-burning fire, and there was a small table close to it where I could sit and get warm. I sat there and looked out the window until my beer was gone and then I ordered another one and then another after that, and then my money was gone. I sat with my last beer and watched it get dark outside the window, watched the snow float down. The door opened, and the deputy prosecutor walked in. She was all by herself, and the sight of her set a spark off inside me, but the spark felt old, and I didn't try to smile, just lifted my hand in a wave. She waved back at me with one finger, the expression on her face not changing, still full of the cold outside. I watched her sit at the bar and lay down her purse and order a drink, her back turned toward me. She would never speak to me again, I knew, and I felt like I was off in a little corner of my mind somewhere, trapped in some small space and hidden even from the rest of myself, locked away so that I would never have to fall apart like Andy had, crying for what I had lost. And I knew that for the rest of my life I would always feel the same, always be in that same place. But as I watched her there, sitting on the bar stool with her legs crossed, sipping her drink, empty seats to either side of her, I knew the testimony that I had wanted to finish, that I would not go sit next to her and tell.

It was a story about how Jeremy and me would sometimes lie awake in the dark and he would tell me about the one thing he really wanted, which was to become a pilot. He started telling me the story in the dark when we were thirteen years old, and he never really finished it, it went on for years and years. When we were thirteen the story was always about what it would feel like to fly the planes, and I could feel it too, lying there across the room from Jeremy, the way he described it, floating through the clouds. Then when we were older the story was about the steps one had to take to prepare, about how to get a license, how to get into commercial flight school, and how Jeremy intended to do these things, and I would get sleepy listening to this story because I'd heard it too many times and no longer had any encouragement to offer, and because Jeremy would have been an awful pilot, always worried and nervous and scared. And so I would stay quiet and wait for him to be quiet and soon he would, and once he was quiet I knew that in his mind he was flying the planes the way he imagined himself, steady and sure at the controls thousands of feet above the ground, and then, while I fell toward sleep, I could be glad for Jeremy that he wanted to be a pilot, because I had never really wanted to be anything. And then I would hear Jeremy move in the dark, and I would know what he was doing, even long after I quit bothering to look—he was lying in the moonlight, placing his hand over his heart, making sure it was still beating there.

# Camel Light

For once, Rick Steuben was home alone. Maggie was gone to her Native American beadworking class, and their fifteen-year-old daughter, April, was downtown with some friends, and their eleven-year-old son, Austin, was at the neighbor's playing video games. It was Saturday, and it was May, and the sun was shining, and the lilacs were in bloom along the back fence, and the leaves were out on the maple tree, and the air outside the screen door was filled with the twittering of sparrows. It was, in other words, a perfect day in Rick Steuben's small hometown in Idaho, and Rick was trying to figure out what to do with it, considering the question at his leisure. Such an opportunity was rare, something he could ordinarily only dream of. And when he dreamed of such an opportunity, such a fine chance on such a nice day, the dream usually taking shape while he sat at his desk at the insurance office shuffling idly through his stack of applications and claims, he imagined reading a good book in the hammock, or getting his old turntable and record collection down from the attic, or taking out his 9-iron and chipping some balls across the yard, or drinking a beer on the

deck, or watching a baseball game on TV, or organizing all his
old college photos in the album he'd bought for that purpose,
or at the very least taking a restorative nap. But now he did
none of those things, just sat at the kitchen table in an almost
vegetative state, idly staring at the daily newspaper. He wanted
nothing more at the moment than the simple right granted to
Muffy, the house cat over there on the couch—the right to be
lazy. Lazy was good. Lazy, sitting there in his sweatpants. He
might do nothing but sit there for the whole hour until Maggie's return.

Or he could make a second pot of coffee. That would require
effort. He looked at the coffeemaker, there on the counter. He
saw something on the floor, in the crease where the tile ran
under the dishwasher. It looked like, could it be . . . a cigarette? It looked like a cigarette. But how would a cigarette get
under the dishwasher? He and Maggie had quit smoking sixteen years ago, when they got the good news about her pregnancy. April had been until lately an almost eerily perfect teenager, not a good candidate for an infraction of this sort, and,
yes, Austin was a handful, but smoking? At eleven? And none
of their friends smoked, other than Valerie, the wife of Rick's
best friend, Martin, and Valerie and Martin hadn't been to the
house in at least a week—in fact they were on vacation in the
San Juan Islands. There were benefits to not having children.

But the thing looked like a cigarette. It *was* a cigarette, it had
to be. Rick grunted and got up from his chair, his knees sore
from jogging yesterday, and went over to investigate . . . the
damn thing was a cigarette, there under his dishwasher. He
picked it up and rolled it between his fingers. Camel Light.

He took the cigarette back to the kitchen table and resumed
his seat. He folded up the newspaper and placed the cigarette

in front of him and almost immediately he wondered—big, huge, waving red flag—where some matches were. Amazing. He hadn't held one of the things in his fingers for sixteen years, but its psychological power was obviously immense—his last cigarette might have been yesterday, the physical memory was so clear. But he wouldn't smoke it, of course not.

The question was, whose cigarette was this? The most likely culprit, if you just looked at it logically, was April. She was at that age. But April was the smart one, April was the achiever, April was the type-A personality, the math whiz, the class president, what have you. Smoking didn't fit the profile. Though problems had begun to surface recently, hadn't they? There had been a downtick in April's enthusiasm for schoolwork— a sprinkling of Bs on her report card. Lackluster responses to suggestions for outside reading—a sudden indifference to *Pride and Prejudice* and *Of Mice and Men*, both of which Rick had tried to foist upon her lately. Rick himself had been a big reader as a kid, and in fact had wanted to major in English and become a teacher, but his father had refused to pay for an impractical degree, etc., etc., there was no sense dredging all that up again. Of course the fact that he had always loved to read didn't explain why he wasn't reading now, out in the hammock on such a nice day, starting *War and Peace*, which he'd been intending to read for the last ten years. It was the longest running of his many self-improvement projects already—why not get started? Because of the cigarette, which had ruined his mood on this fine spring day. Because of April, who was now smoking, apparently. But no, it just didn't fit. Was it possible, was it really *possible*, that *Austin* could have taken up smoking? The kids he hung around with seemed to be good kids, basically, a little restless and bored, addicted to the god-awful

Xbox, which Rick had held out against for the longest time, but basically good kids from good families. They were, like Austin, simply unmotivated to do anything. Could you actually picture them huddled up in the woods outside the elementary school during lunch break, puffing away on Camels? And sure, there had been all the arguments—*fights*, you'd have to call them, Rick guessed—over the past few weeks. Fights over homework, fights over the poor reports from Austin's teachers, fights over Austin's lack of interest in virtually anything the universe contained that was nonelectronic. Austin had taken to screaming, to crying, to calling Rick and Maggie names. Austin was becoming, in a word, unmanageable, and it was just last night that he and Maggie had broken down and lifted Austin's restrictions for bad grades and bad behavior, because, honestly, they couldn't stand the prospect of having their youngest child, whom they both loved, in the house with them for the entire weekend. Austin had won. But now there was this other possibility, *smoking*, and my God if that were the case just *imagine* the hysteria and the fighting that would ensue, and the whole new round of restrictions, and rebellion, and misery. Why, why, *why* would a kid that age have to go off and do something so stupid?

And yet, Rick reminded himself, it didn't mean that Austin was a horrible kid, that there was nothing but trouble ahead where he was concerned. He could sometimes, still, be nice to his parents, nice to his older sister. He could sometimes enjoy family vacations and outings and meals. There were times when he resembled the happy child Rick and Maggie had imagined having when they'd gotten news of the second pregnancy. The truth was that Austin had been an accident.

The intention was to have just one child, and for Maggie to go back to work after April had reached school age. Maggie had, after all, a PhD in psychology, and she wanted to use it, which Rick could understand, but then there was this new pregnancy, and this new son, and maybe some of that stress and frustration had revealed itself to Austin somehow, despite everyone's best intentions, and it had made him a bitter and angry child, with some secret misery coiled inside him, and it had led eventually to this new thing, smoking. Rick twirled the cigarette in his fingers and shook his head. No. Austin wasn't the brightest bulb on the tree, but he wasn't the dimmest, either. There was flat-out no way he would be dumb enough to bring a cigarette into the house.

So how had it gotten here? The house was empty now during the days, April and Austin off at school and Maggie having in fact started up her practice, leasing office space in a building next to the hospital, where she spent a few hours a day now, pretty much every day now it seemed to Rick, even though she had, to date, only a few clients. What if it were Maggie's cigarette? What if she had taken up smoking again after sixteen years? And why—out of boredom, anxiety? Her practice wasn't making enough money yet to pay for the office space, but Rick made a wad of dough. He'd *better* make a wad of dough for the shit he had to put up with, the indignity of being an insurance salesman when what he really wanted to be was an artist or, he didn't know, a *thinker*, a *learner*, a quester after knowledge, someone who spent his free time reading *War and Peace*, even though he wasn't doing that now when he had the opportunity, but still, he would get up and go do it here in a minute, as soon as he got done figuring out the cigarette. He didn't think Maggie would start smoking again simply because the practice had been a bit of a disappointment thus far. In fact it hadn't been a disappointment at all, really, had it? Maggie was happier these days than he'd seen her in a long time.

It didn't seem to matter so much, actually, that there weren't patients, that the townsfolk hadn't come running when Maggie hung her sign out by the road, clamoring for advice regarding their various problematic habits and addictions, demanding explanations of their deep-seated fears and desperate longings, etc. No, it had seemed quite enough to suit Maggie that she simply *had* a sign to hang, business cards to order, stationery to print, a fax machine, a postal box, an intercom system that played preprogrammed music.

True, it had been a struggle for Maggie—the snarl of red tape with the application process, the difficulty of passing her examinations after all those years away from school. She'd had to, somehow, demonstrate to the state board "upstanding moral character." But none of that explained why she might be smoking, if in fact she was, if, hypothetically, it was her cigarette instead of someone else's, which Rick doubted, but you never knew. What in her current circumstances could drive her to resume such a nasty habit, so long forgotten, so thoroughly stored away in their shared memory of the people they used to be that they had not even mentioned *wanting* a cigarette for years?

Maybe he had overestimated her will power. Maybe he was the strong one instead of the other way around. After all, there he was down at the insurance office all day, 8-to-5ing it, and what was to stop him, at any hour of the day, from going out on the rear walkway, hidden from the street, and having a cigarette

with Sarah Amandine, who smoked back there all the time? Or
J. J. Wheeler? Although he would rather have a cigarette with
Sarah Amandine, who had a so-so face and not-so-big tits but a
great ass and very shapely legs for a woman of thirty-five. What
if he took up smoking and talking to Sarah Amandine? What
were the chances of anything happening between them? Best
not to let his thoughts start going down that road.

The thing to do was put the cigarette away somewhere and
go out to the hammock and start reading Tolstoy. Or, well, come
to think of it, if he was going outside, he could find a book of
matches and smoke this cigarette himself. Hey, look, *someone*
had already broken the rules around here, so why shouldn't he?
His heart beat quickly as he turned the weightless filter back
and forth in his fingers and imagined what a cigarette would
taste like after all these years. Either April had broken the rules
or Austin had broken the rules or Maggie had broken the rules;
if it was April or Austin, then obviously all these years of not
smoking had not had their intended effect, so what was the difference? He might as well. And if Maggie were smoking, then
there had been a serious breach in the trustworthiness department, a serious failure to respect the rights and privileges and
freedoms and expectations and what-have-yous of the *other*
in the relationship, and so in this case he was well within his
rights to go out on the deck and torch it up.

Unless the cigarette had somehow just gotten there by
accident. Then his going out on the porch to smoke would
look really bad. Ha ha ha, a small misunderstanding, an odd
sequence of events, a cigarette ends up getting dropped in his
kitchen, the dishwasher had needed repairing, let's say, Maggie had forgotten to tell him, and the dishwasher repairman,

on his hands and knees, butt crack showing from the back of his jeans, had lost a cigarette out of the pack hanging from his pocket. Ha ha, what a joke, but . . . and then there would be Rick's guilt at having smoked the cigarette. No, no, no . . . this was not a trap to fall into. This would have to be considered carefully, all the angles. He checked the clock. He had a half hour yet, he could afford another fifteen minutes or so of good, thorough, investigative work, some clear and logical thinking on the subject, before he decided whether or not he would actually have a smoke.

He went into the bathroom and took a leak and washed his hands and came back out and took his seat at the kitchen table and stared at the cigarette again. He gave it a good roll or two along the table with his index finger, admiring its perfectly cylindrical shape.

The world went on outside the window. Across the street, workmen were pounding the shit out of the McGoverns' house, making a racket. For five years now they'd been "improving" the house in the hope that it would become a place where they actually wanted to live. In front of the McGoverns' walked Mrs. Snell and one of her dogs, this time the basset hound. She had four dogs and she walked them each in turn, all day long, around and around the neighborhood. She wore a little flowered hat, and when she walked the next dog there would be something different about her—she would change the hat, or her blouse, or her shoes. She was a stumpy woman who wore her hair in a tight bun. Her legs were hard and thick like drainage pipes.

The more he thought about it, the less it seemed likely to be April's cigarette. She just wasn't that kind of girl. Or Austin's. He just wasn't . . . well, he was only *eleven*, for Christ's sake.

So, Maggie.

He checked the clock again. Maggie would be back in fifteen or twenty minutes. To save time, just in case, he rummaged through the junk drawer until he found a pack of matches. Then he sat back down at the table with the matches and cigarette in hand. He was now ready to smoke if he decided to.

The phone rang. He let the machine get it. Austin's friend Paul's mother What's Her Name (she identified herself on the machine only as "Paul's mother") said that Austin and Paul and Grayson and Hunter were finished playing *Call of Duty* and now they were outside shooting each other with airsoft rifles and not to worry because they all had the protective goggles and anyway could Austin please stay one more hour. Call her back. Rick would let Maggie do that.

Maggie and a cigarette—what was the likely scenario? They'd been married for eighteen years. By now Rick should be able to read her like a book. But he couldn't even recall what she looked like when she'd left for beadworking. Had she put in her contacts this morning, or was she wearing her glasses? She'd gotten her hair cut and styled just last week—how was it different from before? But certainly he knew her likes and dislikes, her passions and her proclivities. Come to think of it, though, they hadn't talked about those things recently, not since the conversation that resulted in Maggie starting to study for her licensing exams, which would have been . . . Christ, over two years ago? Who knew, then? He had no idea how she felt, really, these days. Let's see—she was excited about the practice, and she seemed less concerned about Austin, and she had missed April's exhibit at the science fair . . . that was all he knew. Again, she seemed *happy* lately.

A couple of weeks back he'd been driving after work past the hospital and he'd seen Maggie's car in the parking lot, and on a whim he'd turned in to pay her a visit. He found her standing out on the sidewalk with one of her few patients, a guy named Clifton Moody, he'd later learned. Clifton Moody had just concluded his scheduled appointment, and now he and Maggie were winding up the day, shooting the breeze. Clifton Moody had just said something to make Maggie laugh, and when she saw Rick her laugh faded to a little chuckle and then a faint sigh. Then there was the introduction, the handshake.

That night, Maggie told Rick all about Clifton Moody. Clifton Moody was an interesting case, the most interesting she'd come across yet. Clifton Moody was clinically depressed, not because, as Rick might have been, his family was a wreck, or he hated his job, or he felt like he'd never gotten all he deserved from life, but because of the state of the world in general. He was depressed especially because he felt that the human race had wasted its vast potential. A corner had been turned, it was too late to go back now, we were witnessing (this was the metaphor Clifton Moody used) the last ticking seconds of human history. Clifton Moody was deeply ashamed, given the apocalyptic circumstances, of his material comfort and well-being (which was a joke, since it turned out he lived in a cabin in the woods with no electricity and only a hand pump for water). He was seriously troubled, perhaps distraught, by the knowledge that he had not been able to spark any positive change through—get this—his chain saw art, but instead spent most of his time carving bears and geese and trout to sell to wealthy transplants from California or New Jersey. The only thing that kept him alive was his one great project; he was carving out, from the massive trunk of an old-growth Douglas fir that he had "rescued" at substantial cost from a logging operation— get this—a *Douglas fir*, in all its glorious miniature detail, which was supposed to be some kind of ironic representation of the supposed regenerative powers of nature—the thing would *look* like a live tree, but it would be dead, or whatever. No wonder the crazy guy was depressed, in other words. But here was the thing—in thinking about how happy Maggie had looked in that moment when he saw her on the sidewalk with Clifton Moody, who apparently could crack a joke to impress his therapist when the situation called for it despite his awful depression, Rick realized that Clifton Moody had been *smoking a cigarette*. Rick could see—right now, vividly—Clifton Moody putting it out with his shoe.

He was stunned for a moment. He hadn't thought Maggie capable of such a thing—an affair. He understood on some basic level that his marriage was no longer *exciting*, that there was nothing fresh or surprising in it, but the thought of one or the other of them creating such a possible disruption, a real rending of the fabric in some potentially disastrous way, was something he rarely considered and always quickly dismissed. And he wasn't even quite ready to consider it seriously now— only there was the cigarette, and how did it get there, scrunched up in the crease under the dishwasher?

He began to play through the scenario, still a bit idly, still to some degree with the purpose of reasoning out the cigarette. One day this past week—let's say just yesterday, *Friday*, mere *hours* before now—the kids are in school, he's at his office, and maybe Clifton Moody has a scheduled appointment. Maybe things get interesting, the conversation. Maybe Maggie is through for the day and says to Clifton Moody something like, *Why don't we continue this conservation someplace else, someplace more comfortable?* Maybe they go to lunch, maybe they have a drink or two. It's still a couple of hours before the bus will bring the kids home from school. Maybe they aren't through talking. Maybe Clifton Moody asks, *Where do you live, anyway?* Maggie says, *You know the neighborhood back behind the city park, where they have the tennis courts?* No, Clifton Moody doesn't know it, or he's not very familiar with it. After all, Clifton Moody lives in the frigging boonies. *Let's swing by*, Maggie says. Maybe she says something like, *Why stop now? I'm having fun. It's interesting to talk to you.* Maybe she even adds a little humor—*I mean, in a nonprofessional capacity.* At the last minute she thinks of how it will look to the neighbors. *I'll drive my car and you follow me in your truck.* Clifton Moody probably drives a truck, an old panel truck that he can haul his chain-saw art in. It will look like he's at the house to work.

Now they're inside. The idea is that Clifton Moody will just be there a minute, so they stand in the kitchen. Maggie offers him a beer. (Had any of his beers been missing? He'd bought a twelve-pack when was it—Tuesday? There were three left for tonight—he checked first thing this morning. Did he drink nine beers during the week? He couldn't remember.) Maybe Maggie even has one herself, wondering if he'll miss two beers. Clifton Moody lingers. He's not talking about his depression now, he's talking about his chain-saw art, or about living out in the woods, how he feels *close to nature.* He's describing to her a little waterfall that's just a short walk from his back door. How peaceful everything is. How the deer come in the morning to his porch, where he's put a salt lick. *Wonderful*, Maggie says.

*Fascinating.* Clifton Moody is no longer a screwed-up crazy guy but a burly individualist with a beard, sufficient unto himself but deeply saddened that the rest of the world can't see what he sees, know what he knows, understand what he understands. He suffers not on his own behalf but on that of other people. Principles and ethics and that sort of thing, stuff he actually *lives* by. Clifton Moody walks the walk.

Now Clifton Moody would like to have a cigarette. Maggie tells him he can go out on the deck. The neighbors won't see him back there, most likely. She studies his rough hands as he draws a cigarette from the pack he keeps in the pocket of his flannel shirt. Maybe it is the hands that draw her toward him, one step, two. She takes hold of his hand and examines it and says something about how she's always admired hard work, men who work hard. Then he moves his hand up her arm and draws him to her and they kiss.

And the cigarette falls to the floor, where it gets nudged under the dishwasher by someone's shoe.

He didn't imagine the rest, or not much of it, though he couldn't stop an image of Maggie naked, her face and neck flushed, moist between her legs, coming quickly underneath Clifton Moody as soon as he got inside her. Right there in the damn bed where Rick slept every night. And this could have happened just *yesterday*. Awful, awful, awful thought, and he thrust it away as if it had bitten him.

Now he *needed* a cigarette. But he was too upset at the thought of Maggie and Clifton Moody to get out of his chair. If it were true, his marriage was a joke, his life a shambles. And how would he ever know for certain? How would he bring up the subject? What did he have to go on, what evidence to confront Maggie with when she returned from the gym? The cigarette. He looked at it on the table. He tried to remember if the cigarette Clifton Moody put out with his shoe had a tan filter. And would Clifton Moody smoke a light cigarette? Wouldn't he smoke a Marlboro or a Lucky Strike? Maybe he was trying to cut out the habit gradually by reducing the amount of nicotine.

The thing to do was assume he had the evidence, negotiate Maggie toward a confession by bluffing his way. *I know there's something going on. I've got evidence. Might as well go ahead and tell me.* What else did he have to confirm his suspicions? The look on Maggie's face when he saw her talking to Clifton Moody. That was the real kicker. A look. A glance. He'd accused her of infidelity only once before, several years ago, and it hadn't gone very well. That time it had been with his best friend, Martin, and it had been the same thing—a look he thought he saw passing between them one night, some sense of secrets shared. But Maggie had laughed at him. She said his suspicions were based on the fact that *he* fantasized about sleeping with *Valerie* and so assumed that she must be sleeping with Martin. A classic case of projection. And she was right, actually. Maggie didn't have a PhD in psychology for nothing.

But things would be different this time. This time he intended to get to the bottom of things. He had the cigarette, after all, and how would she explain it? She couldn't deny any knowledge of it—that would throw suspicion on April, and if Rick knew anything about his wife it was that she wasn't unjust or cruel. No, she would have to fess up, he was going to root it out of her through sheer persistence—and then what? If there was an affair with Clifton Moody, Rick's life would be altered entirely. There would be a divorce, for starters—Rick wasn't the sort to put up with philandering, especially when he'd walked the straight and narrow for so many years. An uproar with the kids, and it pained him to think that he wouldn't be living beneath the same roof with them anymore. Austin, especially, needed him now, even if he pretended otherwise. And now he would be . . . what . . . living in an apartment somewhere in town, or at best a small house, maybe a two-bedroom with a small yard, there'd have to be someplace for the kids to stay when they visited him. Maybe in the long run, when the facts had come to light and the court proceedings were over, he'd end up with the kids and the house and Maggie would have to live elsewhere, but he'd be the one to move out first. Rent to pay on top of the mortgage. And what about Clifton Moody? Would Maggie end up out in the boonies with him? Rick couldn't see it. In fact, he could see just the opposite—Clifton Moody, the hypocritical bastard, would decide he liked the idea of a hot shower and an indoor toilet. Six months from now, a year from now, Clifton asshole Moody could be sitting here in this very chair, rolling a cigarette just like this one between his fingers before going out to smoke on the deck.

Which Rick was getting ready to do right now, goddam-mit. Why not? What was stopping him? He might as well start smoking again all the time. He wouldn't smoke inside the new apartment/small house, but he could smoke out on the porch all he wanted to. And he would start smoking with Sarah Amandine at work. He'd start Monday. *Mind if I have one with you?* Very cool and nonchalant. He could just see the look on her face. She'd always had a thing for him, he knew. Always a hint of flirtation. He'd *sleep* with Sarah Amandine—that would give Maggie something to chew on.

He was starting to like the idea, this whole new life thing. Think of all the free time he would have now to pursue his various interests. He would buy a sailboat or a motorcycle. He would read Tolstoy. He'd let his hair grow long and start showing up to work in sandals. Holy shit, he could write his *novel*. He'd always wanted to write a novel, he *knew* he had it in him. His life had been pretty damn interesting before he ran into Maggie. All the craziness of his college days. What a great group of guys he'd hung out with. And *women*! He'd had to beat them away with a stick back then. You couldn't swing a cat without hitting a woman who wanted to sleep with him. And the trip to Canada with the gang! Damn, he and Martin had told that story at the reunion, and everyone had laughed their asses off. People would love to read about that—a crazy journey with a wild plot and fascinating characters, a coming-of-age story shot through with a vein of nostalgia and reminiscence, kind of a *Catcher in the Rye* or *On the Road* set in the Canadian wilderness. You'd be talking best seller. He'd have to look into finding an agent. Mornings sitting at the keyboard with a cup of coffee, pounding out the chapters, going outside for a smoke while he thought up what came next, and then, when he'd exhausted his store of inspiration for the day, he'd go back to the bedroom where Sarah Amandine would be waiting for him, naked under the covers, inviting him in.

The thought of it was enough to get Rick up out of the chair, cigarette in hand, and out onto the deck, where he was pulled up abruptly by the sight of Lee Fink starting up his riding lawnmower next door. Now if Rick wanted to smoke, he'd have to go out to the garage. And he was getting ready to do that, but then he wasn't sure of the time, so he ended up back in the kitchen looking at the clock on the microwave, seated again in his chair.

Why did he have to worry about the time? What difference did it make if Maggie caught him smoking? He was going to confront her anyway, and if his suspicions were correct, smoking a cigarette would be the least of anyone's worries. And why was he so concerned about smoking in front of Lee Fink, who was just some asshole on city council? He wouldn't have the guts or the persistence to do any of it, would he? The new life in the apartment/small house writing the novel, the fling with Sarah Amandine? He'd start smoking again for real and he'd stop exercising and he'd get fat and die from diabetes or emphysema. He'd putter around all day doing nothing. He'd probably lose his job. There wouldn't be a novel. There wouldn't even be a decent paragraph, just a blank ream of paper and some stupid how-to books on publishing and agents. There would be no Sarah Amandine. The only thing he felt sure of at the moment was that there would be a divorce, that he would be without Maggie, without his kids, without his house, without his self-respect. He already felt inferior to a man like Clifton Moody, some crazy nut job who needed a shrink. If he smoked this cigarette it would just be the beginning of the long spiral into self-pity and worthlessness. And yet he wanted to smoke it and get it over with. Why were cigarettes so awful? Because when you looked at someone smoking, you saw them dying right in front of you.

But what else was there? He could see it now, how he'd been tricked into wasting his life. Boy meets girl, boy marries girl, boy and girl produce more boys and girls, buy a house, buy two cars, buy a home entertainment center, pay for college tuition and medical insurance. Boy's life is over, boy isn't boy anymore, boy doesn't belong to himself but to all these other people. It had all been a sham, a trick, he had fallen for it, and it was too late to go back now. With a piercing clarity he remembered that trip to Canada, a moment when he'd sat with his buddies by a clear alpine lake, startlingly blue, and the conversation and the jokes had died into a brief silence, and there was just the sun on the water and the breeze swirling down the mountain peaks and the dripping water from the bluish underside of a glacier right behind them.

He breathed heavily and realized that he was close to crying. None of it was fair. He'd taken on all these burdens, he'd labored like a beast in the hot sun, burning and thirsting, and they'd kept adding more, hadn't they, one weight after another until he was crushed beneath the load. And what had been his compensation? Three people that he loved, three people he would walk through fire for, April with all her accomplishments, Austin even with all of his dark troubles, and Maggie . . . he didn't know who she was or what she wanted, never had, not really. She had struggled beneath her own burdens and now she was setting herself free. And now that she had broken him, now that he had been broken, none of the things he had broken himself for would be there to sustain him, and his old pre-broken self was gone, faded to a point of light he could find only in memory.

Clifton Moody was right. What was the point, when you got right down to it? What could a human being, one human being, do anyway? Change the world with chain-saw art? A novel? What could you reasonably expect, toiling away on your parched piece of ground? What if you were the president, even?

Start a war, negotiate a peace—nothing but a tick on the clock of human history. Stick your finger in the dike just to find that there's no more water. Global warming, shrinking ice caps, expanding oceans, extensive flooding, widespread drought, mass starvation, a whole species on its way to becoming fertilizer or fish food. It was right there in front of him. You could read the signs in the daily paper.

Alone at the kitchen table, he sat crying quietly when Maggie's car turned into the drive. How nice it looked out there in the sunshine, the gleaming black Volvo wagon he had just washed yesterday. Maggie emerged, carrying a new beaded handbag. She'd worn her glasses today. He remembered that now, could see them in the moment she'd walked out the door an hour ago. She was approaching the house. He didn't want her to see him crying. He wiped his eyes with his hand and the hem of his T-shirt. He grabbed the cigarette off the table and retreated to the bedroom, where he hid it in his sock drawer for future reference, in case he needed it or decided to mention it someday.

# What I Want from You

You would remember Jim, wouldn't you, if you were here? The squirrel without the tail, the one Ryan and Conor watched in the yard from the window, the one they befriended? You didn't pay enough attention to the things you should have, but you would remember Jim. What I want to tell you is that Conor and I buried him today.

There was one day, one day at least, I remember, when you hadn't gone to the office yet for whatever reason, and Ryan lay on the couch beneath the blanket (the yellow blanket, you remember? the one he said didn't chafe his skin), and you sat with him and stroked his thin hair. He loved you, looked up to you to such a great degree (because you were calm and rational? because you knew so many things?). You didn't know how pleased he was that morning just because you sat with him, because you touched his hair.

It was early spring, remember, and still cold enough outside in the North Carolina morning for me to insist that Conor wear a sweatshirt. So Conor was outside in the yard, little Conor, holding some cereal in his hand, edging closer and closer to Jim, who darted around under the dogwood tree, and we could see, you remember, Conor moving his lips, having a conversation with Jim, because Ryan had taken to pretending that Jim could talk, that Jim said all sorts of things that only he, Ryan, could interpret, and Conor of course believed him. So Conor was talking very earnestly to Jim, this poor squirrel with just a stump for a tail, trying to coax him over to eat the cereal from his hand. And you got a kick out of that. You didn't know we had so much fun in the morning, that even with Ryan dying there under the blanket we had interesting things to do. Ryan and I had watched Conor do this same thing on countless occasions, it was our routine, but to you it was new, and you laughed so hard that I thought there was something wrong (and there was, of course), but Ryan laughed then, too, you remember? Laughed because you were laughing, because you were happy for a moment.

We were coming back from a walk today, coming back up the little alley we used to watch you disappear down every morning on your way to work. I would stand with my cup of coffee, facing the window, and Conor would be up on his knees on the couch, his arms folded on top of the couch back, and even in those last weeks when we brought him home from the hospital to die, Ryan would insist that we prop him up with pillows so that he could see you walking away, carrying your briefcase. Sometimes, just before drifting out of sight behind the neighbor's house, you turned to us at the window, an empty grin on your face (a failed attempt at heartiness), and waved your hand. And Conor would smile and rub his thumb across his teeth the way he used to do. And Ryan's blue eyes would focus, half shine from their dark hollows, as if he'd received at least some part of what he wanted, of what he could ask for then.

We walk up and back the alley most days now, and I think about what you were thinking. The petals of the gardenias are turning brown now, the kudzu crawls the fence line. But on the day you died there were dogwood blooms and wisteria, yellow daffodils lining your way. I try to think of you walking up this alley in the spring.

Because what have you left me? An insoluble riddle. Were you thinking on that morning about the essays you had to grade, about the students who would come by your office, about the faculty meeting you would attend before coming home that afternoon? Or were you thinking how you would say that you needed to go to the grocery store, how you would instead drive miles and miles, speeding far away along narrow back roads until you found the courage, as you would probably call it, to press the pedal hard enough to miss the curve? Did you plan it or did it just happen?

But I wanted to tell you that we found Jim run over in the street when we got home from our walk today. I saw the body as we approached the house, and I hoped harder than I had hoped for anything in a while that it would be some other poor squirrel. Because Jim had become Conor's only friend, really. But as we drew closer I could see the little stub. And so we stood there over Jim, over the eye that had popped from his skull and the blood that trailed from his tiny mouth and the flies that had settled on him already, though he could not have been dead for half an hour. And I looked at Conor, expecting him to cry, and I felt my body grow heavy, my arms grow heavy and tired in the way they do now when I feel somebody's need. But Conor took it like a grown man, because he's a little boy, and because he knows already what there is to know about death, how the dead don't come back to you and there's no use in crying.

Do you remember how we first became acquainted with Jim? It was you who found him, you know. It was last fall, when Ryan's hair had started to grow back and we spent our time hoping he had gone into remission. We would all watch TV in the living room and Ryan seemed to be getting stronger, he and Conor on the hardwood floor playing games with toy soldiers. We sat on the couch and talked to Ryan about how, come springtime, he would be out in the yard playing baseball again, how we would take a trip to the ocean. And one Sunday afternoon you looked out the window and said, "Good God, what a funny-looking rabbit." And Ryan and Conor left their game to come see. And there was Jim with his stubby tail, his eyes darting and alert, his tiny paws clawing feverishly at the ground, the muscles of his shoulders quivering. And Conor and Ryan stood there half-smiling, looking out the window and then glancing up at you while you maintained your poker face. "Dad," Ryan said, "it's a squirrel," and you laughed then and punched Ryan lightly on the arm. Those were our last good days.

Conor would tell you every afternoon what the tail-less squirrel had done that day—he had run on the telephone wire, he had started building a nest in the pine tree. And one day you came in from work and grabbed an apple from the fridge and sat at the table listening to Conor talk. And between bites you said, "His name's Jim. I had a little conversation with him just now in the driveway." And Conor's mouth hung open and his eyes narrowed. You took another bite of your apple. "Sure," you said. "Jim told me to tell you how much he enjoyed seeing you and Ryan in the window." And Conor stood there with that look on his face.

But you couldn't stay interested in the game. After all, you had your broken life to attend to. You had your failing marriage, your failing career. You had your dying son, back in the hospital soon enough, for the last time, and you had all the days and nights in the cancer ward, the fluorescent lights in the hallways, the soft padding sound of the nurses' shoes, the doctors with their put-on smiles and vigorous handshakes, clicking their pens and putting them in their pockets. You had the coffee and the snacks from the vending machines. You had the little room to share with Ryan, the room that almost seemed alive, trying as hard as it could to look like home, its pictures of clowns and balloons and its pastel wallpaper. You had the days in the chair and the nights in the bed next to Ryan's, you had the hours of Ryan's sickness and his pain, you had the times of Ryan's fear, you had the times of trying hard to swallow your own fear before it swallowed you, looking out the window at the gray parking lot and the hospital sign. You had the moments when your hopes left, floating out into the air of the room. I know. I had all these same things, too.

And yet here I am, and you're not here, and why? Maybe our hearts broke differently. Your heart must have broken at the office, because that's where you always were. One day while you sat at your computer sending e-mails or going over lecture notes, sticking mulishly to a plan that wouldn't work, because there had been no published papers, no conferences, no accolades, and none of it mattered anyway because your nine-year-old son was dying and all your knowledge couldn't help you come to terms with that fact, some thought of Ryan assailed you (how he stared so intently when anyone was angry, how he took such great care to look both ways before crossing the street, how his fingers tapped the chess pieces while he considered his next move, how he could never sit still when he talked, not ever, pacing back and forth and snapping his fingers, and maybe how we used to reprimand him for that), and your heart broke. You were alone, away from us, and you stayed away. And you spooled out further and further into your aloneness until it led you onto a narrow road at dusk and made you go faster and faster until you sailed with your headlights shining through the trees. We never came together with our broken hearts.

But that isn't how to say it, is it? You know what I'm talking about. You were here. My heart broke. I am heartbroken, brokenhearted—it sounds stupid, insufficient. But there aren't any adequate words. There's not a word in any language that equals the dread I feel in the morning at the prospects of the day. I wake most days to the sound of Conor turning on the television, and I look at the clock and it says 9:00, 10:00, 10:30, and I wonder how Conor has kept quiet for hours, and a blackness settles over me at the thought of getting out of bed, making Conor's breakfast, picking out his clothes, cleaning the kitchen, checking the mail, and my head and my arms and my legs are like heavy stones. How am I supposed to vacuum the rug, answer a phone call? Half of my family is gone.

Conor thought it best to bury Jim. He is familiar with the ritual, after all, having been through it twice so recently. The simple preparations exhausted me. We found an old shoe box in Ryan's closet (you never had to stay here with the memories, learn how they hide in places like shoe boxes), and I got the shovel from the garage and a pair of gardening gloves, because I didn't want to touch the body with my hands. Conor shadowed me, his dark eyes watching my every move. When he saw I was headed to the street, he stopped. "It needs some words," he said. An epitaph. And so, my arms feeling heavier and heavier, my legs moving under me as if they pushed through waves, I returned to the house, Conor right behind me, and I broke a yardstick in half and found a piece of nylon rope and a black marker in the junk drawer. When I picked up Jim (Conor standing there over me with his hands on his hips like a man, the look on his face one of what I would call icy determination, there in the hot July sun), there was a sticky sound, and as I placed the body carefully in the shoe box I noticed that one of Jim's black eyes had clung to the pavement. And I'm sorry—it made me think of you, how they'd found you smashed in the car.

It was Ryan who kept up the game you invented, you remember? When you got home from work, Conor would rush to the kitchen and ask you, "What did Jim say?" And at first you would just stare at Conor as if he had suddenly appeared from thin air, a smiling little brown-haired apparition, or as if you couldn't recall his name. "What did Jim say?" And you would say you hadn't seen him. What would it have cost you to answer that question, to pretend? Maybe too much. I'm not blaming you.

So Ryan played the game you wouldn't play. We were all there in the living room one morning (except you, you remember), and Ryan was feeling better than usual, was even pacing around the room the way he used to. Conor was looking for

Jim out the window, and finally saw him bounding across the street from the neighbor's yard. We all gathered to watch him scamper up the pine tree, his tiny stub twitching. Ryan seemed to be thinking about something, and I was feeling that hard pain that always came with seeing how skinny he had gotten. "Jim says winter's a hard time," he said. "He could use something to eat." And so a few minutes later there was Conor in his blue coat, squatting beneath the pine tree with a handful of cereal while Jim chattered at him from the tree. The first few times he had to leave the cereal and come inside before Jim would take the bait, but soon he could stand in the driveway, then the lawn, and then if he stayed very still, Jim would come right up to his feet. "Jim says he wants to eat from your hand," Ryan said one day, and he and I watched while Conor held his hand out with the cereal, and Jim approached, skittered away, approached again and ate. And Ryan smiled as if he'd accomplished it himself. And he had, in a way. Ryan made Jim a part of our family. First thing every morning—Conor still yawning his sleep away while he spotted Jim out in the yard, Ryan usually not up yet, but soon joining us and situating himself there on the couch—"What does Jim say?" Conor would ask.

"Jim says it's fun to be a squirrel, he doesn't have to go to work." "Jim says thank God we're up finally, it's his breakfast time." "Jim says when he grows up, he wants to be a kangaroo." When there were arguments, Jim took Ryan's side: "Jim says shut up and quit humming, Conor, you're driving him insane." And more practical things: "Jim says wash your hands when you're through feeding him." "Jim says don't forget to drink your orange juice." Jim began talking at all times of the day. "Jim says you can have a piece of candy if you try those peas." "Jim says before you go to bed to brush your teeth."

And then Conor asked one morning, "What does Jim say?" and Ryan didn't answer immediately. It was one of his bad days, I could tell. His face was flushed and his eyes looked weak and I could see his heart beat through his T-shirt where he lay there on the pillows. He drew a breath as if he would say something, then stopped, and a sad smile took shape on his face. And what he said then was something you used to say, something you learned from your mother back in your Idaho childhood, that you said to Ryan and Conor first thing in the morning back in the days when there still seemed like possibilities in life and no one in our house was dying. "Rise and shine," Ryan said, and I could see him grit his teeth. "Rise and shine, Jim says."

And my heart broke right then and never got put back together. I felt it break apart and come up into my throat, and I went from them quickly and locked myself in the bedroom and cried.

That night in bed I was still crying, hadn't stopped all day except when I had to, when I was with Ryan. I lay in the dark and cried, remember, and at first you tried to comfort me. I could hear you talking to me softly though I wasn't listening to what you said, and you held me tight in your arms, pressing my back to you. But I kept crying, and somewhere in my crying I felt your words stop and your body loosen, and then I was cold because you had turned away from me. I don't think you ever held me again.

Jim stopped talking on the day you died. I was cleaning the kitchen, I remember, when it occurred to me that you'd been gone a long time. It had been a sunny afternoon when you pulled out of the driveway, and now the streetlights had winked on. I was scrubbing a skillet. I was going to put it in the rack, take off the dishwashing gloves, unwrap the fresh salmon, and start making supper. But I stopped. I sat down at the table, and I quit my constant worrying about Ryan and began to worry about you. And you were already dead by then, I feel certain. You died while I was washing the dishes.

But I didn't know that, and so I worried first that you had gone back to the office, and I thought about why you had decided to leave us so alone, Ryan and Conor and me, and why you had decided that you and I should go to pieces separately instead of going to pieces together, and why we never talked about it. And so I decided to call you at the office and ask you that question, but you weren't there. I worried for a while that you might have found someone else, that you had left me for some graduate student, maybe, and were never coming back. But then I knew you were past the point at which you would find something like that appealing. And so there in the bright kitchen with it so dark outside my thoughts turned darker. I won't say that I knew, because I didn't, but it became a matter of trying to convince myself that what had actually happened hadn't. And I was scared. I forgot for a long time about Conor and Ryan, and when I remembered I found Conor asleep in his bed with his clothes on and the light on and his toys spread out around him, and I turned off the lights and went out to the living room to find Ryan lying in the dark on the couch, propped up on the pillows just how I'd left him, looking out the window, crying without making any sound. And we waited together. And I don't remember, exactly, but I don't think I told him any lies. I don't think I told him that everything would be all right or that he shouldn't worry or that you would be home soon. I sat on the edge of the couch and looked out the window with him at the dark street and held his hand until the phone rang and there was news of you.

When you died, Ryan's heart broke, but I didn't know it at first. There were too many people—your mother and your father and your sister—and the shock was still too new. I dragged myself through the days, and it seemed that everyone else did everything, and the only time I was aware of anything was when I lay in bed at night with Ryan (it was then that I started sleeping in the bed with him), and then I was only aware of his breathing, of his pain, as if it were part of my dreams.

But it was only after everyone was gone and I realized that Jim had stopped talking, that Conor went out every morning to feed Jim on his own while no one else paid attention, that I knew Ryan's heart had broken, too. He spent his time in his bed, and he got worse. There was a night when I knew he was dying, when I could feel something different in his breathing. And in the morning he was still breathing, but I couldn't wake him up. And I didn't want Conor to know, to see, so I took him to the kitchen and boiled water for his oatmeal, and when I went back to Ryan he had stopped breathing. Didn't you know that he would know why you died? Couldn't you have stood it a little longer? But I'm making assumptions I have no grounds for.

We buried Jim in the backyard, in the far corner by the fence, under the tulip tree. I dug the hole in the red earth, put the lid on the shoe box, put the shoe box in. I covered it up. I planted one half of the yardstick in the ground, tied the other half in a cross with the nylon rope. "What should it say?" I asked, and I felt I knew what Conor would ask then—"What does *Jim* say?" But he didn't say that. He didn't say anything and I didn't say anything and maybe because there weren't any people this time, none of the distraction of preachers and mourners, we just stood and let this death sink in. "Jim died," Conor said after a while. "Only a little squirrel." And so I got down on my knees and wrote that with the marker, the first part across, the second part down. And we stood there then, Conor and me.

Let me tell you about Conor. You know that he starts first grade in the fall. Unlike Ryan at that age, he can't read and he can't add or subtract and in fact he doesn't know his alphabet or his numbers very well at all. Sometimes I have trouble remembering who he is and where he came from. It seems to me often that he's a child who conjured himself. He doesn't talk much, and when he does it's usually about practical matters—"I want some juice, please." He rarely mentions you anymore, but he sometimes talks about Ryan. His memories of Ryan are deeply ingrained, and they are different from my memories. He and Ryan found a snake in the yard. He crashed on his scooter and "broke his neck" and Ryan fixed it. There's an old grievance concerning who punched whom on a particular occasion. Do you remember any of these things? I sometimes don't remember anything, I sometimes don't even remember that Conor is still here. I remember Ryan, and, to a lesser extent, you. Conor is sometimes just a sound to me: the sound of the television, the sound of his feet in the hall, the sound of the basketball as he bounces it up and down the driveway. The only time I really see him is when he goes out to feed Jim in the morning, when

I watch him from the window. I see him talk to Jim. But he won't do that tomorrow.

And me? I wake up each day, though it's doubtful I will ever rise and shine.

And here's what I want to know from you, what I would like you to tell me. I'll never know about you driving up that road. I'll never know where you thought you were going so fast. But what I would like you to tell me is something about that last moment—not the thoughts going through your head, not whether that failed turn was a decision or a surprise, but whether in that last moment when the wheels left the road, when you were released into the air for an instant, you felt light, you felt free?

I rubbed the dirt off my knees. I started back to the house. It was hot outside, and I was so tired. But Conor didn't follow me. He was still standing at Jim's grave. I went back to him, and I tried to think of what to say. "Maybe it's all right," I said. "Maybe Jim is in a better place." But Conor kept standing there. I thought of what you might say. I thought of what Ryan would say. "We can leave now, Conor," I said. "Jim says it's OK."

And then he turned and looked at me. His face was red and streaked with dirt and sweat, his hair matted to his forehead and hanging down into one eye. He had a scrape on his nose and scabs on both knees and his shirt was on inside out, and he had taken off his sandals somewhere. In that moment I knew that I should hold him tight and tell him it was all right to cry, and I knew that I should want someone to hold me and tell me the same thing, but it seemed as impossible as making your car not miss that turn, as making Ryan not stop breathing.

But Conor seemed to read my mind. His mouth stayed in an even line and his eyes stayed squinted at the sun, but he held his arms out suddenly, his fingers flapping like little wings. "Carry me," he said.

I looked at him. I looked at Jim's grave. "It's just up to the house, Conor," I said. "It's nothing."

He held his arms out. "Momma," he said. "*Carry me.*"

# Guests

This is when we were working swing shift at the Toulouse Hotel in the French Quarter, Beebo and me, way before management demoted us to the parking garage, back when we still had jobs in the lobby, when we were still considered responsible and presentable based on our status as recent college graduates, before they figured out we really didn't give a shit and would just as soon as not pack our bags and head back to Idaho where we came from, which is exactly what we did, eventually.

I was the concierge and Beebo was the desk clerk. That meant I sat at my little table with all my brochures for swamp tours and plantation tours and city tours and restaurants, and Beebo stood behind the marble counter where the guests checked in. It was summer, the slow season in New Orleans, and there wasn't much to do but look at each other. They made us wear these forest green jackets with beige collars and it was hard not to giggle constantly. We worked with Carlos the bellman, this kid from Honduras who never giggled about anything, at least not until we taught him to later on, as part of his American education I guess you could say.

So there were me and Beebo and Carlos, each in our respective place, looking at one another, when a limousine pulled up out front. This fact, the black limousine at the curb, the driver emerging and hustling around to open the rear door, wasn't of much importance, except possibly to Carlos, because people arriving in limos tended to tip a little better than the families who pulled in after picking up summer discount fliers at the rest stops on the interstate. But it made no difference to me, since folks who rode in limos tended not to be much interested in swamp tours and riverboat rides, which meant no ticket sales commissions. And to Beebo a limousine meant nothing more than a pain in the ass, because guests who arrived in them usually returned to the desk with complaints soon after check-in.

The driver opened the door and a duck-shaped woman emerged, wearing jeans and a T-shirt—not at all what we'd expected. Her companion, though, sliding across the seat now with a show of thigh underneath a white skirt, was something to see. She got out and brushed herself off and shouldered a purse and held out a bill discreetly to the driver before he'd even gotten the bags to the curb.

"A ten-spot, at least," Carlos said. He had a limited knowledge of the American idiom, except when it came to money, where he had mastered a variety of terms. Beebo's project was to introduce Carlos to the language and culture through the medium of song lyrics, a plan that seemed to be working well. Earlier that afternoon, while he hustled some bags onto the elevator, I'd heard Carlos singing, "If the boys they want to fight, you better be letting them." Sound advice, for sure.

Carlos went out and loaded up the bags and followed our guests into the lobby. I got a good look at the woman in the white skirt while she went through check-in with Beebo. About eight or ten years older than we were, I was guessing. She was slender in an athletic way. Her hair was brown and curly and a little blonde around the edges and she had a rich tan and her skin looked lightly freckled. She had a warm smile and a nice laugh and I liked the way she stood so loosely and casually, one sandaled foot behind the other. In short, I was spinning quickly into that fantasy life I sometimes spun into there in the hotel lobby, three thousand miles from home and ripe for dreaming. This had happened with the sorority girls who came to town over spring break, it had happened with the young professional women who gathered in the hotel bar on weekday afternoons, it had happened with the wives of big-shot businessmen in town for conferences at the Hilton, who tipped five bucks just for hailing them a cab. Nothing ever came of it. I was handsome enough, and young enough, but I worked in a hotel lobby where they dressed me funny, and I was too painfully aware of the situation. Back in Idaho, I could have waded right into the deep water, but not here. The women in the Toulouse Hotel knew poverty and social gracelessness when they saw it, and they weren't in the market for either. Thus my mumbling, thus my averted glances, through which I sometimes caught something a little sad in the faces of these spoiled girls and stylish women, a sort of unbreathed sigh for what could have been in my case, if I had learned long ago to play by rules that I never knew existed.

But Beebo, who didn't think of such things, plowed straight ahead, and for all the rebuffs he suffered there was the sweet compensation of the few victories—like the coed from Charleston back in March, the wife of the TV producer in May. He performed this kind of Cary Grant/Charlie Chaplin shtick—a line of patter smooth as cream combined with clownish antics. I was starting to hate him already on this latest occasion, with his *Welcome ladies I'm Brian but you can call me Beebo and let me say what a treat it is to have you here and I know I speak on behalf of the rest of our staff as well Dave who you see there at the concierge desk and Carlos who assisted you so adeptly with your luggage when I say that we will do anything* anything *in our power to make your stay here at the Toulouse Hotel as delightful as you dreamed it might be when you were back home in let's see La Jolla California it says on your reservation a beautiful place I hear*, when the phone rang.

I knew what was coming. Beebo was about to do this thing where he pretended to walk face-first into the closed door to the back room where the phone was, using his foot to hit the door at the bottom and make the sound of his face supposedly receiving a good smack. Then he would cover his nose with both hands and pretend he was in pain. The women at the desk would gasp. Then Beebo would uncover his nose and smile. The women would laugh. Beebo would go answer the phone. He did it, the door-smacking thing. They gasped. He smiled. They laughed. He answered the phone. I was about as depressed as I'd ever been in my life. Beebo had been pulling this same stunt since our freshman year in high school, and I could never believe how it made adult human beings laugh. I was sure no one would laugh if I tried it. But there was something about Beebo you had to like, for some reason. He had a certain charm, I guess. I hung around with him because we'd been best friends since we were ten.

Beebo finished with the phone call and came back and checked the reservation again and handed the guests the key to room 312 and told them Carlos would take them up in the elevator. I saw Carlos's face fall. Room 312 was tucked into a gloomy corner next to the ice machine, which made a lot of noise, and there was a stain on the carpet, and you couldn't see the courtyard from there, either. Everything about room 312 suggested bad tips. Beebo saw Carlos, too, and with his typical dramatic flair and brazen disregard for hotel policy he swept the key back from the desktop, plopped it in the drawer, drew out another one, and said, "Room 418. You'll like it. Our friend Carlos will show the way."

Carlos and I stood there with our mouths open, like mutes performing a chorus—and if we *had* been performing a chorus, these are the words we would have chanted: *Room 418 is the presidential suite. Room 418 goes for a thousand dollars a night. The last person to stay in room 418, a couple of months back, was Nicole Kidman. You never, never, never upgrade guests to room 418.*

Carlos looked shaky as he wheeled the bell cart to the elevator. Beebo grinned and winked. On the way past, the woman in the white skirt paused at my desk and ran her hand over a brochure. She looked at me and smiled. Her eyes were a deep green with flecks of gold. I remembered them that night lying in bed, with Beebo across the room there snoring in his sleeping bag.

~つC~

Her name was Priscilla Burke. I'd perused her registration slip, learned that she would check out on Wednesday. I'd monitored her phone calls, the blinking red light on the switchboard. I'd seen her having drinks in the courtyard. I'd watched her come and go. Click, click went her shoes across the lobby's parquet floor, going and coming, coming and going, and every time she came or went she smiled at me but never said a word.

On Sunday, their third day in the hotel, she and her friend stopped at the desk to talk to Beebo. They were wondering, politely, why there hadn't been any maid service in room 418. I was across the lobby talking to Mario, the maintenance man. He was from Venezuela. He liked to tell dirty jokes and he sweated profusely and he was a regular guy through and through. I liked Mario. Right then, he was watching Priscilla Burke while Beebo explained to her that, well, technically, they weren't *in* room 418, if she understood his meaning, they were in room 312, but he could procure some towels and supplies from housekeeping, and if they liked he could come up and make the beds himself, and oh no no, they objected, that wasn't necessary, and thank you thank you, they loved the room, it was like a palace. Beebo stood at attention behind the desk, like a dashing cavalier. Mario whispered to me what I knew he would: "We start the pool with that one, heh?" He poked one of his big fingers in my chest. It was a habit he had. "You, me, Carlos, Beebo, heh?" Mario was a betting man, and "the pool" was his way to combine betting with his other interest, sex. We were each supposed to ante up five bucks, and the one of us who slept with the guest in question took the pot. Nobody ever won, except Beebo that time with the TV producer's wife. After the Nicole Kidman pool failed to turn up a winner, we quit bothering to put the money in, even, so ridiculous did the whole thing seem.

"Sure, Mario," I said. "Crank up the pool." Right then, Priscilla Burke smiled at me on her way out of the lobby, like she always did.

Mario raised his eyebrows. He poked his finger in my chest again. "Maybe you win this time," he said.

∼ᗡᢕ

So then it was Monday night. That meant we got free food from the owner of the Maison Rouge across the street, in exchange for our recommendations. Usually Carlos went to pick it up, but he was waiting on an airport cab. When I passed him on the sidewalk, he sang softly, more or less to himself, "They are the egg man, I the walrus, goo goo gajoob."

Inside the restaurant I sat on the little chair by the entrance, where I wouldn't get in the customers' way. I'd been sitting there a while. I figured the food would be ready soon. Priscilla Burke and her friend walked in. Priscilla Burke was wearing some kind of light summer dress that came to just above the knee. I don't know what her friend was wearing. I hoped to God they wouldn't see me, but they did. I watched, horrified, as Priscilla Burke approached me. I'd never felt stupider in my forest green coat. They made us wear the fucking things even in summer, even when it was ninety-five degrees.

"You're David, right?"

David, not Dave, she'd said. "Yes."

"From the hotel," she said.

"Yes."

"You're the one who sells the tours?"

"Yes. Swamp tours, city tours, plantation tours, riverboat cruises. Yes."

"Plantations," she said. "We'd like to see one." She looked over at her friend, who nodded eagerly, as if she were even more anxious than Priscilla Burke to do whatever Priscilla Burke wanted to do. It struck me that this friend played the role of me to Priscilla Burke's Beebo. It hadn't been that way in Idaho, but it was that way in New Orleans, for some reason. "Let me start over," she said. Apparently some time had passed. Apparently I wasn't doing very well with my end of the conversation. "I'm Cilla," Priscilla Burke said to me. "This is Becky."

"Hi, Cilla," I said. "Hi, Becky."

"Do you have a car?" Priscilla Burke said.

"Me?" I said. "Yes. No. I have a truck."

"Do you ever take a day off, David?" she said.

"Yes," I said. "Tomorrow."

She smiled at me. "We were hoping you would take us to see a plantation."

"Yes," I said. "I would."

～つC～

In the morning I shaved more carefully than usual and put on my best pair of jeans and a collared shirt. I looked at myself in the bathroom mirror. As I walked out the door, Beebo watched me from his sleeping bag. He got the sleeping bag because I'd come to New Orleans first. It was my apartment, technically. "Chop chop," Beebo said. "Make haste, Jeeves."

I waited for them in the lobby, talking to the day crew. The day crew wanted to know what I was doing there, so I told them. They were impressed. They had been monitoring Priscilla Burke, too. In a few minutes she appeared in the lobby, by herself, wearing a sleeveless blouse and a tight skirt. "Becky decided not to come," she said. "It's just you and me." She reached out her hand and touched the collar of my shirt. "You look nice, David," she said.

When we were out the door, I heard a low hooting sound from inside the lobby, followed by laughter. Priscilla Burke took my hand and squeezed it, looking straight ahead.

By the time we'd crossed the river on I-310, I'd heard most of her life story. There was a husband back in La Jolla. An alcoholic, the husband, unemployed. They were high school sweethearts but had drifted apart over the years. It was a tolerable situation, though, what with the beach house and all. She was a jewelry designer. I wasn't good at noticing stuff like that—jewelry. If I had been, I would have noticed earlier the rings and necklace and bracelet, the emeralds and sapphires and whatever they were. The necklace alone, a kind of delicate gold fishnet thing with stones dotted all over it like raindrops, must have cost twelve million bucks. Her designs sold in exclusive stores along the West Coast and the Pacific Rim and Asia. She'd traveled all around the world, but she'd never been to New Orleans. Now she was here.

Then it was my turn. We drove along the River Road, Highway 18. There were sugar cane fields and oil refineries and mobile homes and suburban developments and the levee always to our right, people walking along it, doing whatever it was they did in southern Louisiana on insufferably hot days like that one. Priscilla Burke was folded neatly into my passenger seat, her skirt halfway up her thigh, her tan legs crossed, her eyes as green as the emeralds she wore. It was right about noon. If I was going to talk, I needed a drink. There was a little roadside joint a few miles from Vacherie, and I pulled in, the truck tires crunching over the white shells they used for gravel around New Orleans. We drank Dixie beer in sweat-beaded glasses and played pool, which she turned out to be pretty good at. The old guys at the bar tried to offer her pointers, and she understood their accents better than I did. I told her about my four older brothers living back in my hometown and about my father who worked at the Chevrolet dealership and my mother who was a secretary at the junior high school. I told her I'd never been anywhere except college and New Orleans. I told her about Beebo and me. I told her how his father died in an accident at the sawmill when we were twelve. I told her about how we used to listen to his father's old country albums in his basement, and how we learned to play guitar. I told her how we wanted to start up a duo and play Lefty Frizzell and George Jones. We did that, too, started up the duo, before we left New Orleans. We played in every dive that would take us.

But that hadn't happened yet. Right then I was pretty much occupied with Priscilla Burke and how she moved around the pool table and how she bummed cigarettes off the old guys at the bar and how she seemed to get along with everyone so easily, and how she'd told me she was thirty-five years old, and how I didn't care. We had a good time at that bar outside Vacherie.

From there it was just a few miles to Oak Alley Plantation. I had a pretty strong buzz going. When we got back in the truck

Priscilla Burke sat in this kind of lotus position with her legs crossed, her skirt riding up pretty high, her hands in her lap with the palms upturned and her index fingers and thumbs held together. I guess I looked confused. "I'm centering," she said. "It'll take just a minute." Soon she was done centering and she said, "You know why I wanted you to take me here, don't you?"

I looked over at her and she was staring at me with those green eyes. I said something about being the concierge and knowing about the plantations.

"No," she said. "Is that really what you think?"

I told her that was really what I thought, insofar as I thought anything.

"What did you think that moment we first looked at each other, David, in the hotel lobby?"

I told her I'd thought she had the prettiest eyes I'd ever seen in my life.

She said that was the wrong answer, a result of my consciousness being unformed. She said that, at that moment, we'd looked into each other's souls. She said that what I thought of as her physical beauty was actually a spiritual beauty, and that she'd recognized the same thing in me, though the beauty in my soul was still in its formative stages. "It's your aura," she said.

"My aura," I said.

"Your aura," she said. "Yes. Not that I could see it. I don't believe that the aura is visible. I believe that those people who 'see' auras are deluded. But I can sense an aura's presence, and I sensed yours."

I said, "Oh."

"You're a Sagittarius, aren't you?"

"No."

She guessed about six other signs. Then she got the right one, Taurus.

"Taurus," she said. "Hmm. Astrological signs are only one of the indicators." I wasn't supposed to be a Taurus, evidently. There were more important indicators, though. Before she'd left on this vacation, she had visited her spiritual advisor, and her spiritual advisor had told her that she would meet an important person from one of her past lives, and then her spiritual advisor had led her through a regression, and during the regression she had discovered that in a former life she had been an Indian maiden, living somewhere on the Great Plains, beating buffalo hides with sticks and whatnot. She had married an Indian brave and they had lived together happily for many years. Then he had been killed in a skirmish with the U.S. Cavalry. Despite the sad ending, this had been one of her best former lives, because she and her husband had been very much in love. "When our eyes met in the lobby, David," she said, "I knew that we had known each other before, that we had been intimate. I'm sure it's you whom I was supposed to meet."

It was kind of a lot to take in while turning the truck into the parking lot of Oak Alley Plantation, but that's where we were all of a sudden. She got out of the truck. She didn't act like anything unusual was going on. She looked at the long line of huge oaks leading to the plantation house. "It's gorgeous," she said. It was, but I was having a hard time concentrating. I took my time locking the doors and let her go on ahead of me. She looked great, but was maybe a little nuts. In Idaho, we had a natural suspicion of Californians, who were always moving to town and opening arts and crafts stores. To us, Californians were people who had lots of money and wore expensive jewelry and asked for your astrological sign and talked about auras. Well, so, Priscilla Burke.

By then she was hungry, so she bought me lunch at the restaurant, which was outrageously expensive, and we drank mint juleps, which weren't too bad. She didn't say anything else about our being soul mates, and I was starting to wonder if maybe there hadn't been an ironic intent, some kind of joke I was missing. After lunch we went to the gift shop and looked at the various gimcrackery, then I explained at the tour desk how I was the concierge of the Toulouse Hotel, and that got us a private tour with some old guy dressed like a cross between a Confederate cavalry officer and Colonel Sanders. He showed us around and told us about the architecture and the furnishings and explained how it wasn't really so bad being a slave there, what with it being such a nice place and all, inhabited over the years by so many kind and wonderful people. All this time Priscilla Burke had seemed normal, but when the guide showed us the plantation's prized possession, a photograph of a supposed ghost standing at one of the windows, she went a little nuts again, wanting to know the whole story in minute detail. The ghost was thought to be the daughter of the original owner. She'd received a cut on her leg while being chased by a drunken suitor, and the leg had developed gangrene and was subsequently amputated and then buried somewhere, so that they could dump the daughter in with it after she'd died, which they did. But no one knew where the grave was. But Priscilla Burke, no matter how much the guide swore otherwise, was sure that it must be an unmarked grave in the plantation cemetery, which was just across the River Road, which meant we had to go there.

The wrought-iron gate to the cemetery was locked, so we had to climb over. There were only about five graves, and one of them was the final resting place of a family pet. None of them belonged to the legless girl. Priscilla Burke was disappointed, and sat down under an oak tree in one corner of the cemetery. Even in the shade it was pretty hot, but the gnats and mosquitoes weren't too bad there. I sat down and we looked into each other's souls for a minute, I guess, and then Priscilla Burke took my face in her hands and kissed me, and then her hand was in my pants and when she was satisfied that all was in working order she got on her hands and knees there in the patchy grass, hiked her skirt up above her waist, pulled her panties down to her knees, and waited quietly. What was I to do? The whole thing took about three minutes, and I can say with some confidence that we both enjoyed ourselves. It was a most uncomplicated sexual encounter. I guessed that was how they did things in California.

When we got back to the hotel, Priscilla Burke kissed me again. She told me that she wanted me to come back that night and stay with her in the presidential suite. She told me she wanted me to pack my belongings in the truck, quit my job in the morning, and move to La Jolla. She would ride with me. She would pay for everything.

∽)C∽

So I was a little confused by the time I returned to the hotel that evening. I stood in the lobby, waiting to talk to Beebo. There was an older woman complaining to him about the flagpoles on the hotel façade. "All night they clank, while I'm trying to sleep," she said. "Clank, clank. Like that."

Beebo gave her a firm nod. "I understand, ma'am," he said. "The clanking of the flagpoles. I'll send someone out to stop that wind for you right away."

"Thank you," the woman said, and walked to the elevator. All you could do was shake your head. I motioned Beebo to come outside. Mario was across the lobby screwing in a light-bulb, and he'd be wondering whether I won the pool.

Out on the sidewalk Beebo lit a cigarette. "How'd it go?" he said.

"Bear with me on that one for a minute," I said. I stared across the street at the lighted windows of the Maison Rouge throwing a soft glow into the dusk, while I did a little center-ing. "It went OK," I said. "I took a married thirty-five-year-old woman out of town in my truck. I was drunk by 2:00 p.m. In a former life, I was an Indian brave, and she was my squaw. I have an unformed consciousness but an emerging aura, invis-ible to the naked eye. A Confederate officer showed us around a plantation. We went looking for a ghost without a leg, but we didn't find one. We had a quickie in a graveyard. I'm staying in the presidential suite tonight. My bags are packed because I might move to California in the morning."

Beebo flicked his cigarette away with his thumb and middle finger. It landed in the street and rolled slowly down toward the curb. "You definitely had a more interesting day than me," he said.

"I thought some advice might be in order," I told him. "I'm three thousand miles from home and odd things seem to hap-pen here and I'm a little bit confused."

Beebo nodded. "You like her?" he said.

"I like her fine. She's probably insane."

Beebo nodded again. "Why do you say that?" he said. "She sounds like a lot of fun. I'd do her in a heartbeat."

I said, "I think you're missing the point."

He puffed up his cheeks and blew out air and scratched the side of his head. I could hear the phone ringing inside, but he either didn't notice or didn't care. "OK," he said. "You want me to be serious."

"Yes," I said. "For a minute. Please."

"Go. Don't go. If you're worried about me, don't be. I'm fine either way. None of that's the problem."

"What's the problem, then?" I said.

"The problem, Dave," he said, and he looked at me, "is that you don't really want to be happy."

I thought about that for a second. "I do want to be happy," I said.

"You don't," he said. "You're only happy when you're knocking on the door of happiness, just imagining things. You don't really want to be let in, because it might not turn out to be what you expected. You just want to stand on the doormat and wipe your feet. You're a doormat dweller," he said. "Perpetually."

It was the longest character analysis I'd ever heard from Beebo. I was surprised. Sometimes you forgot about his father dying and how he'd probably had to think about some things. "That's not true," I said. "It's just that I tend to think about future happiness, and I don't see what Priscilla Burke has to do with my future happiness."

"Well, here's how that works," Beebo said. "At some point you have to start being happy *now*."

Carlos came out from the lobby. "I answer the phone," he said to Beebo. "Again the woman with the flags."

Beebo rolled his eyes and went back inside. I stood there with Carlos for a minute or two. Neither of us said anything. We watched the people coming in and out of the Maison Rouge and saw the delivery guy from St. Ann Deli ride by on his bicycle and we could hear the Dixieland jazz band start up at the bar down on the corner of Bourbon Street. An old bum with no shoes sat down on a grate up the block a ways, and I knew I'd give him a couple of bucks for food, even though I'd given the same bum money before and he had come back five minutes later with a beer. It was hotter than hell even with the sun going down, even without my green jacket, and there was something I loved about the whole place, the whole thing, about standing there with Carlos and not talking, just looking at the narrow streets of the Quarter and all the strange people, knowing it must have been just as strange to Carlos, this eighteen-year-old kid from Honduras who lived with his sister in Gentilly, as it was to me, and probably stranger. But I wondered whether I could ever be happy in a place like New Orleans or anywhere other than my Idaho hometown, where two or three of my brothers would be gathering now at the Tamarack Tavern for beers. It had been a long day, and I was tired, and I wanted to be at the Tamarack Tavern myself, pulling up a stool, maybe even having finished my dead-end job for the day just like my brothers and my father, maybe even having a wife and a couple of kids and a place to go home to, where I could sink into the same couch I sank into every night and count myself a failure in all the ordinary ways. Maybe that wasn't happiness, but maybe it was an unhappiness you could be comfortable with.

Carlos unfolded his tips from his pocket and started to count the bills. He was mouthing the words to a tune, but I couldn't tell what it was.

"Well," I said, "I'm off to spend the night in the presidential suite."

Carlos pulled a bill from the others and showed it to me. "I know," he said. "She tip me fifty big ones just for bring champagne to the room."

I walked off, gave the bum his two bucks, and made my way around the block to the parking garage, where I could sneak up the back stairwell to room 418.

~⌒~

I'd never seen room 418, but I'd heard stories. Without going into detail, I'll just say that it was very opulent and not the sort of place I thought I could get used to. Priscilla Burke and her friend Becky sat in what I guess you'd call the parlor working their way through a bottle of expensive champagne. There were two more on ice. Later, Carlos would be called on to bring another. It was a real wingding. I sat on this huge sofa with Priscilla Burke and she rested her hand on the back of my neck. It felt good, like I could go to sleep with it there. I don't remember much of the conversation. It wasn't about anything important. I remember Priscilla Burke told a story about some monastery on the coast of Italy where they let guests stay for free. She'd gone there when she was young and didn't have much money. I didn't figure I'd ever see the place, so her description of the rocky cliffs and ancient buildings didn't mean that much to me.

Then it was getting late and Priscilla Burke went to run a bath and she told me to join her in a few minutes. I sat there with Becky. She floated her hand out above her head and made this curlicue gesture, like she was the queen of somewhere. "I believe I shall retire for the evening," she said.

"OK," I said.

She sat there looking at me. I felt like I was getting looked at a lot that day. "Cilla feels pretty strongly about you," she said.

"Right," I said. "Sure. I knew that." I was nodding my head vigorously and clasping my hands tight in front of me, like I was acknowledging a gift I didn't deserve. "Why do you suppose that is, exactly?"

Becky shrugged. "She senses things about people."

"I'm very interested in that," I said. "I'm very interested. Because she certainly does seem to be an unusual person." I could hear the water running in the bath somewhere. I was hoping I could follow the sound. It was that big a place.

"You think she's crazy," Becky said. She was this dumpy woman sitting in a chair. She didn't look like someone who belonged in my life at age twenty-three. I had a hard time understanding why I was there in that ridiculous room with all the gold and the mirrors and the plush furnishings, talking to her.

"Oh, no, I wouldn't say that," I said. "I didn't think . . . *is* she?"

"Crazy like Donald Trump, maybe," she said. "Bill Gates. She's a genius. Do you know how much her designs sell for?"

"Right," I said. "How much?"

"Let me put it this way," she said. "She pays me a nice salary—an *extravagant* salary—just for being an assistant of sorts.

And her best friend. She's rich. She's generous. She's committed to the things and the people she believes in. You're lucky."

"Right," I said. "That's what I was thinking."

"So go," she said.

I went. I found the bathroom that Priscilla Burke happened to be in. It was huge. The tub was the size of a small pond. She was in the water up to her neck and she had her hair piled up on her head to keep it dry. What happened next was a lot like fantasies I'd had in the lobby.

∽つC∼

Then we put on the his-and-hers bathrobes in the closet and walked out the French doors onto what I guess you'd call the veranda. It was too big to be called a balcony. We stood there leaning on the wrought-iron railing and looking out at the Quarter. To our left were the neon lights and shifting crowds of Bourbon Street. Ahead of us were the steep old roofs of the Quarter and the spire of St. Louis Cathedral. To our right, far off, were the river and the boats passing slowly.

"You're not going with me, are you?" Priscilla Burke said.

"I don't know," I said. I didn't. I was liking her a lot better and she didn't seem so crazy. You couldn't help building up some hopes staring out over the roofs and the scattered lights of the French Quarter. It was like something you could imagine happening in your life, something that you might be able to rise to and keep on going, up and up.

"You don't say much, do you, David?" she said.

"I do," I said. "After a while."

"I know you do," she said. "You're not exactly in your element here, are you?"

"Maybe not," I said.

"Then I'll talk," she said. A breeze came up and loosened a few wisps of Priscilla Burke's hair, and I heard the flagpoles clanking and I thought of Beebo down in the lobby, and then I knew that his shift was over and he would be back home already, or out at the bars on Chartres Street. "This seems sudden. But that's how things happen. I don't know a lot about you and you don't know a lot about me. But I can sense this much, David—that you could come to California and we would be happy getting to know each other and we would stay happy for a long time."

I could see that. Maybe she was right. "How would it work?" I said. I was thinking of the husband, specifically.

"I'd rent you an apartment," she said. "I could help you get a job, if you wanted one. You wouldn't have to work if you didn't want to. And my marriage isn't an issue, believe me."

I didn't have any particular affection for work. That part sounded good. And I was young. I had a lot of years to play with. Here was the door being opened for me, like Beebo said. I was being invited into a life I couldn't have in Idaho and I couldn't have in New Orleans, either. But I kept not saying anything, kept not putting my arms around Priscilla Burke the way she wanted me to, maybe.

She leaned over the railing and looked down at the street, brushing one bare foot across the bricks of the veranda. She watched a mule pull a carriage of tourists toward the river. She hugged her arms across her chest, seemed to draw into herself.

I thought of the way her skin felt when we were in the bath, how you could tell she was older than the girls I'd been with. I had liked that feeling, found it calming and settling.

"If it makes you uncomfortable," she said, "please forget what I mentioned about knowing you in a former life." Her head was down and I saw that her eyes were closed. "That's my own belief, and it's not what's important," she said. "This seems strange to you. But I'm older than you are, and I know things about people more quickly. It's like an interpersonal shorthand you learn after a while. You have a big heart, David, the kind I can attach myself to." I'd never been told that I had a big heart, but I was willing to consider the possibility, and I wondered if that might be why I had such a hard time with things. "I can't say anything to convince you, can I? The only thing I can say is that you'd just have to trust me." She turned and walked back to the French doors that opened into her bedroom. "Wait here," she said.

I did. While she was gone I stared out over the rooftops and thought about the two of us in my truck headed down I-10 toward Texas.

She came back carrying her wallet. She stood very close to me, her head almost on my shoulder. "There's one more thing," she said. She undid the clasp on the wallet and took out a photograph and handed it to me. I had to angle it to pick up the light from the bedroom window.

The photograph was of a boy in a wheelchair. It was taken in a beach hut, with the ocean in the background. The boy had curly brown hair like Priscilla Burke's, but that was the only similarity. His head was too large for his spindly limbs and he wore thick glasses and his mouth was open. "That's our son.

He's a wonderful boy. He's bright and sharp in his own way, but he'll never be able to take care of himself. He needs someone with him almost constantly." She took the picture from me and looked at it and smiled. "See his eyes?" she said, and she laughed a little. "He was excited that day." You couldn't see his eyes at all, unless you were his mother. "I'm sorry. I don't normally bring this up, but you should know. I don't want people to feel sorry for me." But I did feel sorry for her, for the way she handled the picture so carefully, for the way it made her smile.

She put her hand lightly on my chest inside the bathrobe. "That's it," she said. "Now you just have to decide." Then she disappeared inside the huge space of the presidential suite, preparing herself for bed. I went inside and lay down and waited for her. She was naked when she came back, and I looked at her in the light from the lamp, and then she clicked off the light and got in bed, and she curled up next to me and fell asleep.

I slept off and on through the night, and when I wasn't sleeping I thought in a dreamlike way about Priscilla Burke's husband and her son. I thought about how they were there now in the beach house in California, maybe sitting on the couch together watching TV, and how Priscilla Burke was there with me. I thought how I would live in California and how I would see Priscilla Burke every day but how I would probably never see her husband and her son, how I would be part of a separate life for her. And I thought about how she probably deserved a separate life like that, because her life wasn't what it seemed like on the surface, happy and carefree, but I couldn't work myself into the hazy pictures I formed in my head, couldn't find myself in the middle of her world where, for some reason, she wanted me to be. And yet I believed at the same time what she had told me—that we were two people who could have made each other happy. And it seemed to me in thinking about it, curled up there with my arm under her neck, that I could even see why she thought there had to be something more between us, in the future or the past, than that one day.

But I woke up in the morning and looked at her face on the pillow, and I slid my arm from under her neck and dressed quietly and walked out of room 418.

～ﾠC～

The next afternoon I was back at the concierge desk, where I would keep putting in my time until they exiled me and Beebo to the parking garage, and Priscilla Burke was on a plane. When we'd taken up our usual positions, wearing our green jackets same as always, Beebo handed me a letter Priscilla Burke had left for me at the desk. It was a much nicer letter than I deserved, considering. I read it out on the sidewalk, and I wrote her back later that night from a bar near the hotel—the first exchange of what would be many letters over the next few years. But she never came to New Orleans again, or to Idaho after I moved back home, and I never made it to La Jolla.

Just before we got off shift that night, I stepped outside to read the letter another time, under the flickering gas lamps at the hotel entrance. Carlos came out a minute later to join me, and I folded the letter and put it in my pocket. We stood there for a little while, watching some drunk wearing a football helmet stagger along the sidewalk past the Maison Rouge. It was the kind of thing you got used to seeing in New Orleans, and we didn't search for any explanation. It was just another slow night in the middle of the slow season.

"So you have a good time with her?" Carlos said.

That seemed a little bit personal to me, and I gave Carlos a sharp look, but he was watching the guy in the football helmet. Carlos had these sad, dark eyes that made it hard to be angry at him anyway. "Yeah," I said, "a pretty good time."

He smiled kind of vaguely. "You win the pool?" he asked. He was concerned about his five bucks, I thought.

"I suppose," I said. "But you don't have to pay me."

He shook his head. "No, I am thinking only." He glanced my way quickly, then looked down at the sidewalk. His lips moved a little, as if he were testing out words. "You like her pretty much?" he asked me, nudging at a cigarette butt with his shoe.

I thought about Priscilla Burke arriving at the airport in San Diego, going home to see her husband and her son, and I wondered if she was thinking of me. "Yeah," I said. "I guess so." But even as I saw Carlos slowly nod his head I knew that it didn't matter so much that I liked Priscilla Burke, who was perhaps, after all, in need of a little better centering. What mattered was how Priscilla Burke liked me, how she felt so certain of me, in a way that I was never certain about myself anymore. And I knew it was that gap in our thinking and feeling that had kept me from getting in the truck and driving to California. Priscilla Burke knew that everything would be all right and I was afraid that it wouldn't be, that I wouldn't be able to share in the feeling she had about me, that I would still be on the outside of the feeling looking in.

And here was Carlos, who wanted me to tell him about this feeling, apparently. His hands were in the pockets of his forest green jacket and he glanced shyly in my direction, wanting to ask something more, wanting to know something more about what it felt like to be with a woman like Priscilla Burke, whether I was happy, whether I had suffered any injury. But unlike Beebo, with his careless talk and his song lyrics, I wasn't someone Carlos could approach that easily, and I had come out as far as I was going to to meet him. He could feel the door closing between us. I offered him a tight smile and he offered one back, having learned by now to give what he got, and he turned back toward the hotel doors, mouthing the words to a song that he kept to himself.

And there I was at the end of my shift, standing beneath the gas lamps, looking at all the happy people in the warm light of the Maison Rouge, while the moon in its mysterious circuit ascended above the rooftops, slowly, surely, knowing right where it belonged at the end of that particular evening.

# *Ayudame*

Douglas "Deeder" Mumphrey was wakened from a dream of the record shop in Haight-Ashbury by his ten-year-old daughter, Grace, who was, surprisingly enough, standing by the side of the bed dressed and ready for school. It was Deeder's turn, not his wife's, to get Grace ready for her car-pool ride, that much seemed sure, based on the fact that Grace stood by his side of the bed, not Theresa's, and based on her serious and rather tired expression, which said several things to Deeder, such as "Dad's lazy," and "Dad's forgetful," and "Dad had too many beers last night," and "I had to make my own breakfast," all of which were true, more or less, not to say that the various truths contained in the expression didn't annoy the hell out of Deeder, because they did, because why the hell should a ten-year-old girl be right about so many things when he himself, Deeder, a forty-one-year-old man, was rarely right about anything.

Deeder glanced over at his wife, her hair in the band she wore to keep it out of her face while she slept, soft snores coming from her puffed-out lips, and he was reminded of the argument they'd had the night before, and he wondered how she could sometimes look like such a peaceful, easygoing person, and then he whispered "Sorry" to Grace and dragged himself out of bed, still smelling somewhere in the back of his head the incense he burned in his record store, the one he never had, back there in the Summer of Love when he was just born.

In the kitchen he brewed a pot of coffee and ran through a couple of spelling words with Grace to see if she was ready for her test, which she semi-was, not for lack of effort, but Grace wasn't much of a speller. *Rapture, censure, preacher, adventure*— three out of four. Her forte was personal grooming—he marveled now at the way she'd managed to pick out the blouse, the pants, the matching socks all by herself, the way she looked so *neat*, her straight blond hair brushed *just so*.

There was Mrs. Adkins, pulling into the drive. He waved out the window, hoping she couldn't see he was in his boxers. He made Grace give him a kiss on the cheek. "You stink, Dad," she said. He watched her set her pack carefully in the back of the Adkins' Aerostar, watched her climb in, smoothing her pant legs under her to keep them from wrinkling. Monterey Pop, the family's black Lab, was lying with his head on his paws over by the sofa, wagging his tail slightly. Deeder poured some more food in his bowl and watched him come over and eat.

The next order of business was to remember why he was still here at such a late hour, why he hadn't set the alarm, why he wasn't at work already, roofing the . . . what . . . the fourteenth house in the new development north of town. The month was October. Yesterday it had been unusually hot for eastern Washington, daytime high in the 70s. He'd worked shirtless all afternoon. His toe had hurt like shit in his boot, so he could barely walk by the end of the day—the ingrown toenail, that was it.

He had a doctor's appointment at 8:30, in forty-five minutes. Time for two cups of coffee, time to luxuriate a little. He could feel the toe throbbing, but it was worth it, no matter that his brother Marlin, the foreman, thought he was being a pussy. The motherfucker hurt. He deserved a couple extra hours of R&R today.

In the waiting room he got lost in the dream again, the vividness, the texture, it had felt very real this time. There was his record store, right there on the corner of Haight and Ashbury, in the same place he had dreamed it since he was a teenager. He was taking records out of a shipping box. Jefferson Airplane, Quicksilver Messenger Service, Big Brother and the Holding Company. He could feel the slick plastic wrap in his fingers. He didn't know, actually, whether records had plastic wrap in 1967, but they did in 1976, when he'd started buying records. What was he left with by then? Boston. Styx. A rip-off. A shame. He'd missed it all. The incense, the patchouli—he could practically smell it. Owsley was dropping by the store to deliver a hit of acid, the Dead's "Golden Road" was spinning on the turntable, he had hash pipes and rolling papers for sale, and there through the beaded doorway into the back room stood a girl with long brown hair swaying her hips suggestively while she studied the front cover of *Surrealistic Pillow*, and outside on the street thousands of flower children were tuning in and dropping out, and the Diggers were feeding the masses, and the sun shone down on the proceedings benevolently, a cloud or two passing in the marmalade sky. What a drag to wake up in 2008.

They called his name and he unglued himself from his seat and crossed the waiting room slightly hobbled, past the balding old lady thumbing through a copy of *Self*, past the chicken-

poxed kid battling his Game Boy, the mother busy sending a
text message, past the TV tuned to Fox News and the crash-
ing stock market, and a dark mood descended on him so hard
that it came out in a protracted groan, and he saw a reception-
ist glance up at him, probably wondering if he was a terminal
patient.

Then he sat on an examining table in the doctor's office
reading the posters about high cholesterol and heart disease,
prostate infections and STDs, healthy foods high in fiber,
warning signs of Alzheimer's, the facts about menopause, the
link between diabetes and obesity, and he read five times the
framed cross-stitch about how God might grant him the seren-
ity to accept the things he could not change. Finally he settled
for watching a beta darting up and down anxiously in what
looked like an oversized pickling jar. The doctor was a fifty-ish
man with a squat body and chubby pink hands, not the same
doctor he remembered from the last time he'd been in after he
slipped on wet shingles and fell off a roof and broke his arm.

This doctor got right to work, making Deeder take his boot
off and lie down on the examining table before he'd even said
hello. Yep, he told Deeder, that toe was infected all to hell, and
he got out some instruments and asked Deeder if he wanted an
injection for the pain, and added that most people didn't need
one. So of course Deeder didn't either. But then he wished he
would have, other people be damned. The pain was pretty considerable, if not downright excruciating, and although Deeder
didn't actually look he could feel blood and pus erupting from
the toe while the doctor gouged down into the meat to reach
the offending toenail, and to keep from shouting Deeder began
doing a kind of *doo doo doodle doo doo* thing with the open-

ing strains of "White Rabbit," rather softly, rather under his breath, or so he thought until the doctor, pressing hard into the infected toe so that Deeder began to knead the padding on the sides of the table, said, "That's a good one. One of the best."

Did he mean the toe? Did he mean the song? "What?" Deeder asked.

"I saw the Jefferson Airplane play January 14, 1967, at Golden Gate Park. They were terrific, I think. I don't remember much."

This announcement had a curious effect on Deeder. He was experiencing quite a bit of pain, and his arms were involuntarily reaching out now toward his foot, but the pain was getting confused with something else in his head, which was a date he had long since memorized, January 14, 1967, the Human Be-In at Golden Gate Park, Ginsberg and Leary and Grace Slick, everything right on the brim of the Summer of Love, simmering there in wait for the warmer days, when the world would burst open into the flowers and the sandals and the peasant skirts, and there was also the new work of recalibration going on, the redefining of this doctor, whom Deeder had taken to be a bit younger and a lot more stuffy, but who was now being transformed rapidly into a personal hero, and in the turmoil of this synaptic overload Deeder found himself saying, "Wait a second, wait a second, *stop*, for Christ's sake!"

The doctor stopped. He sniffed. He squeezed Deeder's toe with a piece of gauze. "Yes?" he asked.

The pain was gone instantly, and Deeder took a deep breath. "Can we just . . . hold on for a second?" he said.

"Certainly. I realize that it's painful. If you clip your toenails correctly, it won't happen again."

Deeder waved one hand back and forth, as if to dismiss the gruesome sight of his toenail and the subject of its proper care. "You were *at* the Human Be-In?" he asked. "You were, like, *at* the original Human Be-In?" He was looking at the same doctor, pudgy-faced, white-coated, bespectacled. Clearly this was an elaborate disguise.

"Yes," the doctor said. "You've heard of it?"

Deeder shook his head in bewilderment. Had he *heard* of it? "I should have been there," he said. "But I was just born."

"Ah, yes," the doctor said. "You're one of those. I find that people of your generation either highly romanticize or unfairly vilify that particular time in our history. I'm not sure which is worse."

Deeder stared at him, narrowing his eyes.

"Can we get back to your toe now?" the doctor asked. He turned an instrument around and around in his hand.

"Yeah, sure," Deeder said, and the doctor went for the toe again, as if the toe were the most important thing going on here. "But wait, wait, wait . . ." Deeder said, waving his hand again.

The doctor sighed—almost, but not quite, inaudibly. "You want to hear about it," he said.

"Yes," Deeder said. "Yes."

The doctor pushed up his sleeve and looked at his watch. "I've got time for the short version," he said. "Not the long one."

"OK," Deeder said hopefully. "The short version, then."

The doctor pushed back the folds of his coat and put his hands in his pockets and leaned against the sink. "I finished college at the University of Washington in the summer of

1966. I had been involved in the Civil Rights movement, but it had progressed far enough by then that we weren't much help anymore. Down South they were going after blacks with fire hoses and attack dogs, much more provocative stuff than some white kids sitting around singing "Kumbaya." So things turned to Vietnam. Everybody was going down to California. I went. It was exhilarating at first. There was a camaraderie, a feeling that everyone was involved in some sort of profound change. You knew famous people. You hung out at their apartments. You did drugs. You met interesting women. Right around the time of the Be-In it was probably best—it felt revolutionary. The country was watching us. People were appalled or inspired, depending, but they paid attention either way. Then it got to be too much. People poured in. Some of them were serious, some of them weren't. It turned into a zoo. Runaways, prostitutes, media types, tourists with cameras. The war was escalating, and I was afraid I'd get drafted, so I went back to Seattle to attend medical school. By the time I left, I was glad to get out. People were strung out and hungry and dirty and depressed. The predominant smell was urine." The doctor leaned away from the sink and took his hands from his pockets, twirling the dastardly instrument again. "That's it. End of story."

Driving to the job site, Deeder was still in a bit of a whirl. He'd never actually met anyone who was in Haight-Ashbury during the Summer of Love. His wife's aunt had been a hippie down in California then, but she was a loon. All of her stories were about the men she dated at the time, nothing interesting. The doctor had been there for the good stuff. His cynicism was a bit deflating, sure, but Deeder attributed it to the doctor's current lifestyle—having sold out long ago, there was nothing left for him now but bitterness. Deeder had been tempted to invite him outside for a spliff, the makings of which he had in his glove box, but the mood hadn't been right. He'd have to save the story and the spliff for Rudy, the Mexican he shared most of his time on the roof with.

And soon that was where he was, on the roof with Rudy in the warm sunshine, his toe free of pain. His brother Marlin was hanging around today to keep an eye on things, which meant he and Rudy couldn't go on the back side of the roof away from the road and torch one up, plus there were the two Mexicans laying out frames for the sidewalk, so it probably wouldn't have been a good idea anyway. They'd have to wait until lunch, which, fortunately, due to his visit to the doctor's office, was only a couple hours away. It was shaping up to be a good day—Marlin hadn't even given him shit about his toe yet.

"So the doctor he was a hippie?" Rudy said. He was nailing down shingles methodically but quickly, like always, not looking up but listening with interest to what Deeder said. Rudy was the only one of the Mexicans Deeder could talk to. His English was good and he was friendly and he knew, surprisingly, a hell of a lot about the '60s and rock and roll.

"No," Deeder said. "He was a guy who used to be a hippie but sold out to the man. That's my point. That's why he was so negative about everything."

"Maybe, maybe not," Rudy said. "Maybe he just like things better nowadays."

Deeder humphed at the suggestion. "Who could like things better nowadays? You're the one who's always talking about how fucked up everything is." In addition to music, Rudy had a passion for politics. His principal concern, of course, was

with immigration laws, but he could range on any given day—
whether on the roof or at the local bar after work—from immigration to the economy to the Middle East conflicts to human-
rights abuses in sub-Saharan Africa. Deeder had picked up a
lot of talking points, actually, from Rudy.

"Some things better, some things worse," Rudy said.
"Depends on your perspective."

Deeder glanced around to see if Marlin was in the vicinity,
and when it turned out that he wasn't, Deeder shifted to his
rear end, put his feet out in front of him, and lit up a smoke.
An unscheduled break seemed to be in order. "What's better?"
he said. "Tell me." Deeder looked out over the development,
the trees cleared for acres and acres, the thirteen already-
constructed homes standing naked along the empty cul-de-sac.
Deeder couldn't believe they were actually still building the
damn things. Was the developer crazy? Could anybody afford
to buy one of these houses anymore? And why would anyone
in his right mind buy one, anyway? What a way to live. The
only thing within walking distance was the Super Wal-Mart
over there along the frontage road, and it was the only thing to
look at, too, if you didn't count the mountains in the distance,
which after all never changed. Deeder thought dreamily of his
record store.

"In the Summer of Love," Rudy said, "would I be up here
working on the roof with you, making the same amount of
money?"

Rudy didn't make the same amount of money as Deeder—
after all, Deeder was, for better or worse, the foreman's brother,
and he was a citizen of the United States—but Marlin had
warned him many times that Rudy didn't need to know that.

"OK," Deeder said. "Muy bien, amigo." In addition to making Deeder more politically savvy, Rudy was trying to make him bilingual. Deeder knew most of his colors and his numbers up to twenty and the names for various work-related objects—*casa* meant house and *tejado* meant roof and *martillo* meant hammer and *clavo* meant nail. Music was *musica*. Rock and roll was just *rock and roll*. "You've got a point there, Rudy. But you cover it well with your hair."

Rudy rubbed his head and smiled to show he understood the joke. This was Deeder's contribution to Rudy's education—an assortment of colloquial phrases. *What am I—wood? Were you born in a barn?* Deeder's favorite moment in recent memory came when Marlin had tried to convince Rudy that it was OK to go without a curbing system on a custom skylight for a low-pitch roof—an obvious attempt to cut corners because they didn't have the right materials on hand. Rudy scowled and rubbed his chin. "Marlin, you do not know shit from Shinola," he said. He would have gotten fired if Deeder hadn't convinced Marlin that Rudy didn't understand it was an insult. That plus the fact that Rudy was the most reliable worker on the crew.

Rudy had finished a row of shingles butting up against a plumbing vent and Deeder passed him over a flange. "But you're right," Rudy said. "In the '60s, the government of America it sucked. But the people did important things. They made the government do things different in Vietnam and here in U.S. They should be proud. And there was excellent music—Dylan, Doors, Hendrix, Carlos Santana." Rudy's overestimation of Carlos Santana was a subject of constant debate. Rudy wanted to place him in the first order of the pantheon, while Deeder insisted he belonged in a second tier with, say, Canned

Heat or Little Feat. At the moment Deeder decided to let it slide. "The thing to understand is that the grass is not always so green as you think."

"I guess," Deeder said. He snubbed his cigarette out and tossed it off the roof. "But I listen to that music and I think about the stuff that was going on and I imagine having my little record shop and I think, Jesus Christ, man, I missed the fucking boat."

Rudy stood up and turned his face toward the sun for a moment. It felt good on the roof in the warm weather and Deeder just sat there, not ready yet to pick up the shingles and the roofing nails. "What about Theresa and Grace?" Rudy asked.

"Oh, I'm not saying that," Deeder said. "Don't get me wrong. I wouldn't change a thing in the long run. I'm just saying I missed out. Man, I'd have been there dropping acid and wearing my tie-dyed shirt and getting teargassed by the cops, the whole fucking nine yards. I'd have been there for all of it, believe you me." He felt a surge of anger. "That doctor was a dumbass. That doctor was full of shit. What a fucking ingrate."

Rudy laughed. "You're good fun to work with, Deeder," he said. "Bit lazy, *más o menos*," he said, wiggling his hand back and forth, "but good fun. Good man."

"You too, asshole," Deeder said.

Rudy laughed again and Deeder laughed too, and then Deeder saw what Rudy was looking at, a corner of the flange that was slightly turned up, something Deeder wouldn't have bothered with but he knew Rudy would, and sure enough Rudy leaned down and took a step, but the toe of his boot caught somehow, and as Rudy pitched forward Deeder extended his hand, as if the gesture could somehow perform a rescue. But there was the slap of Rudy's elbow hitting the shingles and he somersaulted over on his right shoulder and skidded briefly at the edge of the roof, grabbing at it, and then he was gone.

"Holy shit," Deeder said. He was surprised, most of all, at the moment, to find himself alone on the roof. Then he shouted, "Hey . . . hey!" But there was no need. The guys framing the walk had already started running, and Marlin had appeared from his truck parked out on the road, dropping a Styrofoam coffee cup in his haste and grabbing at the cell phone in his pocket to call 9-1-1, and Deeder hightailed it to the ladder and got down quick. When he reached the ground, his initial thought was that, based on what he had learned in conversation, this was the first time Rudy had fallen from a roof. Deeder had fallen twice. Rudy now trailed Deeder in roof-falling by only one.

One thing Deeder knew from past experience was that all men who fall from roofs look more or less the same right after landing. It was difficult to predict the severity. He had once seen a man fall from a two-story roof, land on the roof of the garage, do a backflip over the edge, land on the packed dirt of what would soon be the driveway, and get up to his feet in less than a minute, acknowledging the crew's applause, suffering nothing worse than a strained Achilles tendon. He had also seen a man who fell no more than eight feet while descending a ladder wind up with a broken back and a collapsed lung.

At first glance as he came around the corner of the house, Deeder's impression was that Rudy was either dead or completely fine. There was no blood but no movement, either. He had missed the sidewalk framing and landed on the hard topsoil a few feet from a drainage pipe. The two other Mexicans on the crew stood to one side and Marlin stood to the other, already talking to the 9-1-1 dispatcher. Rudy did not appear to be speaking and it also appeared that, strangely enough, no one was speaking to Rudy. Marlin spoke into his cell phone and the Mexicans stood there quietly. Deeder waded into their midst, squatting next to Rudy, hovering over him, watching his chest rise and fall jerkily.

"Don't move him!" Marlin ordered. He went back to talking to the dispatcher.

"I know not to move him, dumbshit," Deeder said. Rudy's eyes were open, staring straight up into the morning sunlight. "*Rudy,*" Deeder said. "Rudy, how you feeling?" Rudy's eyes flickered over toward Deeder, the eyelids blinking fast. "It's Deeder," Deeder said. At that Rudy raised his hand from the ground and Deeder took it, holding it in an arm-wrestling grip. The hand was surprisingly strong, squeezing tight. Deeder took that as a good sign, and it occurred to him for the first time that he *really* didn't want Rudy to die here, that he *urgently* wanted Rudy to make it through this, as if it were, say, Grace or Theresa who had fallen from the roof, and Deeder wondered why this might be, and he concluded to his own surprise that it was because Rudy was the only person he could even talk to nowadays, that Rudy was, in the current context of his life, his best and almost his only friend.

Rudy tried to say something, but Deeder couldn't hear it because the Mexicans had chosen that exact moment to whisper among themselves. "Ssst! Ssst!" Deeder said, waving his free hand anxiously at the Mexicans. "He's trying to say something." Marlin was through talking to the dispatcher for the moment but he held the phone in his hand and the three of them, Marlin and the Mexicans, placed their hands on their knees and leaned in toward Deeder and Rudy.

"Rudy, you hang in there," Marlin said. "An ambulance is on its way. How do you feel? Where are you hurt? Can you move?"

Rudy's eyes rolled wildly and then settled on Deeder's face, and the hand squeezed Deeder's again. "I ooda may," he said, and started to cough, and he winced in pain and his chest jerked upward.

Deeder squeezed his hand back in response. "I'm here, buddy," he said. "What's that you're saying?" He seemed to be talking in English, which was another good sign, probably, because if you were losing consciousness or you were incoherent you wouldn't have the wherewithal to speak in your adopted language, would you? And two of the words—*I* and *may*—were clearly English, though the middle word was troubling. *Ooda?* That must have been Spanish, but what could it possibly mean? What kind of word would you stick between *I*, which was a noun, and *may*, which Deeder suspected was a verb? And even if you took the *ooda* out, what was he saying? *I may* what? May *die?*

"OK, Rudy, *Jesus*," Deeder said, and he lowered himself to his knees, holding Rudy's hand against his chest. There was a troubling sort of rattling in there, like Grace when she had the croup last winter. "We're not gonna die here, OK? We're not gonna fucking die here at this stupid fucking empty house falling from this stupid fucking roof, OK? You with me on this, Rudy? You with me?"

Rudy nodded his head vehemently and he squeezed Deeder's hand again.

"OK," Deeder said. "OK now. Not dying. We're agreed on that, right?" Rudy made no response. "Rudy?" Deeder said, and he held Rudy's hand up and shook it a little. Rudy nodded. "OK," Deeder said, taking his free hand to pat the back of Rudy's hand. "Not dying here. Not *even* fucking dying here. Now what are you trying to tell me?"

"I ooda may," Rudy said, and his eyes closed tight.

"Hey, *hey*," Deeder said, and he patted Rudy's hand hard and shook it and Rudy opened his eyes and they swam for a second and then locked back onto Deeder's face. "Eyes right here," he said, "eyes right here, buddy," and he made a motion with his index finger connecting Rudy's eyes to his own.

Rudy nodded again and kept his eyes on Deeder. "I ooda may," he said again, and this time he choked and a little drop of blood burbled up from his lips and went down his chin.

"Oh, shit," Marlin said. "Fucking *shit!*" He held the phone back up to his mouth. "Where the fuck is the ambulance?" he yelled. Deeder heard a voice on the other end trying to calm Marlin down. "Get the fucking *ambulance* here!" Marlin said. "This guy's in *bad* shape." A voice on the phone again. "Bleeding internally," Marlin said. "Get the fucking *ambulance* here."

"I ooda may," Rudy said, looking right at Deeder, squeezing his hand, only more softly this time.

Deeder held one hand out to the Mexicans. "What is that?" he asked. "What's he saying? What's *ooda?*"

The Mexicans spoke to each other and shook their heads.

"*En Ingles?*" Deeder said.

The Mexicans shook their heads and one of them held his hands out and said, "*No sé en Ingles. No sé.*"

"Shit," Marlin said.

The Mexicans had only been on the crew about a week and Deeder didn't even know their names. They got all their instructions from Rudy. They didn't speak English at all, and so now they weren't any help, what with Rudy speaking some kind of hybrid of English and Spanish and saying the same thing over and over again while looking into Deeder's eyes, as if Deeder were supposed to help him in some way, and the Mexicans not understanding or not being able to tell anyone other than Rudy what they did understand, and Rudy not talking to them but only to Deeder, and Marlin yelling into his cell phone as if he could make the ambulance come faster by abusing the 9-1-1 dispatcher, and Deeder not understanding anything, and it started to seem like that Bible story Deeder remembered from when he was a kid, the one where the people built the big city using all the available technology and science but God didn't like the city, and he made everybody talk different, and the people got confused, and the city fell apart, and that seemed to be what was happening here. The only thing that seemed to work, the only line that was operational, was the line from Deeder to Rudy.

"OK, I want you to listen to me, Rudy, and I want you to keep your eyes right here." Rudy nodded again, making an effort to keep his eyes lined up with Deeder's, and Deeder leaned in still closer to help Rudy do that, and he saw blood on Rudy's teeth and noticed how dry Rudy's dark skin looked, the black stubble in little patches on his cheeks. "I want you to think positive here, Rudy. I want you to think about something nice." Deeder looked up at the cloudless sky, felt the warm air snuggling up under his shirt sleeves, but that didn't seem right—*look on the bright side, it's a beautiful day!* "The ambulance is going to be here in a minute," he said, and he realized that he was listening all the time for the siren coming from town, but still it wasn't there. "Just think about the ambulance. It's gonna be here in a minute and you're gonna take a ride to the hospital and they'll have you fixed up in no time and you'll be back to work . . . hell, probably tomorrow, you tough son of a bitch." Rudy was breathing hard through his nose and his chest was jumping and he was holding on to Deeder's hand and trying his best to look in Deeder's eyes. The ambulance needed to get there quick. Deeder pictured loading Rudy into it and riding with him and arriving at the hospital to meet the hippie doctor, the one he'd visited that morning, he had been summoned to the hospital and would be the one there on the scene, and Deeder would say, Doctor, you've got to do something for him, this is what you gave it all up for, to help people, right, to *help* them? And he thought of his dream the night before. "Rudy," Deeder said. "*Rudy*, I want you to think of something else." He squeezed Rudy's hand and shook it to get Rudy to pay attention, because there was a listlessness in his eyes and in his grip that Deeder didn't like at all all of a sudden. "I want you to think of my record store, man—*our* record store, I'll go in halves with you." Rudy's eyes were back now, and Deeder almost thought he saw him smile. "There we are in San Francisco, buddy, and it's the Summer of Love, and we're listening to the best music in the world and smoking the world's best dope, and holy shit there's Carlos *Santana*, man, Carlos Santana just walked in our record store and he's carrying his fucking guitar!"

"What the *fuck* are you talking about, Deeder?" Marlin said.

Deeder took a deep breath. He could see the scene clearly in his head—the store and all the records and the customers in jeans and T-shirts and the beaded curtain casting its colors all around, he and Rudy behind the counter and Monterey Pop, even, lying in a patch of sunlight on the floor. But Rudy wasn't seeing it, he could tell. Rudy's eyes were going away again. It wasn't the same thing to Rudy as it was to him. "Shut the fuck up, Marlin," he said. "Leave me the fuck alone and I mean it." Marlin left him the fuck alone. Nobody said anything. "OK, Rudy," he said. "*Hey!*" He slapped Rudy's wrist and Rudy looked back at him, not seeming to understand why Deeder would hit him, and it pained Deeder right in his heart. "Sorry, buddy, but you've gotta stay with me." He took a deep breath again. "OK, I want you to picture *your* dream place, Rudy, whatever it is—someplace in Mexico, maybe with your family. You're back home in Mexico, and all your family is there to see you, it's the place where you grew up, where you were a kid. What do they have there—cactus?" He looked up at the Mexicans but they just stared at him oddly. "Do you see it, Rudy? Do you see it?" In answer, Deeder felt a light pressure on his hand. Rudy's eyes were still open, but now they had moved away from Deeder entirely and the sky was in them, something very far away. Mexico. Deeder had no real idea of Rudy's family or where he grew up, only that he had two children back in a town called Oaxaca where they had a pretty cathedral. "You and your sons, Rudy. You and your sons in Oaxaca," Deeder said, and he was surprised to find that he was crying. It was the light in Rudy's brown eyes, something beautiful there. Deeder heard the ambulance now, and it sounded like music, but he didn't say anything to Rudy, just let Rudy dream, sitting there holding his hand and thinking, suddenly, of the only time he had ever actually been to San Francisco, when he was seven-

teen with his friend Todd, they had lied and said they were
going to stay with Todd's brother in Spokane for a few days
but they had driven to San Francisco, arriving in the afternoon,
New Year's Eve, 1984, and on their way to Haight-Ashbury they
had come across Panhandle park, and Deeder thought he'd hit
a time warp, it was all still happening, it was still going on
*right now* and why had nobody told him. There were the flower
children, hundreds of them in headbands and tie-dyed shirts,
smoking weed and playing guitar, they were spread out all over
the place, and he and Todd had joined right in, and when they
were good and stoned they'd noticed people going around trying to sell tickets, tickets to what, they'd asked, to the Dead con-
cert that night, they played every New Year's Eve and the kids
dressed up like flower children and came to the park beforehand. So it was just a show, Deeder discovered, like Disney-
land, and they didn't have enough money for tickets, and when
they'd wandered on down to Haight-Ashbury it had been a disappointment, a chain drugstore on the corner where his record
store should have been, and everything ugly and dilapidated,
there was no Haight-Ashbury anymore, but still he'd had that
golden hour when he thought it was all true, that was his real
memory of San Francisco. And now there were Rudy's eyes, off
somewhere in his own dream to someplace real or imagined,
he wasn't there with Deeder anymore, and the ambulance on
the way with the siren getting louder but it wouldn't be soon
enough for Rudy, blood all down his cheek now, Deeder leaning in to wipe it off with his shirt and patting Rudy's hand to
comfort him, poor goddamn Rudy who wouldn't be there on
the roof anymore, not there anymore with Deeder, Deeder all
alone, and no one would care, not Theresa or Grace, not really,

because Rudy was just a man they knew through Deeder's stories of working on the roof, which was something he did for them but which they had no interest in, and because they were generally indifferent, to Deeder and the world, the world where Deeder had long ago come back from San Francisco, a microscopic dot moving on the surface of the big dark Earth, a planet turning through the vast universe in the tiny light of a medium-sized star. He and Marlin and the Mexicans and Rudy were little pinpoints on that planet in the faint light of that star, and in other places there were also people dreaming, people struggling, people dying, their eyes like Rudy's, their breathing shallower and shallower, in the Middle East and sub-Saharan Africa and even right here in the USA, and Deeder couldn't or wouldn't be there to help them, only this one pinpoint, just this one hand he was connected to, that voice saying *I ooda may I ooda may* over and over, those eyes gone off to Mexico or some other place Deeder didn't know, and as the ambulance pulled into the driveway and the paramedics approached, Deeder and Rudy held on, their clasped hands like a bridge, the touching skin and the light exchange of pulses, how terribly *present* life was, how awfully *now*, and as a hand on his shoulder urged him to move away, Deeder leaned over Rudy and looked one last time into his eyes, to make sure they still knew each other, that they were both still here.

# Harmonica

Taylor Rue buys a pack of cigarettes at the convenience store on the corner of Euclid and Pine. There are some goth-looking kids in the parking lot. When Taylor comes out the door, they stare at him and lower their voices. He doesn't have anything against the kids—it's just that they look so strange and he doesn't know what they think or what kind of shit they're capable of.

That has something to do with why he touches his wallet in his back pocket. That has something to do with why he doesn't light up till he's around the corner and a little way down the street—he doesn't want them asking for a smoke, crowding around him.

So he's on Euclid when he opens the pack, takes out the foil, taps the pack hard on his hand. Right when he gets the cigarette to his mouth a guy pulls up on a motorcycle. It's a beat-up motorcycle, not anything you'd want to have, particularly. And the guy who cuts the ignition and puts down the kickstand and steps to the curb isn't the kind of guy who can be too picky about what he has or what he doesn't. He has what he has.

"Hey, buddy," the guy says. Taylor isn't his buddy, and the guy knows it and Taylor knows it. The two of them know that much. "Bum one of those?" the guy says.

And he's approaching too fast, coming too close to Taylor. It's dark on the street, only the faint shine from a streetlight halfway down the block. Taylor has had trouble in his life before, and this looks like some. This is a lanky guy, a stringy guy, and he seems a little wild, a little reckless. He comes right up to Taylor, gets in his face there on the dark street, and his hand starts fidgeting with something in his pocket. Taylor's cigarette is lit by this time, so he says, "Sure," and jabs the cherry in the guy's eye.

The guy drops to his knees. "Motherfucker," he shouts. "Mother *fuck*." Taylor kicks him once in the neck to make sure he stays down. The guy does. Taylor walks on. He doesn't have any place to go to. His ex-wife and his kid live on this street but it's not like he's going there. He's just walking. He's just out to see the stars.

A truck pulls up. It's an old, dented Dodge Ram, Taylor thinks, though he can't see it well in the half dark. The driver gets out and talks to the guy there on the ground. They know each other. That much seems clear. Taylor isn't a coward, but something tells him he should be moving faster. He turns up an alley and starts to jog, just steady, not too fast. He bounces along on the gravel between the toolsheds and the fences, and a dog barks, and another one, and in a few seconds the alarm has spread through the neighborhood. When he gets to the next street, the headlights are swinging fast into the alley. Taylor turns the corner and ducks behind a fence. It reminds him of Halloween, how they used to throw eggs and hide from the cops. But the cops don't beat you or knife you, and these guys will, very likely.

He hears the crunch of gravel and the truck skids to a stop ten feet away from him, on the other side of the fence. He tries to see the driver through the wooden slats, but he can't very well. "Fuck," the driver says. The lanky guy on the passenger side is still moaning in pain. It almost makes Taylor feel guilty. What if the guy really just wanted a cigarette? If so, then he needed to learn a better way of approaching people. The truck spins out of the gravel and makes a hard right, the tires chirping when they hit the pavement.

Taylor considers his next move. He wishes his heart weren't racing, but it is. A thing like this shouldn't upset him. He stands up from his place behind the fence, winces for a moment at his aching knees. Getting older. The best plan might be to walk back up the alley. They won't check the alley again for a couple of minutes. There are the dogs, but with so many barking all around that won't tell them where he is. And if he sees the lights, there's always someplace along the alley to hide. So that's the plan, walk up the alley, but after he's gone just a few steps he feels compelled to run again and it makes him angry, at himself and at the assholes in the truck.

He's listening for the screech of tires but he doesn't hear it. Maybe they've given up. He's winded, slows his pace, soon is just walking again. The alley is familiar. Back when he lived in the house on Euclid with his ex-wife and his daughter, he would walk the dog, Stanley, up this way. Good old Stanley. He wonders if Stanley is still around.

Maybe he should go by the old house. He could say it's an emergency. And it is, isn't it? Two guys in a truck are after him.

But it's hard for him to believe that at the moment, there in the dark of the alley, the millions of stars above this small town in Idaho, the summer night air cool and crisp under his shirt collar. And it isn't the sort of thing he'd want to show up on the doorstep and tell Sheryl. And then there's the inevitable fight about child support to consider. And the husband, Justin. The last time Taylor went by the house to visit Courtney, his daughter, two years ago now it must be, he and Sheryl had gotten into that easy kind of talk, where they kidded each other and laughed about things, and this Justin had lost his cool, smashing a beer bottle on the floor and trying to work up the nerve to punch Taylor. When the host starts threatening the guest, that means it's time to leave, is Taylor's feeling on the subject. He'd gotten up calmly and said his good-byes and gone on his way. That was the important thing—the necessary calm, the necessary quiet, a balance to all the noise.

Now he comes out the other end of the alley. Things are pretty quiet on Euclid Street, just a cat scurrying up the sidewalk at Taylor's approach. And there's the guy's bike at the curb. It's just an impulse, and he knows there must be a way to resist impulses, but he's never been very good at that. He bends to the shape of things, almost always. And so now he's sitting on the bike, making himself comfortable on the vinyl seat. An old Yamaha 650 Special. It reminds him of the Yamaha he used to have, not the same model, but close enough. Those were the days before Courtney, when he and Sheryl would just take off sometimes, whip down the highway.

He can't remember how much noise the guy's bike made. He hops off for a second, checks the muffler to see if it's bored out, but it isn't. Theoretically, the thing should purr like a kitten. He looks up and down the street for headlights. The truck seems to have disappeared. He turns the key, flips out the kick-start with his foot, then raises in the seat and steps down hard. The thing comes to life right away, surprisingly, and it's as quiet as he could hope for. Then his shirtsleeves are rustling with the breeze and he's out of the old neighborhood, past the convenience store with its bright lights over the gas pumps, still riding slow, easing off the throttle. But on the other side of town he lets it loose and feels the engine push him into the backrest.

He'll go to Big Dave's Place, away from downtown. A dozen bars they could choose—what are the odds? The guys in the truck are the type who would hang out at Dave's, but he's never seen them there. Odds one in ten, one in twenty? Better odds than he gets most of the time. He forgets about the guys in the truck and enjoys the ride.

He leaves the bike in a dark corner of the parking lot. He figures he'll bum a ride home. He sits on a bar stool. The clock on the wall says 12:30. He's got four bills in his wallet, and he's hoping one of them is a five or a ten. He doesn't really want to look, so he plucks out two, both singles, and puts the wallet in his back pocket. He orders an Oly in a can. He lights a smoke and sits there.

At one time he would have known every person in Big Dave's Place. But now he sees no one he knows, not even the bartender. All these new people have moved to town, and the people he used to know have gotten old and gone home.

It's open mike night. The evening has worn off on Taylor Rue and he stares dumbly at the man with the guitar and the harmonica player. But then after a minute he knows the harmonica player.

He knows the harmonica player, but he can't think who he is. An older guy, thinning hair, hard creases around the eyes. Maybe, really, he's about the age Taylor is now, but Taylor has a hard time thinking of it like that. The guitar player strums some casual chords, lets the harmonica player have his way. And the guy's blowing the thing, and Taylor has heard better harmonica players, but this guy Taylor Rue thinks he should know from somewhere is pretty good. He's playing a sweet, sad tune, but a little rough around the edges, too, like Dylan would do it, maybe, not so clean that it makes you embarrassed to listen to. Then the guitar player is back on the chorus and singing, and the harmonica player finds just the right spaces in the music to fill, just the right spots to make the silence move. It makes Taylor Rue feel like he used to in the old days, hopeful about things, light in his thoughts, and as the song ends he tips up the last of his beer and orders another.

And just like that the harmonica player is standing next to him and buying his round, and Taylor Rue can still hear the music he was playing. He takes a look at the face again. The harmonica player holds out his hand for Taylor Rue to shake.

"Holy shit," Taylor Rue says. "Stewart Busby."

The harmonica player is Stewart Busby, a guy Taylor went to high school with. They worked on a salvage crew together for a few days. Once they stole a case of beer from a delivery truck at the bowling alley and drank most of it sitting in the high school parking lot. They talk about those things. Stewart Busby asks Taylor what he's been up to. A little of this and a little of that, Taylor tells him. Construction mostly. Last week he was roofing. This week he's building a fence for a rich Californian his uncle knows. What's Stewart Busby doing? Logging with

Richie Fink. It's funny that Taylor and Stewart haven't seen each other in years, here in this small town. Sure is.

In the quiet that follows, Taylor Rue watches the guitar player pack up his case. It's almost closing time. The song comes back to Taylor Rue. It sounds even better now that he's not hearing it. There was Stewart Busby, there on that stool, playing the harmonica. It fills Taylor Rue up somehow, the rise and fall of the notes, Stewart's silver harmonica flashing, and Taylor Rue begins to sway back and forth and he slaps his leg and laughs. "Holy shit, Stewart," he says. "Holy shit."

"What?" Stewart Busby says.

Taylor Rue motions to the empty stool on the little stage. "That was you," he says. "I was watching," he says, "and . . ."

"What?" Stewart Busby says.

"Man," Taylor Rue says, "that was *you*. You were blowing the shit out of that thing. You were playing a fucking *tune*."

"Oh," Stewart Busby says. "Right. Yeah."

"Jesus H.," Taylor says. He reaches out and pats Stewart Busby on the arm. He pulls his hand back and scratches his ear. "I mean," he says, gesturing with his hands. He's trying to make a shape, something that will indicate to Stewart Busby what he doesn't seem to understand, that he took the smoke-filled air of Big Dave's into his lungs and blew it back out in a wonderful stream, but there isn't a way for Taylor Rue to explain it with his hands. "That was *good*, Stewart. That was good." He shakes his head. "I don't know anyone who plays music. How'd you learn to do that?"

"Oh, I don't know," Stewart Busby says. "Picked it up here and there."

Taylor kind of stares at Stewart Busby, who seems like just a regular guy, a guy you might run into anywhere.

"Shit," Stewart says, and laughs. "Come here." He leads Taylor over to a table and shows him his harmonicas. There are a bunch of them. You have to have different ones for different keys, Stewart Busby explains, but Taylor doesn't know what he's talking about. They don't cost much. Taylor could buy one and learn. Stewart Busby recommends that Taylor start with a C. "Well, shit," he says. "Here." And he hands Taylor Rue one of the silver harmonicas. It glows red in the bar light.

"You want me to blow on it?" Taylor Rue says. His heart thumps like it did back in the alley.

"I want you to keep it," Stewart Busby says. "Old times," he says, and raises his beer. "But yeah," he says, "blow on the fucker, why not."

Taylor Rue closes his eyes. The harmonica is small and light in his hand. He brings it to his lips and tastes the nickel plating. He hears in his head the song Stewart Busby played. It goes like this. But when Taylor blows on it the sound is nothing, just a *hoo* and a *wah* and a *hoo*.

"You keep that," Stewart Busby says. "You take care."

The harmonica is in the pocket of Taylor Rue's jeans as he walks out to the parking lot. He's thinking about how Stewart Busby learned to tame it, to get the sounds to come out right, to shape the dead air into music. He can do it, too. He'll start learning how tomorrow. It doesn't matter if he misses work. The fence isn't going anywhere. It's just a fence, taking up space at right angles to the ground, filling the air with something you can't see through.

Then it occurs to him that he forgot to find a ride. So, the motorcycle. He's on it again. Like Stewart Busby said, go ahead and blow on the fucker, why not. He figures he'll leave it where he found it and walk on home.

When he gets back to Euclid, he's in a good mood. He makes the turn, the motorcycle's headlight shining briefly in the windows of a house across the street, and what he thinks about is how he'll go home and crack open a beer and sit on the couch and start learning how to play the harmonica. Why wait until tomorrow? Maybe he'll put a little Dylan or Neil Young on the stereo to help him out. Or maybe he'll just try to listen in his head to the tune Stewart Busby played. But as he's getting ready to pull up to the spot where he took the bike, what he finds now is the truck with the two men inside. For a moment he eases off the throttle, not quite believing what he sees. The truck is just a bad memory, something from an earlier time in his life, back a couple hours ago when he didn't have much hope. It shouldn't be here, not now when he has something he's so looking forward to. How stupid, he thinks. How fucking dumb. And then there's nothing to do but hit the throttle. The wind goes faster and faster through his hair and the headlights are behind him.

They're on one of the county roads soon. The problem with the bike, Taylor finds, is that it won't stay in gear, keeps kicking out, throwing Taylor forward in the seat while the engine whines. He ratchets on the shift, gets the bike to kick back in, but he can't get any distance on the truck, the headlights always creeping up and swallowing him. But he knows a quick right and a quick left and a quick right that will take him onto a deserted stretch of road. He's lived here all his life. If they haven't been around awhile, don't know the place, he'll lose them. The odds are still pretty good, still in Taylor Rue's favor.

The quick right and the quick left but when he makes the next right the bike won't hold the gravel road, shitty tires, that's the thing. He's sideways, turning into the skid, but headed for the ditch anyway. And then he no longer feels the hum of the bike between his legs, he's in the air, and the ground hits him hard, his head in the damp weeds and swimming. And then he seems to be dreaming under the stars, dreams of music and engines.

It's a while before he figures out what the light means. He's in the cool sharp late-summer air, and he can see a clump of white snowberries. The lights mean the truck is in the ditch, too. They've driven into it right behind him. Taylor Rue stands up. The stars whirl and the mountains in the black distance right themselves. Two figures in the weird lopsided headlights. Silhouettes.

He's still shaky on his feet, so he plants his legs wide as the silhouettes come near. He shields his eyes from the headlights, but it doesn't help much. "What can I do for you?" Taylor Rue says. Stupid talk, a dumb thing to say.

"Well, I don't know," one of the men says. His voice sounds funny, kind of high-pitched and nasal. "You got a tow truck handy? You got a cell phone on you so we can call the cops?" He's waving something in his hand, something Taylor doesn't like the looks of.

The other guy starts rubbing his eye, so Taylor knows which one's which. "Hey, Curtis," the eye-rubbing guy says. "Let's make him help us get the truck out of the ditch. I can go to town and get the cops while you wait here."

To Taylor Rue, that's starting to sound like a good plan. But Curtis stays put, just stands there. "No," he says. "I want to hear what he has to say about this." His voice is high, like sing-ing. "You got anything to say you better say it."

Taylor Rue doesn't have anything to say. What he thinks he'd like, what occurs to him that he ought to do, is to pull out the harmonica. It seems to Taylor that he could play the harmonica perfectly at this moment, just the way he hears it, and he'd like to let the music do the explaining.

But there isn't time. A flash and a ripping sound, and he's on the ground again, the thick damp weeds, the earth bunch-ing up his cheek.

He listens for a while. *Asshole*, he hears someone say. He remembers how he'd been nervous about something earlier. What was it? The goth kids. But these aren't them. These guys could be anyone in the world. He thinks of how he saw them there through the fence, how he'd almost felt bad for the one guy. He thinks, too, of Courtney and Sheryl in the house on Euclid Street. It's time to get up, but there isn't any. Isn't any-thing. He isn't moving. The lights are going out. The sky is a million miles wide.

Was an asshole. *Was*. He hears them. Now what do they do with the bike, the truck. Will the bike start? Shit. Mother fuck. They're in the middle of nowhere in the middle of the night. There's a dead guy now. It is somebody's fault.

Taylor Rue thinks he might as well relax. Whatever's hap-pened has already happened, and there's not much he can do. He might as well go to sleep.

But he's soon wakened by the two men going through his pockets. What will they find there? His cigarettes and his lighter. His wallet. Two dollars. A useless credit card, a few phone numbers of women he knows, the phone number of the kid who sells him pot. A receipt for his new power drill. A picture of Courtney on her sixth birthday, long ago. The harmonica, which he had planned to learn how to play. He feels it come out of his front pocket, hears one note fill the air, no more. The harmonica Stewart Busby just gave him is now someone else's. He's never been able to hold on to anything.

He's drifting again. Behind his eyes there's nothing but the whiteness of the stars. He hears things, though, the swaying of the evergreens, the whisper of the weeds. And the men, first dumping the bike behind the snowberry bushes, then trying to get the truck out of the ditch. The engine roars and the tires crunch through the undergrowth and the men yell and cuss at each other, and Taylor wishes they would shut up, quit panicking, be still. Half his life he's been besieged by pointless noise, the series of bosses with their do this, do thats, and the pounding of hammers and the pocking of staple guns and the squealing of saws, and Sheryl, good God, all the yelling and yelling and yelling. He's never had a decent stretch of quiet to sift through, it seems, and he wants that now, but here are the men again, this time dragging him along the ground, smashing him into tree trunks, goddamn shit motherfucker, they say. Finally shoving him into some bushes.

A little later he hears, far away, the truck shifting gears out on the road. And then it's quiet. He can hear the trees, and he can hear the soothing sound of water. They've left him near a stream. Taylor Rue has thought a lot about dying. He's always thought that, even if he never managed to make anything out of his life, never had any money, never made many friends, never shared enough love with a woman to make it work, never managed to be the father he wanted to be to the only child he ever had, never learned something as simple as how to make music from the air like Stewart Busby, even, never found any harmony at all in any thing, he could at least bear up when the time came, face death with calm and dignity. But it's easy to die, Taylor Rue is discovering. Anyone could do it. You just have to lay there.

Out on the highway is a man named Dillard Rains, riding shotgun and blowing on a harmonica. He's sure it bothers the hell out of Curtis, the driver, but Curtis is a dumbfuck for shooting that asshole, and Dillard Rains's burned eye feels like it's drilling a hole through his skull, and the blowing helps to force the pain away. He wishes he'd never come to this town, wishes he'd never met Curtis, wishes he hadn't fucked with the asshole over a cigarette in the first place. It's all gone to hell for him and he doesn't know why, and he has to wonder if there's anything out there in the world that makes it worth all the trouble and the wait. He better just blow on the harmonica and watch the road and the world outside the window, a world that seems to be changing now as he pipes his crude tune, stars dripping like wax into the trees on the mountainsides, a dead man's face in the purple moon. The time is bound to go by slow. By the look of things, there's still a lot of night to get through, and then a whole lot of morning.

# Visitation

These are the rules as I understand them at the outset of this story: Guests may not steal things—my houseplants, my stereo. They may not enter my house with the intention of carrying off my computer or my TV. They may not dig my coin collection, stuffed into an old sock, out of the top drawer of my dresser. Though my parakeet cage is empty, they may not appropriate it. They may not enter my home in my absence, even if they mean to do no worse than watch the tropical fish. I have valuables; they are mine, not my guests'.

While these rules are not posted in my house, are not nailed to the door or magnetized to the refrigerator, I feel they are understood, *should* be understood, by every person who enters here.

Then there is James. Unbeknownst to me, while I am attending church, this James decides to violate the rules. He decides to enter my house, the door of which is never locked, in order to take something that is mine—namely, fifty dollars that lies on the coffee table. He knows the fifty dollars is there, on the coffee table, because, on the previous evening, he had for the first time been a guest in my house, at a housewarming party during which I had paid for three cases of expensive beer, and had been reimbursed, partly, and had chosen to leave the money on the coffee table. In one sense, you could call this story "The Gall of James."

I come into my new house. I have been to church. I close the door behind me. When I turn around, there is James. He is caught in the act, and, at least for a moment, the look on his face reflects this fact. His complexion is pasty. His mouth forms the shape of the letter O. The bills crinkle in his hand, as if they cry out for justice or mercy.

I am alone. My first thought is, does this James have a weapon. James does not. The look on his face makes this clear. He is not in control of the situation. I am in control. It is my house.

This James is skin and bone. I had noticed this the night before. He is refugee skinny. He is also shorter than I am. Quickly, I run through the numbers. I am six feet tall, and I weigh one hundred and ninety pounds. This James, placed on the rack, might stretch to five foot seven. With the heavy boots he wears, he might, on a good day, tip the scales at one hundred and ten. I could break him up like kindling.

Had I been in a different state of mind, had there been no extenuating circumstances, had this James begun by saying something else, we might have proceeded without violence.

I said, "What are you doing here?" I thought perhaps there was some misunderstanding.

"I came to steal this money," he said.

These were the extenuating circumstances: 1) I had, in all good faith, invited James into my home on the previous evening, as he was the friend of a friend, which is good enough for me. 2) While puny enough to pass for a refugee, this James did not look destitute. His hair was freshly cut, his face was clean, his clothes looked fairly expensive. The boots were sturdy, barely broken in. 3) For the first time in many years, I had been to church, and something unusual happened during the service. My mother died.

So I grab this James by both arms—his arms are about as big around, I estimate, as the plastic tubes at work that we secure our precious artwork in—and pick him up and toss him, making sure to bend at the knees. He travels several feet and lands on the hardwood floor, striking his head. Without a sound, he stands up and makes a break for the door. Despite his surprising agility, I am able to snatch his spindly arm as he goes past and swing him, sending him across the room into the wall, where he goes left-shoulder-first into the picture window, shattering one of the smaller panes.

He does not get up right away this time. He busies himself with his shoulder, where blood begins to saturate his shirt. He appears to be smiling, or grimacing. He does not look at me.

I pick the money up off the floor, count it, fold it, and place it in the pocket of my slacks. Loosening my tie, I look around the room for the absence of small items he may have pocketed. But what's to see? The fish food. A baseball cap. CDs fanned out around the computer. My iPod. A framed miniature of my ex-girlfriend. Anything else that might be missing I do not care enough about to remember. The rest is bottles and cans, cigarette butts jammed in empty glasses and ashtrays. I take off my tie and toss it on the rocking chair. I unfasten the top button of my shirt, roll up my shirtsleeves, and, for some reason, remove my shoes and socks—I suppose they were hurting my feet. At the advertising firm where I work, we are into dressing down, and I had not laid eyes on these shoes for quite some time, much less worn them.

My options, I decide, are these: 1) Continue to toss this James around until he loses consciousness or dies. 2) Call the police. 3) Talk the situation over with this James first, then decide whether to call the police. 4) Do nothing, and wait for my father and/or my younger sister to arrive. My father and/or my sister were bound to arrive shortly. They were there too, at the church, when my mother died.

Here is the sequence of events culminating in my mother's death. First, there was her insistent invitation. She called me at work on Friday, suggesting, *begging*, that I attend church with the family on Sunday because "something special" was in store. It is this "something special" that is important to note; nothing special occurred during the service except my mother's death, which leads me to believe that her death was, in fact, the "special" thing, that she *willed* herself to die there in the pew. So, I agreed—I would attend church with my mother and father and my younger sister and her husband and their two young children, all of whom attended church regularly. Then, at the housewarming party I threw Saturday night, I made fun several times of attending church. I made jokes about hangovers and vomit. And it *was* the case during the service that my head hurt badly, an ice-pick pain right above my left eye, and my mouth was parched, and I thought constantly of a glass of water. I sat at the end of the pew, along the outside aisle. I have an enlarged prostate, an unusual condition for a man my age, and though it was not troubling me at present, I intended to use it as an excuse, an opportunity to escape for a few minutes during the most tedious point in the service. But my mother held my hand throughout, *clung* to my hand like there was no tomorrow. She looked at me significantly during the service, and I assumed this meant that I should be extracting some meaning from the pastor's sermon, which was of the "I shall fear no evil for thou art with me" variety. I heard not a word of it, though, really; instead, compelled by the feel of my mother's wrinkled hand in mine, this sixty-some-odd-year-old hand that I had not remembered being old and wrinkled before, I thought over the relationship we had shared all these years, something I had not paused in my life to do up until that very time. As a mother, she was of the zealous variety—a warm-sweater knitter, a VapoRub administrator, a balanced-diet monitor, a *don't go out there without your boots on* caretaker, a *when you come home late I can't get a wink of sleep* worrier, a *we miss you so much, when are you coming to visit* devotionalist, a *does this new girlfriend treat you any better than the last one* loyalist— all in all, it goes without saying, a saint. Put in a curious mood by this remembrance, I looked at my mother, her hair done up just so, her cheeks rosy with rouge, her lips a glossy but not too floozy red, a little emotional tremble puckering up her chin, and I squeezed her hand. She turned a smile on me, a perfectly vivacious smile of the sort she might have turned on people forty years before, a smile made beautiful by the teary light in her eyes. "I love you," she said, and she squeezed my hand in response, and she died. Her eyes rolled upward, her eyelids fluttered, her chest expanded and then froze, her hand squeezed tighter and tighter, and she went suddenly limp, as soft and formless as the blankets she used to pull up to my neck before walking softly out of my room, when I was a child, at bedtime. She died with a pleasant look on her face. I continued to hold her hand. No one else noticed. I turned toward the pastor behind the pulpit, and the lights of the church blurred. I laid my mother's hand gently in her lap, released it, and hurried up the aisle and out of the church into the sunny, if somewhat chilly for September, day outside.

Then I am in my house with this James, whom I have tossed around unmercifully. I find myself sitting on the couch, barefoot, taking deep breaths. James lingers by the window, hunched and somewhat forlorn. My mood has softened a bit. Without knowing why, I say, "Come sit on the couch," and I pat the cushion next to me. This James does. He sits on the couch, careful not to lean against the back, because it would get stained by his shirt, which is now quite bloody.

"Do you have a towel?" he asks.

I point to the bathroom down the hall. "In the cupboard," I say, and James gets up from the couch and walks into the bathroom, shutting the door behind him. I hear the lid of the toilet plop against the tank, and the sound of James urinating. This he does in intermittent bursts, by the sound of it, and it makes me wonder if we share the same difficulty, but probably he is just nervous. Then I hear the toilet lid drop back into place, the cupboard door opening and after a few moments closing again.

While this James is gone, I turn on the TV. A cable channel is showing a rerun of *Happy Days*, an episode in which Potsie and Joanie seem to play larger than usual parts. I glean this, as if by osmosis, during the subsequent conversation.

James returns to the couch, making sure to place the towel over his shoulder in such a way that no blood will get on my furniture. The towel is bloody where he has pressed it against his shirt. There is really quite a lot of blood.

"I might have to go to the hospital," says this James.

"I think so," I say. "But we haven't settled things."

He nods, a look of nothing more than resignation on his face. No anger, no misery, no panic, no fear. With this nod, he resigns himself to the necessity of talking to me. His nod is sobering, and I rarely look at him again after this, and I believe he does not look much at me. We stare at the television.

"What are you going to do?" he asks.

"I think I might call the police," I say. "But something seems to be holding me up."

"What?" he asks.

"I don't know."

After my mother died, after I left the church, I ran down the avenue several blocks—a difficult undertaking, running, in the suit and the dress shoes—until I was forced to stop from lack of breath and my pounding headache. I stood in the middle of the sidewalk with my arms akimbo, my jacket flaring out around my hands, until I was sure that I would not be sick, and then I moved on, at a much slower, more reasonable pace.

All the way home, the remaining dozen blocks or so, a thought or a feeling nagged me, not by its presence but by its absence. There was something not quite right in my reaction to my mother's death, something missing. There was a stray thought or feeling floating near me that I could not bring inside. As I walked I began to search for this thought or feeling.

My mother was dead. That I knew. I knew from the moment her poor hand went limp in mine. I was not in denial. It was not the knowledge, the full awareness, of my mother's death that I was missing. I was not imagining, for instance, a conversation I might have with my mother later on that day, in which I would tell her the story about how she had died in church and then complain about her behavior. I had it firmly in mind that there would be no more conversations with my mother. And it was not a lack of guilt that bothered me. I *did* lack a feeling of guilt, but I had no need to feel guilty. For what—my lack of regret, the absence of grief? I felt regret, in the last moments before my mother died, when I thought about all she had done for me and how little I had done for her in return. It was regret that made me squeeze her hand. I felt grief, in the moments after she died, when I found myself on the verge of tears and ran from the church. The running seemed to have worked the grief out of me. So there had been regret, there had been grief, and the absent thought or feeling was neither of these. And, therefore, having experienced both regret and grief, I had no need for guilt, either. But *something* upset me. And it was not merely the absence of my mother—the actual physical absence—that I was mistaking for some missing thought or feeling. In other words, what was missing was not my mother's presence. I was telling myself right then, in fact, very rationally, in a steady internal voice, that I did not *need* my mother. I had not needed my mother for years, possibly not since my early childhood, when I was afraid of the dark. I would *miss* her, certainly. I am neither an ogre nor a stoic. This is not a tale of uncaring offspring. But I did not miss her right at the moment, it was true. And yet it was not the absence of this missing, either, that irked me. I was content to know that I would miss my mother later. No, it was some other lack or absence, one that I couldn't name.

And this James was interfering with my inquiry. "You're keeping me from thinking about my mother," I say to him. "My thoughts are divided, and it's difficult to decide what to do."

I have no idea how this surprising statement strikes James at first, because my eyes are on the TV, on a scene at Arnold's Drive-In in which, again, Potsie and Joanie figure prominently.

"You planned on thinking of your mother today?" he asks. His voice does not betray any opinion he has on the matter. His voice is as plain as air.

"My mother died today," I say. "In church."

For several seconds there is laughter from the television.

"I'm sorry to hear that," he says. He speaks plainly, but the absolute dryness of the statement lends it credibility. I believe he is sorry.

"I need to go to the hospital, though," he says. "You need either to call the police or give me permission to leave."

How old is this James, I wonder. I look at him again, at his painful thinness and his drawn face. I am glad he has not removed his shirt, although he must have done so in the bathroom to examine the wound. I would guess he is twenty, a rather remarkable twenty.

"What would you tell the police?" he asks.

I stare at the TV. "That you broke into my house. That I caught you stealing my money."

"And here's what I would say," he says. "That I met you last night for the first time and came over to see you today. That you were grief stricken at the death of your mother, that you lost your temper with me for no reason and threw me against the window."

"You don't seem like a person who lies," I say.

"Not habitually," he says.

We watch the TV. Only the images on the TV move in the room—the images on the TV, and the bubbles in the fish tank, and the fish. The only voices come from the TV—from the TV, and, more distinctly than before the small pane was broken, from out the window on the street. I am cold suddenly. My sweat has dried, and the crisp fall air has gotten into the house. Today would be the first fall day to turn on the heat. There is an upside, at least—the broken window has aired out the stale living room.

"This is the one where Joanie falls in love with Potsie," this James says.

And why so? The question occurs to me. I understand now the expanded roles of these minor characters, based on his explanation, and indeed Joanie is at this very moment professing her love for Potsie, and Potsie is attempting to ease her adolescent pain. But why? Why this particular plot, why introduce it for development? An advertisement, no matter how clever, is only successful if it calls attention to the product, and the *product* here, in the case of this show, as I understand it, is Arthur Fonzarelli. Arthur Fonzarelli posters and Arthur Fonzarelli lunch boxes and Arthur Fonzarelli leather jackets. It was Arthur Fonzarelli that people back then tuned in to see, not Joanie and Potsie.

"Do you think Joanie and Potsie got together and demanded more airtime?" I ask this James.

"I don't know," he says. "She falls in love with him after—"

"No," I say, "did the *actors* make *demands*?" On the screen Joanie and Potsie are engaged in dialogue. They seem happy with the larger parts they play. "Or do you think the producer and the director and the writers felt sorry for them, and that, out of the kindness of their hearts, they decided these two supporting actors had earned this episode, that it was their just dessert for all the years of hard work?"

From the corner of my eye I see that James is thinking. His right hand presses the towel down onto his shoulder, and his face is set in a way that suggests the wound may be really hurting now. "I'm not sure," he says. "Maybe."

But this James knows more than he lets on, I am convinced. He has some insight into the matter, could tell me more, if he chose, about what's happening here.

"Can I go, then?" he asks. I am not looking at him, but I sense this time he might be looking at me.

"Not just yet," I say. "I want you to help me understand something about my mother."

The TV has gone to a commercial. I watch in the same vague way I study all advertisements, with my ears pricked, so to speak, but without real interest or enthusiasm. I am immune to the power of suggestion.

"Like what?" he asks.

"Well," I say, "don't you find it odd that I'm not crying?"

"No," he says.

But that won't do. I can wait all day, or at least until my father and/or my sister arrive, while this James's situation—all the bleeding—is more urgent.

"Don't you think it's strange," I say, "that I—a man whose mother has died no less than an hour ago—would be concerned about your taking a measly fifty dollars, or that I would sit and talk to you about a TV show?"

"Maybe you had issues with your mother," he says. "How do I know? Maybe you weren't a very good son," he says, though the last words float slightly upward on the air, into a near question.

"I wasn't a *bad* son," I say. "I loved my mother. I never did anything to hurt her. I tried to make her proud of me."

"I'm sure she must have been proud of you," he says. "You seem to have done very well." I could take this as a tactical maneuver, an attempt to improve his position through flattery, but I read it instead, coming from James, as a bare statement of fact, based on the knowledge that while I am not that much older than he, I am a college graduate who owns his own house and is gainfully employed in his chosen profession. I stay quiet, waiting for him to continue. "I mean, I'm sure you hid the things she *wouldn't* be proud of, and she was proud of the things you let her see," this twenty-year-old James says. "That's more or less how it is with all of us, right?"

He is thinking of the housewarming party on the previous evening, no doubt, all the drunken foolishness, and how I would not have wanted my mother to see, and he is right, of course.

"If she was so proud of me," I say, "then why did she kill herself?"

His feet shuffle on the floor momentarily. *Happy Days* is back from commercial break, and there is the laugh track again. "You didn't say she killed herself."

"Her death was intentional," I say. "That much was plain. She saved it up for a special occasion."

And, all at once, everything is clear. This James has helped me to see. For a moment, I had been fooled. I had warmed up to the subject of my mother's purpose, the *why* of the matter, as if that were the missing component. I would never know *why* my mother had chosen to die the way she did, whether she believed that God had called her, for instance, or whether she was suffering and wouldn't tell me. When she suffered, she did so quietly, always, by herself—and perhaps it was this failure to confide, this question that would always remain unanswered, that bothered me, that seemed to hover.

But no. I know now, very clearly, sitting there next to James on the couch, what it is. Those words—*special occasion*—were the same words, exactly, that I had used in forming an excuse for not inviting my mother to visit my house. *I'm waiting for a special occasion*, I had said. But what occasion could be more special than a housewarming? And yet I had still not invited my mother, had not even told her the event was taking place. It would have made her happy, my mother, to see my house. But I had bought it just a month before, and it was the first house of my very own, and I did not want her in it, for some reason, not yet. Perhaps the bottles and cans. Perhaps the dirty ashtrays.

And for a few moments, that is all I can think of: *I did not invite my mother to my house. She would have liked to see it.* Immersed in that thought, and that thought only, I understand—and the understanding pulls me out of the thought—what had been wrong up to that point. It was not a particular thought or feeling that I lacked, but a *totality* of thought and feeling. Until I became lost in the memory of that non-invitation, I had not been occupied entirely with thoughts of my mother and her death. The death of one's mother is a singular occurrence, of tragic proportions, at least for the bereaved child if not for others unconnected to the death, and one should lose oneself in contemplation of the fact, should trudge blindly into lampposts and step in front of moving vehicles. But that was not happening to me, even while I ran down the street. Until the several seconds when I thought of how I had not invited my poor, aging mother to visit my house, and that thought absorbed my attention, so that I forgot this James who had tried to rob me and was at that very moment saying something I didn't hear, and forgot the TV show and the bubbling fish tank and the noises outside my window, I was failing to experience my mother's death completely, and what kept me from doing so was that very feeling that some thought or feeling was missing, which was the only other thought or feeling I had that did not relate directly to my mother's death, and which was keeping me from this feeling of *completeness*, which was the very missing thing. When one's mother dies, one should think of that alone, and it was this feeling that there was something else that stood in the way of my doing so. It was a very real and curious conundrum that I had become lost in.

No longer, however. I had become preoccupied with thoughts of my mother, if only for a short time, and I felt better for it, and ready to go on. And I have, in anxious moments during these few days following my mother's death, returned to that moment of focused abstraction several times, summing up the experience with those same words: *I did not invite my mother to my house. She would have liked to see it.* It is a neat package in which to place everything.

So I sit there with this James, who has helped me, through his conversation, to resolve my dilemma. And by this time I feel a certain tenderness toward James. He has been beaten up. He is refugee skinny. He looks like he could use a break. "You can go now," I say. "I'm not going to call the police." Strangely, as soon as I speak these words, I feel the need to urinate, as if my prostate has been waiting patiently for me to straighten out my thoughts and has now decided to assail me. Unlike this James, though, my prostate is rarely honest; it is a difficult business to ascertain, and I choose, for the moment, to ignore what my body, falsely or not, is telling me. "I'm sorry I hurt you," I say.

James rises to his feet and places the towel on the coffee table carefully. The towel is covered with blood, and so are his shirt and his hand. He is prepared to walk out without saying anything more, and I am sad at that. I would rather he didn't leave.

"Did you think you needed the money more than I do?" I ask him. "Are you more needy? More deserving?"

He stands across the coffee table from me, looking out the broken window. "No," he says. "I didn't think of that at all. I don't need the money. I don't know about you."

"Why take it then?" I say.

He shrugs with one shoulder only, looking out the window. "You said last night you never lock your doors. You said you were going to church at thus and such a time. You left the money on the table. I thought it would be nice to have fifty extra dollars today." He glances at me then, and smiles. "But you came home early," he says, "because your mother died."

My mother died, never having been invited to the house I bought recently. Before that I lived in a series of apartments, and before that I lived for a long time in my mother and father's home, and we were happy there. This is not the tale of an unhappy family.

"My father and my sister will be here soon," I say. "You should go. You can leave by the back door if you don't want anyone to see you. There's a gate behind the shed."

"Thanks," he says. "How will you explain the window?"

"Grief," I say. "I was distraught. I broke the window."

He nods. "Just one thing," he says. He looks toward the back of the house, staring at the swinging door to my kitchen.

"Walk right back through there," I say, pointing. "The back door's past the pantry. What's the one thing?"

"Promise not to move until I'm out of here," he says.

I nod back at him. We are two people who understand each other well, me and James. He is afraid I will beat him up some more. "OK," I say. "I won't move a muscle. I'll sit right here."

And I do. I sit there, ignoring the false testimony of my troublesome prostate. I sit there long after James leaves, even after my father and sister leave. I do not even show them, my father and sister, around my house, not even after we have all calmed down, first about the condition they find me in and then about my mother.

James takes two steps toward the kitchen and stops. The TV is laughing again, though it's now on a different program. During his two steps, James has thought of something, clearly. He looks at me, stands there looking for quite some time, and I avert my eyes, to give him ample time to think. This James is a smart young man, and he is beginning to understand things. There are signals in the air, passing so quickly that neither of us can be sure exactly what they mean. But James is beginning to understand that I am no longer in control here. I have ceded control. I have promised not to move a muscle. I have promised to sit right here. This couch is my province. Everything else belongs to James. It is his house now.

Still James hesitates. I look at him once again. We stare at each other, and his eyes search mine for confirmation. His eyes ask the question *How secure is this promise, to what extent does it hold true?* And with my eyes I try my best to tell him, *This pledge will not be broken, I will not move a muscle, I will sit right here.*

And my message appears to reach him. He glances out the window, then comes around the coffee table to the couch again. I do not move a muscle. I do not say anything. James rests his left knee on the couch cushion, leans across with his right arm, very calmly puts his hand into the left front pocket of my slacks, and removes the fifty dollars. From the TV, there comes a cry of voices. James smiles, and I smile back.

Again he prepares to leave, takes his knee from the couch and stuffs the money in his pocket. And I am ready for him to leave now. But he stops. He has thought of something else, and, watching his face, I feel betrayed, as if what will happen next is not part of the bargain we struck between us.

But there is little time to think. James stands before me, and he lifts his leg and brings his heavy boot down on my bare feet. The pain is nearly unbearable, and I *do* break my promise—my legs jerk upward, my body tenses, my hands rise slightly before he closes his fist and slams it into my chin.

This does not hurt so much. James hits me for all he's worth, over and over, but he is small and weak and out of breath already, and though I taste blood, the blows he deals out feel soft and light. He is pummeling me with fluffy pillows. He is tickling me to death with a feather duster, and the TV roars with laughter, but I will not laugh with it. I close my eyes and listen to the laughter. I wish, though, that I could hear James instead, that he would blubber like a baby while he hits me, or tell me secrets about his mother like the ones that I told him. But James is quiet, and the TV is enough. Its noise comes ever closer, until finally I am there inside the laughter, all the way in, as if out of the kindness of someone's heart I have been invited to come among these people and play a role, participate in their benign story. A pleasant breeze blows over me, and I imagine swirling curtains, a patch of moonlight in a dim room, and there are faint voices out a window, and the light sound of a bell ringing. I feel a sense of infinite completeness. I am being rocked to sleep.

My eyes open when the rocking stops. There is James, gliding softly out of the room in whispered footsteps, casting one last careful glance over his good shoulder as he slips through the doorway and leaves on the light.

# Tired Heart

M y journey started in South Carolina, in what's called the Low Country, along the coast. It would end in an old Norwegian fishing village on the western shore of Puget Sound. On my way I was supposed to stop at six locations, always on the back roads, to pick up packages for a Mr. Griffin, who had called me one night from New York. Mr. Griffin understood, he said, that we intended to relocate, my wife and I. He understood that she would fly to Seattle and then rent a car to take to the small fishing village, and that I would drive out with our belongings in a U-Haul to meet her there. He understood that we had sold our car to help pay for the move and that we didn't have any plans to implement or any opportunities awaiting us once we arrived. He offered me a pretty substantial sum of money to pick up his packages, enough money to pay for the entire move and then some, so that we'd be able to settle in comfortably and spend some time determining how to get by. I would be paid in full once I delivered the packages, which I would not be allowed to inspect, to Mr. Griffin, who would meet me in the fishing village, at a location that I would learn when I arrived. Mr. Griffin assured me that he ran a legitimate business, and he did in fact send paperwork to support this claim, along with a contract for me to sign. I was satisfied with the arrangement. My wife knew nothing about it. I wanted the money to be a surprise.

So on the day I was scheduled to leave I drove across the Savannah River into Georgia and then through the small towns and the surrounding cotton fields. It was a dark day with heavy clouds and a steady rain, right at the height of fall, when the leaves are their most colorful. The cotton in the fields was ready for picking. The bolls were plump like oversized snowflakes, very pretty in the gray light, and many of the fields had already been reduced to stubble, and at the edge of these fields the cotton stood in huge rectangular bales covered with tarps. The roadside was lined with white fluff blown from the trucks, gradually turning dirty in the exhaust and the rain. The U-Haul drove smoothly and was actually much more comfortable than I had expected. I wasn't thinking about how I would miss the South, about how this would be the last time I'd see the cotton fields, because that sort of thing never mattered so much to me. I wasn't the kind of man who spent a lot of time dwelling on the scenery, and I didn't care too much what kind of place I lived in. So I felt fine, rather happy driving along my way.

My first destination was just beyond a small town called Sardis, which had only one street and no pedestrians. The brick-faced buildings looked mostly empty, and the town hub seemed to be a convenience store where a black woman in a polka-dotted dress pumped gas and two men sat on the curb smoking cigarettes. The town's tallest structure was a storage elevator. My directions, which were very specific, said that I should drive 3.2 miles past this elevator and turn left onto a dirt road bisecting a wide cotton field. At the left edge of the field, approximately one-tenth of a mile from the turnoff, I would find an oak tree draped with Spanish moss. From the base of this tree, I would step off, to the west, six rows of cotton. Between the sixth and seventh rows I would turn into the field, walk twenty paces, and find a package wrapped in brown paper.

It happened exactly that way. There was the package, rainwater dripping from the cotton onto its surface. The paper wasn't ruined, though; it obviously hadn't been in the rain for long. I looked around the field, but there was no one out there to see, just what seemed like miles and miles of cotton, pretty and white. I picked one of the bolls and rubbed it between my fingers. Back in the truck, I placed the package on the floorboard and the cotton on the dash. I checked my timetable, which, like the directions to the locations, was very specific. I had completed the first pickup three hours and twelve minutes early.

My next pickup was just south of Memphis. I drove on across Georgia in the afternoon, and Alabama, keeping to the back roads as I'd been told to do. I'd driven out the other side of the rain, and the sun was shining bright and clear, and a little mist rose off the wet surfaces of the road and the fields. I drove past collapsed barns and auto junkyards and trailers flying rebel flags and pastures with bony horses and acres that had been cleared for timber and dozens of brick country churches. At times, the branches of oak trees leaned over the roadway, brushing the top of the U-Haul. I thought of my wife in a plane on her way to Seattle, and then in her rental car on the way to the small fishing village. My greatest weakness in life for a long time had been that I was madly in love with my wife and couldn't go very long without thinking of her. I was often a fool where she was concerned. She came from the sort of old Southern family that prided itself on once having been part of the leisure class, and she was used to having things done for her, getting her way. Even when I was on the right side of our many arguments, I forgave her quickly, never waiting for apologies. I was inclined to do virtually anything she asked. When she said, for instance, that she wanted to move away from the South, where we'd both lived all our lives, to the Norwegian fishing village we'd visited on our honeymoon, which I suppose she thought was a more romantic, interesting place, I agreed. It meant squirming out of our lease and giving up my job and starting over, but that was all right. As far as my job went, there was not much to say about it except that it was very routine and not at all difficult, and I was compensated fairly for the mediocre work I performed, meaning I didn't make all that much money.

Crossing the state line into Mississippi as night fell, the open windows sucking up the heavy air, I thought of my wife and how it would be when I arrived at the little fishing village, how I would surprise her with the news of my arrangement with Mr. Griffin, and how we would make love in a quaint hotel room all night and wake to the sound of foghorns, as we had done on our honeymoon. I knew that it wouldn't actually happen that way, that instead she would have a number of complaints—she was tired, and it had taken me too long to get there, and she was bored with the quaint hotel room already, and the Norwegian fishing village wasn't all that she'd remembered it to be—and that my arguments would be feeble, and that we would sleep on opposite sides of the bed. But I loved my wife, and I pretended it wouldn't be like that. I loved her because she had pretty red hair that fell in an even line around her shoulders, and smooth pale skin, and because she was much smarter and funnier than I was, and because she could have had her pick of any number of men and had chosen me, perhaps because of my pliable nature.

In the Mississippi Delta there were almost no lights, but there were as many stars as I had ever seen out a windshield. Looking up at them I began to grow sleepy. It had been a long day. I thought I would pick up the next package and check into a motel in Memphis. The broken yellow line of the road blurred at its edges. I watched it suck back toward my spinning wheels. To wake myself up I stopped at a convenience store in Batesville and bought a cup of burnt coffee and, back in the truck, tried to call my wife on her cell phone, because she'd asked me to keep her updated on my progress. But there was no answer.

Climbing back in the U-Haul, I looked at the directions for my next pickup. Just beyond a railroad crossing 1.7 miles past the first sign I'd see for the Tallahatchie River, I would take a right turn into the driveway of a white farmhouse. I would cut off the lights and walk down the gravel drive until I reached a white fence. I would proceed through the gate and across the pasture to a soybean field. I would walk between the seventh and eighth rows of beans to the left, all the way across the field, and I would find the package on the seat of an old tractor parked there. This procedure seemed unnecessarily elaborate to me, and I couldn't remember seeing it when I read over my instructions before I left. And when I arrived at the farmhouse and saw the lights blazing away inside, throwing a yellow glow over this little patch of the huge, dark Delta, I assumed that the farmer must be waiting for my pickup. The clock on the dash of the truck cab showed 12:44. What else would a man who lived here be waiting up for until that hour? Alongside the driveway was a mailbox, and I thought of how much more reasonable it would have been to simply place the package inside it, or, if there were an arrangement between Mr. Griffin and the owner, how much easier it would have been to simply instruct me to ring the doorbell and ask for the package. But I parked in the driveway and cut off the lights, and while an old beagle barked at me from the fenced-in yard I walked down the gravel drive and swung open the white gate. I had forgotten to bring a flashlight, and I stumbled over the uneven ground of the pasture, which seemed to stretch on forever. Finally I could make out the bean field, and I could see that the bean field, too, went on for a considerable distance, and as I entered it and walked along the rows I began to worry about the time, and how late it would be when I arrived in Memphis, and how I would undoubtedly, now, be wasting my money on a room I could sleep in for only a few hours at best. Even in October there were crickets chirping across the Delta, and I listened to them and to my feet, because there was nothing else to listen to. The place was utterly lost in the night. Finally I came to the other edge of the field and there was the tractor, and there was the package, just as my directions had said. I trudged back all that long way and the dog barked again and the lights of the farmhouse were still on, and there was no indication that anyone had even noticed my presence there, the truck parked in the driveway. But I thought it would be prudent to get a little way down the road before I turned on the light in the truck cab and checked my next destination.

Stopped by the side of the road, sipping my coffee, I looked at my timetable. It had seemed easy enough to keep when I'd checked it out beforehand. But now I saw that my next stop was in Dubuque, Iowa, at 7:18 the next evening. The clock in the truck cab said it was now 1:12 a.m. My road atlas showed a drive of at least eight hundred miles, and I wouldn't have the opportunity to drive on the interstate if I wanted to stick to my instructions. But how would Mr. Griffin know if I didn't? What if I just slipped right onto I-55? That would give me time for four or five hours' sleep.

But as it turned out I slept only an hour, right there on the side of the road in the Delta. The night was warm enough that I had to roll down the windows, and mosquitoes whined in my ears, and the dying crickets whirred their anxious song.

Then I started driving again. I stuck to the back roads, as directed. I remembered that package in Georgia, how the rain had barely touched it, how I suspected someone might be watching me. And so I drove the winding roads along the river, often with the interstate in sight along the chalky bluffs, and at times I had to take other roads that led me out of my way, winding through the hills. I drove in a near daze past the cornfields in the autumn sun. I shifted around on the seat, and I exhaled loudly from time to time, and I thought of my wife, and for some reason I pictured her lying in bed in the quaint little hotel, playing the "Imagine Alice" game. Alice was the child we'd never been able to have. The doctors disagreed about the nature of our difficulties, but I had more or less accepted the blame, because I didn't like to argue. The "Imagine Alice" game involved nothing more than lying in bed and talking about the routine we would have after Alice was born, after I got over my problems, whatever they were, and helped my wife to conceive. I knew my wife played "Imagine Alice" even when I wasn't there.

Approaching Dubuque, I pulled into a gas station and checked my maps and my instructions. Again, I was frustrated by what seemed like the idiocy of the pickup arrangements. This time, Mr. Griffin had me retrieving the package at a rest area—*a rest area off the interstate!* And yet I wasn't allowed to use the interstate to get there. I was instructed to pull off the narrow two-lane road beneath a billboard advertising a local diner and to proceed through *three consecutive cornfields* to reach the back side of the rest area, where I would crawl under the barbed-wire fence, go to the nearest picnic shelter, and retrieve the package *from the roof of the shelter*. This seemed absurd to me. I had checked all the travel plans before signing the contract with Mr. Griffin, and I was sure that I had never signed my name to any agreement stipulating that I climb on a roof. I wondered if, maybe, there were two sets of plans—maybe I had happened upon a provisional set of plans of some sort, for emergency situations, and the simpler, more reasonable set of plans was in the glove box or in my travel bag. I riffled through everything I had in the truck cab, and then I threw open the gate to the U-Haul and checked through our boxes of important papers, thinking that maybe I had packed the real instructions away with other files. But no such luck. I sat there with my legs dangling over the trailer hitch, feeling defeated. The trip seemed long and hard, and I wasn't even halfway done. I had imagined a leisurely drive along pleasant back roads, a chance to take in some of the countryside, which I'd never really paid much attention to. My only worry had been figuring out how to explain to my wife why the journey was taking me so long. But now Mr. Griffin's ridiculous pickup arrangements were making it nearly impossible to keep to my timetable, which was awfully difficult to keep in the first place. I merely drove in a sort of frenzy, troubles and worries seeming to pile up on top of me there in the truck cab, so that I took no pleasure in the various sights, or even the songs on the radio. I tried calling my wife again, and again there was no answer. This time I left a message, saying that I would call at noon the next day.

So then I humped along through the cornfields, and there were three barbed-wire fences to crawl under total, not one, and I had to climb onto the roof of the shelter by dragging a picnic table over and placing a bench on top of it while middle-aged women at the rest stop stared at me. But the package was there, as usual. I scanned the faces at the Coke machines and outside the restrooms, seeing if I could somehow identify the person who'd put the package up there in the first place. What would I have said? That Mr. Griffin was being unreasonable. That I wanted to talk to him about things. I walked rather shakily over to the front of the rest area and stood at the top of a bluff while the sun disappeared, looking down at the Mississippi winding its way peacefully along in the purple light. There were boats on the river, a barge floating timber, a paddle wheeler with tourists aboard, lit from bow to stern with white lights. It was soothing to stand there in the cold wind, but I had to get back to my truck.

My next pickup was at 3:36 a.m. in the town of Worthington, Minnesota. The clock now read 7:32 p.m. I had made my Dubuque pickup by only about five minutes. Again I hauled out the maps, and again I found that the schedule left me virtually no time at all for sleep, unless I wanted to ditch the back roads. I'd been driving for a day and a half on one hour's rest. Something had to be wrong; I had checked out the entire itinerary before signing the agreement, and everything had looked easy. I read down the list of my subsequent appointments: Newcastle, Wyoming, 3:13 a.m., almost a full day after the stop in Minnesota; Bonners Ferry, Idaho, 5:26 a.m., more than twenty-four hours after I was due in Newcastle. That was easy enough—if I could just make it this one last time, just get to Minnesota without sleeping. But this same thing had happened before—it was always the *next* stop that seemed impossible, not the ones following. They only seemed impossible when it was time for me to go there. I had a thought—what if, when I left the truck to get the packages, the man who had left the packages was getting into the truck? What if, each time, he was substituting a new timetable? That was the only possible explanation. I was locking the truck when I left it—the packages were just sitting there on the floor in plain view, after all, so I assumed I had to be careful—but it was definitely not beyond Mr. Griffin's capability to talk the truck rental outlet into issuing another key. But five more keys, one for every stop? Or was the same person following me? If so, why couldn't he just deliver the packages to the small Norwegian fishing village himself? But I was too tired to think, so I turned on the light in the truck cab, took my coffee cup from the dash, dipped my finger in the coffee, and very lightly dabbed a spot between the lines of type on the second page of my timetable. It made a perfect little stain, virtually unnoticeable to anyone who wasn't looking for it.

I thought of my wife again. There she was in the fishing village, reading a book out by a dock. She would hear the blast of a foghorn, and a chill would pass over her, and she would pull the sleeves of her sweater over her cold hands for a moment, and look up from the page, and shake her hair back from her eyes. Maybe she would think of me, driving my truck. Maybe she would wonder why she hadn't heard from me. Maybe her phone wasn't working. It seemed unfair that I couldn't be there already, that I hadn't had a chance to talk to her. I thought of the road I had to get back on. I thought of sleeping. I thought of how, if I could only drive on the interstate, I could take a nap in the truck cab and still make it to Minnesota in time. Who would know? Mr. Griffin in his office in New York? I turned off the light and stared down at my map, the spidery lines just visible, slightly translucent from the light that shined on the billboard. The truck cab was cold now. The numbers on the digital clock sent out a faint red glow. Everything—the trash I'd tossed on the passenger seat, the steadily growing pile of packages on the floorboard, the Styrofoam coffee cup in the holder, the T-shirts and socks I'd thrown around haphazardly, the cotton ball I'd placed on the dash—all of these things were as common to me now as my furniture back home, as familiar as my job, my town, my wife. It seemed like I'd lived in the truck cab for months instead of days, and the rest of the world—the night out there, the car lights going wide around me on the darkened road—felt a little threatening. For the first time I started to wonder if something had happened to my wife, if that was why I'd been unable to reach her. Suddenly, I had a hard time thinking of my wife. Her image came to me indistinctly. I couldn't quite capture the sound of her voice, and strangely enough that felt natural to me. I had the truck cab; that was mine. But letting that idea sink in made me apprehensive. What if I never made it to the small Norwegian fishing village? What if I really never saw my wife again? What if I were lost out here on the road somehow forever, scrambling over fields and onto roofs after Mr. Griffin's packages? What if the list of destinations simply went on and on and the highways never ended?

These thoughts startled me, and I cranked the engine and got the truck in gear. Right then I made a decision. I would drive on the interstate, agreement or no agreement. I would pull off at a rest area and get some sleep. My thoughts were getting jumbled—sleep was the only way to set them straight.

Soon I was on I-90 heading west, buzzing through the flat Midwestern night. I opened up the engine, laid my foot heavy on the pedal. I drove until I began to nod off, then pulled into a rest area and settled my head on a dirty T-shirt against the seat. When I woke the clock said 12:18. I'd slept two hours. Worthington, Minnesota, was 160 miles away. The rest area was mostly deserted, just a trucker wandering back from the restroom, a line of semis across the way, a few other cars spread out across the parking lot, people sleeping in them just like me. The truck cab was freezing. I blew on my hands, started up the engine, turned on the defrost. While the truck warmed up, I kept an eye on the truckers and the drivers of the other cars to see if anyone else was starting up, preparing to leave. When I pulled onto the freeway entrance ramp, I watched for headlights behind me.

Now I ran into serious trouble. I would make it to my stop in plenty of time, as long as there were no delays. But sleep had acted on me like a drug. For half an hour I was fine, but then the desire for more sleep hit me, and I was so overwhelmingly tired that the two remaining hours to Worthington became downright perilous. I drifted onto the rumble strips, crossed the center line. Trying as hard as I could to keep the speedometer up to seventy, I felt nothing but the pressure of my foot on the accelerator, as if what energy my body had left was being channeled down my leg, and in response my eyes would close, my head would wobble as if my neck were no stronger than a rubber band. I turned the radio up until the speakers rattled, and I sang the songs I knew in a raging shout and hummed the ones I didn't at such a volume that my teeth buzzed. I rolled down the window and stuck my head out periodically, into the icy wind. I slapped myself continually—my legs, my face—and I jerked my body around in the seat, trying to keep every part of myself moving at once. The lines on the road and the lights of the cars fanned out like ghosts, seeping past their own edges. I nearly wept when I discovered that the truck didn't have a cigarette lighter. It had occurred to me to burn my fingertips each time I felt my eyes begin to close. Instead I punched myself as hard as I could in the right ear, and that worked for a few minutes. I chanted to myself, moving my lips, *twenty thousand dollars, twenty thousand dollars*— that was the amount Mr. Griffin had agreed to. But then I was falling asleep again. My head fell forward and I slapped myself awake again in time to find myself headed straight for a dim figure at the side of the roadway. I jerked the wheel, and the figure disappeared. I looked in the rearview mirror and there was nothing. My heart, though, was awakened by the scare, and pumped blood where it needed to for several minutes. But then I started to doze off again, and each time I woke I was petrified by the thought that something—a creature, a person—had almost jumped in front of my headlights.

Finally, though, there was Worthington, and as I coasted down the exit ramp I was no longer sleepy at all. The town was nothing much—dusty streets and worn-out buildings, a shallow lake at its perimeter. I stopped in a little deserted park along the shore, and took note of the sign that said no overnight parking. It was a place I couldn't sleep, in other words, and I knew that I would want to sleep again when I had picked up the package, and I was determined to do so—this time, I intended to make sure my timetable wasn't changed.

To my surprise, Mr. Griffin's directions showed that I had come to the right place. I was instructed to stop right there at the little park by the lake. For a moment I felt almost lightheaded with my luck. Since I had arrived in Worthington more than half an hour early, and I had already located the package, that meant an extra half hour of sleep, or maybe even a chance to stop and eat at a place where I could sit down, have someone wait on me. But as I read on I found that the package was *in the water*. I would proceed to a stand of cottonwoods off to my right—I could see their shapes clearly in the moonlight—and standing under them I would look out over the water and see a buoy 150 feet away from shore. The package would be tied to the buoy. The directions did not go on from there to say what I was thinking—that Mr. Griffin was a son of a bitch. The directions just stopped, as if there were nothing unusual about asking a man to swim across an ice-cold lake in the middle of the night.

But twenty thousand dollars was twenty thousand dollars, and once I had this package in hand I would be two-thirds of the way there. And according to the timetable the rest of the trip would be easy. This was it, the last real hurdle. So I lifted the gate on the back of the truck and rummaged through my duffel bag to find a pair of clean underwear and a shirt, and I placed them in the truck cab. I took off my shoes and socks and pants and left them in the truck as well, then I locked the truck and carried the keys with me. Looking around, I saw no cop car hidden behind bushes, no car that might have been following me, no one waiting to unlock the truck once I was gone. Still, I watched the truck all the way to the cottonwoods, and I was upset to find that, down by the shore, I could no longer see the truck through the trees. The buoy was clearly visible, rocking up and down on gentle waves. The wind seemed to blow right through me, and I almost fooled myself into believing that the water would be a relief. It was not, of course. My feet plunged through what felt like a skin of ice, and I could not commit myself to going farther. And the thought came to me right then—it would be at this very moment, when I entered the water, that Mr. Griffin's spy would make his way to the truck. And so I was out of the water again, hustling up the bank in my underwear, emerging from the trees to find . . . nothing. A car whisked by quietly on the road beyond the parking lot, and I watched its lights round a bend. A tree branch snapped in the wind.

The water at the buoy was not over my head, and I stood chest deep untaping the package, which was wrapped in a plastic bag. The night was crystal clear, and I could see the reflections of stars dance on the water. I was colder than I could ever remember being, but despite the cold I stopped for a moment and held still. It was so quiet that I could hear the water lapping at the bank far behind me. Then a train whistle sounded loud across the water; it could have come to me from miles and miles, it could have been anywhere. I felt unusually calm—I wasn't angry, I didn't regret my ordeal. It wasn't embarrassing, to be a grown man out in a lake in his underwear, retrieving a package from a buoy. I felt purposeful, committed to seeing the whole thing through.

Back at the truck I toweled off in the cold air, changed into clean clothes, put on my jacket. I unwrapped the package from the plastic bag, saw that it was undamaged, tossed it on the floor with the other ones. They made a satisfying little pile, a sort of record of my progress and accomplishments. Then I settled in to check my timetable, feeling certain, for once, that it hadn't changed. And, yes, there was the light coffee stain right there on the second page. I was getting warm in the truck with the motor on and the heater running, and my heart beat easy. And so for a moment I doubted what I saw on the page in front of me.

The scheduled stop at Newcastle had been moved up almost half a day. I was now expected to arrive there at 4:32 the next afternoon. The clock in the truck cab said 3:31. I had estimated that a trip along the back roads would take about eleven hours. One hour of sleep—that was all I could dare. One hour of sleep and then back on the road in the dark until the sun came up, when I would buy coffee and then more coffee and drive on through the morning past the barns and silos and cornfields and in and out of the dusty towns, the sky like a piece of blue china overhead, and then into the McDonald's drive-thru or a convenience store where I could grab a bite to eat, and then the afternoon that stretched out like an eternity, the part of the day I had come to dread most, when my eyes stayed at a half squint and my mouth hung open and my head felt full of glue. I would arrive at Newcastle in the nick of time, and then what—another impossible stretch without sleep to pick up the last package in Idaho? For a minute that was all I could think of, just the torture.

Then I started to rebel. To hell with Mr. Griffin's rules—I would take the interstate again. And more than that—I would sleep as long as I wanted to. I would get a motel room right there in Worthington, sleep until checkout time. I would stop for lunch at an actual restaurant, enjoy a leisurely meal. The package in Wyoming would just have to wait. If it was a matter of such great concern, Mr. Griffin's Wyoming spy could stay there and keep an eye out until I arrived. If, when I arrived at the end of my journey, Mr. Griffin refused to pay me, I would refuse to hand over the packages, simple as that.

But there hadn't been any spy in Minnesota. I was staring at the same coffee-stained timetable, not a new one that had been substituted. The only explanation for this was that *the timetable had changed itself*. At that thought I felt my spirit of rebellion evaporate—it literally seemed to steam out my ears from my brain, and I could feel my body deflate with the loss of some necessary energy. My heart thumped, as if it were desperately trying to refill me, but I couldn't move, couldn't really even think. I felt alive only in the way a tree might feel alive, or a weed. My eyes were fixed on the timetable, expecting it to change before my very eyes maybe, and soon I believed it actually had. A section in bold print seemed to have appeared, something I hadn't seen before: **Violation of the terms of the contract entitles the contractor to reduce or eliminate payment to the assignee, according to the contractor's discretion. In addition, the contractor may seek retribution against the assignee as he deems**

**fit and appropriate, whether said retribution should take the form of the assignation of tasks subsequent to those outlined in the original contract, or, in cases of particularly egregious violations, punitive measures not restricted by extant laws or statutes, which may be leveled against the assignee, or the property of the assignee, or persons legally bound to the assignee, according to the desires of the contractor.**

I was close to tears then, there in the truck cab, thinking of my helplessness, thinking of the endlessness of Mr. Griffin's demands, how he would keep me there behind the wheel of my truck hunting down his idiotic packages until I died from exhaustion, or, if he preferred, seek retribution—that frightening word—against my poor wife, according to—that other awful word—his *desires*. But I did not have much time for crying.

Before I got back on the road, I threw open the gate of the U-Haul and rummaged through a box of my wife's things, pulling from it a black blouse I'd bought her for Christmas. Pressing the blouse to my face, I found that I could smell a trace of her perfume, and I closed my eyes and breathed. This was what I needed, something to comfort me as I drove the endless miles. I climbed back in the cab and placed the folded blouse on my lap, and two or three more times as I found a road heading west I raised the blouse to my face and smelled my wife's perfume, though the scent was already fading.

I grew a little calmer. Mr. Griffin's warning had unsettled me, but as I drove along in the usual way, with nothing more out of the ordinary occurring, I began to feel the idleness of Mr. Griffin's threats. That one phrase, *not restricted by extant laws or statutes*, came back to me. Instead of frightening me, the phrase now seemed to indicate a measure of desperation, and

I found myself laughing at Mr. Griffin as I sped along through the night. Surely he didn't expect me to believe that he was somehow above the law, that the normal rules didn't apply in his case, that he had been granted impunity to do whatever he liked. It was a ridiculous threat, an obviously transparent attempt to whip me into a panic so that I would push myself harder to keep to his ludicrous timetable. Well, I would play along for a while. It was probably best to let Mr. Griffin think that he had succeeded.

For at least a hundred miles I turned these ideas around, and I felt better for them, but a tall figure crossed the road in the nighttime, or I imagined a tall figure, dressed in a long coat and brimmed hat, and while this figure passed by mere feet in front of the bumper, my heart stopped and my hands froze to the wheel. I found that my body was absolutely rigid, that I had locked up, couldn't move at all, but my eyes could move; they began to close involuntarily. And then there was a bend in the highway, and with a violent jerk my body started up again to make the turn. And then my body went on working by itself, out of fear, while my mind seemed to sleep. My body did what it had to to stay awake, the coffee and the slapping and the singing to late-night radio again.

And then I was past Wolsey, South Dakota, and I began to feel lost. I knew I was on the right road, but I would lift my wife's blouse off my lap, replace it with the map, and determine for the third or fourth time that I was on such and such a highway. My chest felt tight. Passing north of the Badlands along a highway notable only for its long stretches of barbed wire and the occasional eyes of field mice lit up along the road, I began to worry that my heart would stop. It would not be

a heart attack, no great seizure and intense pain, just a simple stopping, as if my tired old heart had done all the work
it intended to do in the world, had loved as well as could be
reasonably expected and then some, and had nothing more to
offer me or anyone else.

For long moments during that night I would feel that this
was happening, that everything inside me had halted, and I
waited for my eyes to close, for the truck to drift slowly off the
pavement while I faded to my last unconsciousness. But each
time my heart felt like conceding, fear—nothing more—would
jolt me backward in my seat, and I would suck in air like a
drowning man. I was afraid of dying, even though it seemed
like the least complicated way out of my difficulties. I did not
want, when push came to shove, for my life to end by the side
of the road, in a U-Haul truck wrapped in barbed wire. And I
did not want to die and leave my wife in the hands of Mr. Griffin, a man who took pleasure in cruelty, a man who had both
the impulse and means to carry out unspeakable tortures, even
if I doubted he would do so, upon this woman whom I loved
beyond reason. I drove on.

But I had reached a point of nervous exhaustion. With the
sun now well established in my side mirrors, and the bar-
est chance of making my destination on time, my wits failed
me. The road looked impossibly narrow, and each car that
approached in the opposite lane seemed fated to collide with
me. The needle on the speedometer kept drifting down, no
matter how hard I tried to maintain a steady pressure on the
pedal. Soon it stood at fifty, and yet the world seemed to whirl
by at an impossibly dangerous speed. As I neared the Black
Hills, I still had an hour to make my schedule. It was possi-

ble—possible if I pushed the truck far past the speed limit, if I ignored red lights and stop signs, barreled through tourist towns hoping not to hit any pedestrians. This was my plan.

Soon, though, I realized it was hopeless. The more I tried to hurry, the more my panic grew, until I could barely see the road in front of me at all, and my heart seemed to seize up every few moments, like an engine running without a piston or two. Finally I could not breathe or make my heart beat anymore. I skidded the truck to a stop outside a convenience store. Somehow my legs carried me inside to the cooler, where I grabbed a pint of milk with a shaking hand. There were tears in my eyes as I approached the clerk, a teenager who looked shocked at my deranged appearance. My weakness had reached such a point that I intended to give up, to fall on my knees at the register and tell the boy to phone an ambulance and the police. Before I died on the way to the hospital I would tell my story, tell the police to alert the authorities in the small fishing village on Puget Sound, tell them to keep my wife from harm. But I couldn't do that. Calling the police would certainly constitute a "particularly egregious" violation. So I became confused, and stood there at the register in front of a line of customers, muttering the word *dying, dying*. I struggled to reach inside my pocket, and my fingertips felt the rough surface of coins, but I could not seem to extract them, until finally my hand jerked upward and the coins spilled onto the floor and I began to sob. The boy behind the counter held up a hand, his face pale, his eyes fixed somewhere around my chest, and I wondered if my heart had exploded through my shirt. "I'll get it," he said. "Just take the milk."

Outside I sat in the gravel and tore open the top of the carton and poured the milk down my throat in a long stream, feeling it run down my neck onto the collar of my coat, until I succeeded in making myself swallow, and then my hand felt more controlled and I emptied the container in long gulps. I felt better, like I wasn't dying after all, and in a minute I was back on the road, pushing ahead to my next stop even though there was no longer any chance to make it on time.

Exactly 1.3 miles past the high school football stadium in Newcastle, Wyoming, I turned into the parking lot of an abandoned tractor dealership, located the Dumpster behind the building, slammed on the brakes and leaped down from the truck, climbed into the empty Dumpster to find no package taped to the inside wall, no note, no anything. Wearily, I pulled myself back out and stood there in the gravel. The wind swept with a cold hiss across the dry Wyoming plains, and the sun was high and cold in the Wyoming afternoon sky, and a train that looked like it pulled a thousand boxcars wound its way east off in the distance. And yet, there in the absence of anything I found a reservoir of hope. I was a man, after all, and I was still alive, and I had come all that way, made an almost superhuman effort to drive that truck across the country's narrow back roads in almost no time at all, and I could not be faulted. I grimaced into the bright sky and resolved to settle with Mr. Griffin in my own way. I would speed on to Puget Sound to offer my wife my protection. I realized that it was hours past the time when I had told my wife, on her voice mail, that I would call her again, but I also realized that there was no use in calling now. Mr. Griffin had cut off our communication—how else to explain my wife's failure to return my calls? But it made no difference; I was close, it was only a matter of time.

When I reached I-90 and pulled into the westbound lanes
I had already devised my new strategy. Something had happened to the package in Newcastle. I had arrived too late, and
someone had found it before me. Or it had been withheld by
Mr. Griffin's drop-off party because I hadn't met the timetable.
Either way, it was clear that Mr. Griffin had much at stake with
the packages and would still be expecting me to pick up the
last one, which waited for me in an Idaho town not far from
the Canadian border, still a good thirteen hours away, according to the timetable. He would not make a move until then,
because he would risk the loss of the last package. My plan was
to take the interstate, which he would surely discover, by whatever means he had discovered it before. But he wouldn't know
that I had no intention of picking up the package until I sped
right past the turnoff to that little Idaho town, which lay seventy
miles north of the interstate. A seventy-mile head start, I would
have, on whomever Mr. Griffin had sent to meet me. With the
U-Haul humming along as fast as it could carry me I felt that
heightened awareness peculiar to the best moments in life,
those times when one feels slightly larger and more important
than the other objects of the world. I churned straight on into
the lowering sun, thinking pleasant thoughts of the fishing village and how my wife and I would live there happily. We had
been there on our honeymoon, and my wife had fallen in love
with the fog that draped the hills in the morning and the miles
of blackberry brambles lining the quiet country roads and the
sound of foghorns over the water. Mr. Griffin seemed remote,
as if I had not made a deal with him and he had not threatened
me. But I had not slept in a long time. Toward sunset I began

to grow so tired that the bare Montana hills bobbed before my eyes, rolling down and down and then popping up again in their proper places, as if I were watching a TV screen with a faulty vertical hold. There was no reason not to sleep, really, no reason not to pull over at the next rest area and fall asleep in the cool air next to a picnic table with the dreamy voices of families headed back and forth to the restrooms. I was no longer on a schedule. Nothing would matter until I passed the turnoff to that small northern Idaho town. But my foot held steady on the pedal, and at each opportunity to leave the interstate I found myself moving on.

Without intending to, I began to play "Imagine Alice." Imagine Alice being born, the intimacy of the delivery room, holding my wife's hand, the sweat on her forehead, the smile on her face when it was all through and we held Alice close. Imagine Alice coming home, wrapped in warm blankets, to the little house we would have on a hill. Imagine Alice nursing, my wife holding her in a rocking chair on the porch. Imagine Alice going to school, how I would hold her hand going up a sidewalk while my wife sat in the car watching us, calling out last-minute instructions. Imagine Alice on her wedding day, as pretty as her mother.

It had grown dark. I was somewhere in Idaho. At the edge of sleep, I knew I had already passed the turnoff, had failed to notice it somehow. I jerked in the seat and my hands made the motion of turning, as if I had decided I needed to turn. Then, strangely, I was not on the asphalt any longer, was tilted down into the ditch, and in what seemed a long tired motion, an exhausted and comfortable reclining, the truck turned onto its side as if it wanted to sleep as much as I did, as if it were a tired animal, tired of the incessant beat of its own old heart, and I pitched across the seat and came to rest.

I might have slept for days. I remember first the daylight, the feel of the packed dirt beneath my cheek, and a light rain. Sitting up, I looked across a field at a gravel pit, a huge truck rumbling and clanking. Turning, I found the interstate, a semi roaring past, its wind in my ears, mist hissing up from its tires. Not one of the drivers seemed to notice me there in the ditch, and I barely noticed myself. I merely watched the cars and trucks stream by in colorful waves and listened to the hissing tires, which sounded oddly like radio static or the whir of electrical appliances. I thought of nothing—not my wife, not the small fishing village on Puget Sound, not Mr. Griffin and the task I'd failed to complete. My sleep had emptied all thoughts out of me.

It was some time, even, before I discovered that the U-Haul was missing. I remembered the crash, the slow and somewhat peaceful tipping of the truck onto its side, and the way I'd seemed almost to float downward to hit the passenger door. But there was no evidence of the crash anywhere. No tire tracks leading from the shoulder into the ditch, no broken glass, no trail left by a tow truck. I walked up and down the area several times, looking for clues, but to no avail. Not one head in any vehicle turned in my direction, not one person seemed curious about what I was up to. Without the truck heater to warm me, I was very cold, and I put my hands into my coat pockets. There I found my wife's black blouse, folded neatly, and the cotton ball. I checked my back pocket and my wallet was gone. I returned to the spot in which I'd slept, hoping to find the wallet there, but what I found instead, pressed flat to the earth where I had lain, was a note on a sheet of stationery. The letterhead read *Griffin Enterprises*, and the note consisted of one word, in bold black ink: **WALK**.

And so I got on the road again. This second journey would take much longer, and it would be much harder, even, than the first. For what lay ahead of me were the countless miles of ancient floodplain that made up eastern and central Washington, a stark landscape more like the surface of the moon than anything on Earth. What lay beyond that were the fog-shrouded Cascade Mountains, the huge fir trees leaning into the steep slopes rolling up the mountain peaks. Only after I crossed the mountains would I reach Puget Sound, and only after I crossed the sound would I reach the fishing village, and all the time I would not know what I'd find there. What lay ahead was the long, dead trek along the shoulder of the interstate. The crunch of gravel and the sift of volcanic ash beneath my shoes would become so familiar that I would dream it ever after in my sleep.

I obeyed Mr. Griffin's command; what other choice did I have? Not only could Mr. Griffin monitor my actions and my whereabouts, he could also make large physical objects disappear. What other explanation for the truck? And in case I harbored any doubt, it soon began to seem as if *I* had disappeared as well. I was seemingly invisible to the drivers of the cars on the interstate. No one stopped for me. No one honked a horn. No head turned in my direction. I limped along my way—my right leg had been injured in the accident, and there was a painful twisting to my knee at every step—entirely unnoticed. I came to think of myself as a wandering spirit. And yet not wandering—my destination was always clear.

Since no one seemed at all interested in my plight, even on the first occasion when I became hungry I did not hesitate. I marched into a convenience store next to the off-ramp, opened the door to the cooler, and grabbed a soda. From one of the aisles I took a bag of chips and a package of beef jerky and stuffed them in my pockets. Walking out, I looked around, and only one customer appeared to notice—she must have heard the rustling of a bag of chips and was looking on the floor to see if it had fallen.

When I needed a place to sleep, I clambered into the back-seats of unlocked cars or huddled in the corners of service-station restrooms or the stairwells of motels. I took whatever I wanted from the stores I passed along the way—food, a warm hat and a warm pair of gloves, cheap tourist items I thought would amuse my wife. In less than two weeks I covered over three hundred miles. I became familiar with the various car-casses of dead animals—the dogs, the cats, the skunks, the raccoons—and the detritus thrown from windows—cigarette butts and fast-food wrappers and dirty diapers and damaged CDs and ragged T-shirts and beer cans and old magazines. In one strange instance I found a gold wedding band just off the asphalt in the weeds, and a little farther ahead a corsage of some sort, but I could never understand the story of how the two were related, though I felt certain they were. I found a hockey stick and a gas mask and a letter from a girl to her mother. And all the time there was the icy, swirling wind kicked up by the semis. Once I reached the mountains there was the sigh of the evergreens, which I could only hear deep in the night, when fewer vehicles were passing.

And I grew stronger. In the end I walked by choice rather

than compulsion. It would have been easy to slip into the cab of a semi parked at a rest area. The driver never would have known. But I understood that Mr. Griffin would know. I was not invisible to Mr. Griffin. And yet I felt that, even had I been able to avoid his scrutiny, I would have chosen to continue walking.

I thought of my wife now almost unceasingly, because the miles were monotonous and I needed a focal point. I played "Imagine Alice." And something began to take shape out of my new feeling of resolution—a new kind of relationship with my wife, a sense of possibility for the family we had always wanted. I thought of the months after we first met, how she had honestly seemed to feel passionate toward me, and I thought of how that passion had gone away, though I could not exactly remember the passage between the two stages. We had passion, and then we didn't. But I began to see that my weakness had created her change of heart. By acceding to her wishes constantly, I had allowed her to become the worst part of herself, and for that she despised me. She selfishly tried to press her own advantage, and when she met no resistance there was nothing left for her but the selfishness and the accusations, and the accusations were really a sort of plea. She needed something to push against, and when she had it she would stop pushing. I was confident, even, that our infertility would vanish with my newfound strength. I did not think at all, perhaps because avoidance of the thought felt necessary for retaining my strength, about Mr. Griffin. Mr. Griffin I would deal with when the time came.

On an achingly cold day in November, I arrived on the western shore of Puget Sound via the Bainbridge Island ferry. I took some pleasure in violating the spirit, if not the letter, of Mr. Griffin's law, walking back and forth steadily along the deck while the ferry hummed across the water, the tourists and commuters ignoring me. From the ferry landing I walked a series of quiet country roads, the afternoon sunlight warming me a little. Finally I reached my destination, setting eyes once again on the quaint stores and restaurants and old wooden churches of the little Norwegian fishing village my wife had fallen in love with. And walking up the town's main street, looking out toward the sunlit water where the fishing boats swayed softly in their moorings, and seeing up ahead already, on a hill overlooking the sound, the quaint hotel I had stayed at on my honeymoon, I thought of how I was only minutes away from seeing my wife again, and I had a clear picture of how it would be when I found her, how she would see me with a new sort of recognition. My legs felt strong and healthy, and my vision was sharp and clear. I carried the power of the journey I'd put behind me, those long weeks of the road and the weather, and I carried the power of my love for my wife. I felt full with this love to the point of bursting.

But as I began to climb the hill I came upon a little park, the waves lapping lazily on a sandy strip giving way to grass and picnic tables. On the closest table a woman lay with her legs spread wide, her red hair fanned out, and a man in a long coat and dark hat stood above her, the coat hiding his rhythmic movements, the hat pulled down to shield his face. My wife and Mr. Griffin, I knew.

I walked toward them, seeing only, for the moment, my wife's bare legs, the whiteness of them beneath her hiked-up skirt, the way her muscles responded to Mr. Griffin's pressure.

Then I saw the blotchiness of her skin, the cold, and then her face, red and twisted tight, and the fogging of her breath. Her head turned in my direction, but she did not appear to see anything, her glazed eyes staring somewhere past me toward the buildings of the town. Mr. Griffin kept up his steady rhythm, his face hidden behind the upturned coat collar, the brimmed hat. I could see nothing of him at all, and yet I knew him, and I knew what the two of them were doing—they were conceiving Alice.

I wanted to kill Mr. Griffin, grasp him in my hands and break him the way I knew I could now, but he seemed less than real to me, an insubstantial figure, an invisibility inside a coat. There was no mention of the packages, delivered or undelivered, and no mention of my payment. There was nothing from Mr. Griffin at all, not even a glance. There was no need for him to tell me that this was my punishment, this my failure, to see him taking his pleasure with my wife there on the shore of the little Norwegian fishing village. I could see now the lengths that he had gone to, the shady plan that he'd devised to take my place. But at the same time, something told me that he himself was nothing but a shadow. Mr. Griffin was not really there. It was only my wife and me, and if I could somehow make myself known to her, then I would be the one there with her.

My heart pumped hard into my limbs and into my head, and I knelt down on the ground and I imagined Alice, imagined her harder than I ever had, imagined her as the culmination of the love I felt and that my wife would come to feel, the love we were on the verge of having together. From my coat pocket I took the few things I had collected on my journey, and I held them tightly to my chest until I could feel the walls of my heart giving way, and I rose from my knees and stepped forward, closing my eyes to imagine everything better. Without opening my eyes, hearing my wife's breathing coming faster, I held my arms out in front of me, held out the life I'd made from those few lifeless items, a cotton ball and a black blouse, bumper stickers and key rings. "This is for you," I said, still walking forward. "Here's Alice. Do you see? She's right here in my hands."

# Blackout

I should start by saying my name is Bobby. Ten years we'd been waiting for the reunion, all of us—me—Bobby—and my friend Norm who's crippled now because his leg got crushed when he was in the woods working the skidder. That would be, what, seven years ago. His first year in the woods after he quit trying to go to college. He's a good guy, Norm, my best friend really, he hobbles around. Give you the shirt off his back. I saw him get mad once in his whole life, when he punched this kid Darrell for telling Mrs. Harms he cheated, Norm cheated, on his spelling test. He got an F anyway. He can't spell for shit. Then I guess also he got mad once about his crushed leg, a couple years ago, maybe, the summer my wife was being nice to me, I remember. He broke one of the side windows in my garage, but I count that as more a sad thing than angry.

And there's also Gayle; he's got a girl's name but you don't want to tell him that to his face. And Dennis, his father owns the wood shop where they make wooden lighting fixtures, so he's the boss, sort of. I sell cars. I started off after high school just as the kind of gofer and clean-up guy—make parts runs and wash the cars on the lot, shine them up, etc., run the tow truck sometimes, minor repairs, basic service stuff, oil changes and spark plugs and filters, and sometimes keep customers occupied if one of the salesmen was working two customers at the same time, just talk to people about the weather or mention little options they were getting not included in the sticker price. I worked my way up to salesman, last year runner-up top salesman, I sold more Chevy vehicles than anyone at the dealership except one other guy. And Tony, who's not as bad off as Norm but still he's missing parts of three fingers. He works for Dennis at the wood shop where they make lighting fixtures, indoor and outdoor, do lots of mail-order business to folks back East who want to look rustic. Tony gets stoned a lot before he goes to work and he sticks his fingers in one of the saws or the joiner. He'd get fired if he wasn't Dennis's friend. All of us, basically, us guys who stayed around town, we'd been waiting for the reunion ten years. I know some of the people who left, including Abbie, were looking forward to it, too, but you get the feeling they'd moved on to other things.

Ten years, and what I'll be stuck with for the next ten is pissing in the bubble gum. We started off the first afternoon at Jerry's. The first day of the reunion, I mean. Jerry's is a bar, not somebody's house. Did I say I was married? To Sondra. She's all right.

The thing was we were too eager. We'd waited too long. The reunion was two nights, Friday and Saturday. The first night was at the Lakeshore Lounge, by the lake. Then the second night, Saturday, we had a steak dinner at Trudy's. That's a restaurant in town, not a person. Fuck me—who ever said I could tell a story? It was my wife's idea that I get it all out. She went to college for a while. She doesn't know about the bubble gum, though, so if I'm going to put that in she'll never read this. Or the note and the picture. She thinks it was just the blackout, or what she calls the supposed blackout.

It was maybe 3:30 in the afternoon and we were already buzzing. Every one of our bosses had gave us an early weekend. Except Norm, who's on government disability or something, he won't talk about it, not even to me. We were telling ourselves everything was OK but I think we all probably knew we'd get too drunk and make spectacles of ourselves.

That doesn't explain what happened to me, though. We didn't eat anything, either. I knew Abbie would be there, but I thought she'd have her husband with her. I remember the moment I found out, when I talked to her under that canopy thing they had pitched on the lawn. I was nervous. I'd been counting on her husband to protect me from myself, I guess. Then the only other time I remember talking to her that night was when we went to order drinks in the lounge. I told her how I had dreams sometimes of being back in high school and I asked her if she did too, and she said no. Her husband works for the army, but not as a soldier, some kind of other work that involves government contracts, and they live in California. I don't know how I got the note from her or the picture. That's part of the blackout. But I told her I still had dreams about high school, even though I was twenty-eight now, and how I was actually glad to be in high school in the dreams. I don't know why I told her all that. I guess because I expected she would say, oh yeah, me too, like everyone has dreams about still being in high school and is happy about it. I'm just going by me and Norm and Tony and Dennis, though. I hadn't thought about how the people who moved out of town might not dream about it anymore. But I told her too how they would turn into nightmares sometimes, because I would find out there was some class I needed to graduate that I hadn't even been to, and Principal Burton wasn't going to give me a diploma.

We were at Jerry's. We played darts and pool. I was already getting drunk and sleepy before the reunion started. We were too worked up about it was the thing. Sloan, the bartender, though, he invited me into the back room and let me do a little bump, a little of the white stuff, because he said I needed it. We were supposed to be getting some stuff for the second night, too, Tony was, but it never happened, at least not as far as I know.

The last thing I remember was talking to Abbie. She didn't have her husband or her kids with her. Sondra and I had a girl, but she died. Kid cancer. I don't even think about it anymore. I make myself not. It was a fucking horrible thing, just horrible. That poor little girl. I think it was after that that I really started not doing much but look forward to the ten-year reunion.

I remember the whole conversation with Abbie in the convenience store the second night, too. We went there to pick up cigarettes. We were going to smoke them in the parking lot of Trudy's while everyone else ate dinner, but then we didn't. I just went home. That was after I pissed in the gum. End of fucking reunion for me. Ten years before I can hope to clear another space in my head. Writing it down won't do anything.

We talked under the canopy. My wife, her husband, her kids. We renewed our old acquaintance would be the phrase. Things felt just the same. She still looked good. A little muscley, actually. I guess she stayed thin by jogging or lifting weights. I kept noticing how strong her calves looked underneath her skirt. They were attractive. I look pretty much the same. Not so bad, not so good. I don't do anything to stay that way. Sell cars. I'm just naturally thin.

Abbie wasn't the best-looking girl in our high school, just the best-looking and most popular one who paid any attention to me. I played football, but I wasn't one of the best players. She was a jock chick but not a cheerleader, sort of second level, below the cheerleaders really. Dennis was hot shit. She dated him for a while until he dumped her. She always seemed to like me, though. I liked her but I was dating Sondra on and off and then we got married. Me and Sondra was a settled kind of thing. But Abbie and I always had something. Lots of people said so.

So then I don't remember anything. It's just a blank. Next thing I know it's afternoon, and we're back at Jerry's. I honest to God couldn't figure out if it was Friday or Saturday, if it was the first day of the reunion or we'd had one day already. I thought I was going to pass out, I felt just that shitty. All I knew was I was drunk. I got Norm off to the side. I'm fucked up, buddy, I said. He said, What do you mean? I said, I mean I don't know what the fuck's going on. He looked around. We're playing pool, he said. I asked him, Is this today or yesterday?

He took me in the back room and tried to get me a bump but Sloan didn't have any. Instead we started going over the events of the night before. I said to him what happened after I talked to Abbie and he said when was that, and I said at the very beginning and he said well, we left the party to go get stoned and drove around and then came back and went to this guy Allen's motel room to drink some more, but then he seemed to remember I wasn't with him and looked at me like I'd disappeared in some strange way or he didn't know who I was. He said, Where *were* you? I said, That's what I don't know.

And for some reason I reached in my back pocket. I had on the same jeans from the night before. I'd bought a new pair of Levi's. I didn't want to wear my car salesman outfit to the reunion. I wore Levi's in high school. We'd all agreed to wear the same stuff we'd worn in high school. This was something we thought would be cool, but it really just meant me and Norm and Dennis and Gayle and Tony were dressed worse than everyone else. In the pocket of my pants were two things. The first thing I pulled out was this note from Abbie. It said, *I'm so glad you came to the reunion. You've really helped to make the whole experience special. Let's make sure to talk again tomorrow.* It was on a bar napkin. Then the second thing was a Polaroid, one of those old instant-camera Polaroids, of Abbie down by the water, bare-ass naked, mooning the camera. It wasn't just your regular mooning shot. Her legs were slightly apart and you could see quite a bit.

Fuckin' ay, Norm said. He kept holding the picture away from me and looking at it himself. But I couldn't remember it. I didn't have a camera. I didn't remember seeing Abbie with a camera, and certainly not one of those old Polaroids which you wonder why the fuck somebody would bring. It was a mystery to me. I couldn't remember anything.

It seemed like we were at Jerry's for hours. Maybe we were. I kept trying to put Friday night together. I kept trying to remember being with Abbie. I kept trying to remember if I fucked her. I looked at the picture between pool shots, slipping it in and out of my pocket. For a long time I'd had thoughts of hooking up with Abbie at the reunion. But it made me sick, thinking I might have. The whole night was a blank. Me and Norm and Dennis and Gayle and Tony were supposed to have a great time. And they kept remembering things they'd done the night before, and they did seem to have had a great time, but they all sounded slightly depressed, and none of them remembered anything about me. I couldn't remember anything about myself. I had on the same pants and shirt. I figured I never went home, although Sondra says I did. She says I came home early. She says I slept beside her in the bed all night. She says she remembers this, but there's a look in her eyes. She doesn't know how I ended up in the same clothes the next day. She doesn't really seem to know it all too clearly. There's something in her eyes where she wonders. And she doesn't know about the note or the naked picture of Abbie.

Really it's like I disappeared. It's not just a blackout. I've blacked out before, but people always told me what I did. Once I outran a cop in my Camaro. Once I passed out in the snow in someone's yard. There was always someone there to tell me. This time it was like I didn't exist. A naked picture of Abbie. A note. What I'd waited for for ten years.

I was scared. I was scared I'd slept around on Sondra. I kept asking everyone at Jerry's. I remember the convenience store perfectly. We were at Trudy's. I still couldn't remember anything. I thought I hadn't even been home to Sondra. I thought she was ready to divorce me. I was thinking I wouldn't go home that night either. It was like I'd lost my identity. It still feels that way. I'm having a hard time these days being a car salesman.

That's part of why Sondra said write all this down. It's like I don't know who I am anymore because I don't know, after waiting ten years, what I did at the reunion.

Abbie said I had a spirit, that's what was so attractive about me. This is before we went to the convenience store, skipped out on dinner. I really wasn't thinking about getting together with her anymore, I was thinking more about trying to figure out what I'd done Friday night. What kind of spirit, I'd like to know? I don't have any spirit.

Here's the only way I can explain it. It's like I slept through all of it, I was asleep the whole time, I set the alarm for my ten-year reunion and I never woke up. Or I'm asleep now. Sometimes it feels that way. I'm asleep now and the reunion never happened and I dreamed the whole thing. Or it's still *before* the reunion and I've only dreamed of all these things happening. Or, maybe, I *am* still in high school and I've dreamed the last ten years and the alarm will go off and it'll be time for Mrs. O'Connell's first-period English class.

Maybe everyone is sleeping. Sometimes I look at people and they seem asleep. Maybe I'm the only one awake.

Abbie and I were talking so much that we couldn't pick out anything. We came there for cigarettes. I haven't told Sondra anything about the convenience store. I barely even told her I talked at all to Abbie. Here's the reason Sondra didn't go to the reunion: she got fat. Abbie kept saying I had this soul or spirit that was special. I suppose that was an interesting thing for her to think about, and not too different from what I thought about her all those years. Like all those ten years when her life got boring with her husband and her two kids who grew up and now went to school during the day, and she had to run errands and keep the house looking nice—Sondra works as a secretary at a company that makes salad dressings because I don't make enough money for her to stay at home and we've still got medical bills from before our daughter died, when she was so sick—and all that time Abbie could sit around and think while she was vacuuming or running errands that things wouldn't be like this if she'd married Bobby Sullivan back in high school, because he had a soul and a spirit. That's what I think about where she got those ideas.

I kept thinking about that picture. It was in my pocket. Like where did it come from and how did I get it, and what had we done together before or after it was taken and what did it mean. I kept trying to pick up clues in her conversation. She kept wanting to talk about ideas like God, did I believe in God and what kind of God and did I believe in a spiritual life, and questions like why were people so afraid of death. This is while we're looking at bags of potato chips. I know a thing or two about death. There's nothing mystical or beautiful or natural about it like Abbie was saying. It's ugly and slow and it hurts you in places you didn't know you had. I didn't tell Abbie about my daughter. I'm pretty sure she didn't even know I ever had one. People won't tell you their personal opinions if they think it's in an area that actually concerns you.

Our daughter's death didn't have anything to do with Sondra getting fat. To tell the truth, it seems like Sondra was already gaining weight from when I first started dating her. She never said that was the reason she didn't go to the reunion. I just knew. She didn't cry or spend a lot of time looking at herself in the mirror. The reunion didn't seem to mean anything much to her. She wouldn't have even asked about it except she knew I was interested and then how I was so worried because I couldn't remember things.

I don't know why Abbie got hung up on this idea of my fine spirit or good soul. I mean why not Dennis or Gayle or Tony or Norm? I mean, Norm, shit—if anybody's got a fine soul, it's him. How'd you like to hobble around with a leg like a broken fence post? And he's the nicest goddamn guy you've ever seen. All day that Saturday he tried to help me track down what I'd been doing the night before.

We were in the convenience store and we kept talking and picking up stuff and putting it back down again, Abbie because she was so involved in this conversation and me because I kept seeing this picture of her bare-assed naked. I had the thing right there in my pocket, and it wasn't just your everyday moon shot, her legs were spread apart and you could see it all there. It was a very odd thing to have in your pocket in the first place, something that, to tell the truth, I would have been very happy to have just the week before, but now it wasn't turning me on in any way. It was just worrying the hell out of me because I couldn't remember the circumstances or anything about the whole night. I couldn't get a bead on what we had between us, me and Abbie, based on the night before. She didn't seem any different. It was like she didn't even know about the picture or the note, or maybe we had had sex and she was waiting for me to try to straighten things out, maybe say something about going on with our lives and cherishing the memories. But I didn't have any memories.

In fact, there in the convenience store I couldn't tell anymore if I was awake or sleeping, I couldn't tell if I was alive or dead. It came to me that maybe I had died and this was some strange sort of afterlife, where it almost overlapped with the actual life you'd just got done having but not quite. I was drunk, too, very drunk, I'd been drinking, as far as I could remember, nonstop since yesterday afternoon. Abbie was on the other end of the store for a minute, getting cigarettes I think from the cashier, and my eyes were closed and I was sleeping on my feet someplace, I guess I thought I was at home, I thought I was dreaming and maybe I was, I still can't tell the difference, but when I came to there in the convenience store I had pissed in this candy tray that had these little individually wrapped pieces of bubble gum in it, all colors of wrapped bubble gum, and they were floating in this piss and the piss was starting to drip around the tray's edges.

I don't know if Abbie knew what happened. I got away from there but she was coming toward me. I thought she looked in that direction. I could barely walk. She helped me to the car. We didn't smoke the cigarettes, at least I didn't. She took me to Trudy's parking lot and I went to my car and drove home. That I remember.

I waited ten years for the reunion. It seemed like all I had to look forward to. I wanted mostly to see Abbie. I was sort of hoping that the reunion would help me forget the last ten years, but all I forgot was the reunion. I don't know what happened or didn't happen, not any of it. I don't know if I'm awake or if I'm sleeping. I don't know whether the reunion has actually happened yet or not. Maybe I'll wake up tomorrow and it will be the first day and it will all be as fun as Norm and Dennis and the other guys and I had planned it. Maybe Norm will get his good leg back. Maybe Tony will get back his fingers. Maybe I'll get back things I lost and don't like to think of. But what I *remember*, real or not, is those pieces of bubble gum floating in piss. That's my reunion.

The naked picture of Abbie seems real. I still have it. Sondra doesn't know. The card Abbie gave me when she dropped me off in the parking lot at Trudy's seems real. It's like a business card, only it's a family card instead. It has a color picture of Abbie and her husband and their two kids smiling and sitting under a tree. It says *The Simms Family—Jack, Abbie, Bonnie, and Elaine*. And it has their address and phone number. I have a card, too, and I take them out of my wallet and compare. My card doesn't have a picture. It has a Chevrolet symbol and the name of my dealership. It says *Bobby Sullivan, Sales Representative*.

# A Desert Island Romance

Roger never remembered how he had gotten there in the first place. He had a vague recollection of choppy seas, a perilously small craft, an inadequate supply of life jackets, but the actual circumstances were wrapped in a mysterious fog. Nor did he ever learn the whereabouts of the island; this was consistent with his understanding of what it meant to be a castaway—in all the information he had encountered on the subject, the stranded survivor never determined his exact location. So, once there, he set forth with a sort of woozy resignation about the business at hand. As nearly as he could recall, his job was to erect a crude grass hut, learn to live off the fruits of the land and whatever small animals he could snare, spend a good deal of time staring off into the horizon in hopes of spotting a sail.

What he didn't expect was the arrival of Sharon. She was beached a few weeks later after a drunken fall from a cruise boat, and was pleased to find such a nice man (handsome, too) inhabiting the tropical isle. Roger liked Sharon's smile, and a certain dainty way she had of curling her hair behind one ear, and, since she seemed quite taken with him, he began to stare less and less at the horizon and more and more at the flotsam the horizon had sent him.

They took moonlit walks and made love on the beach. They fished and picked fruit during the long, lazy days. They explored their island—learned every cove, every stream, every clump of trees—and began to call it home. They set up house-keeping and started dreaming of a future.

Eventually, they began to talk—seriously, as couples will. Roger told Sharon about his ex-fiancée, Debbie (at least, he considered her his ex-fiancée now), who'd lived with him in New Orleans, and Sharon told Roger about her similarly "ex" husband in Mitchell, South Dakota. Roger was born and raised in Shreveport. His father owned a bar there, and he supported his son's efforts to make a go of it in the big city. Roger was a bartender at the Bayou Pirate on Esplanade and showed every sign of management potential.

Sharon held an anthropology degree (a major she'd selected in all innocence) from USD, and her schooling had made her skeptical of any divine influence in the creation of human beings, a sentiment that she couldn't carry home to her dear mother and father in Mitchell, or to her high school sweetheart,

Ted, a dairy farmer whom she eventually married. They had been on their honeymoon cruise when she fell—Ted asleep in the cabin while she tied one on out of pure grief at their misguided union.

Sharon sympathized with Roger; Roger sympathized with Sharon. They understood each other's loneliness. Soon their walks on the beach took a therapeutic turn. Sharon helped Roger cope with feelings of inadequacy concerning his career. Bartenders were so underappreciated, and the pay wasn't the greatest, either. In turn, Roger did his best to help Sharon overcome the idea that she must downplay her education to soothe her mother's mind; the family matriarch was a good Christian woman, and she believed that Sharon's schooling had diverted her from the straight and narrow path—hence the return to Mitchell on Sharon's part, the marriage to Ted. They comforted each other in these respects.

Eventually, they introduced other friends and family, hobbies, work, the daily pattern of their lives. Sharon thought Roger worked entirely too many shifts, and that his irregular hours could only do him harm. She suspected his best friend, George, was actually a bad influence—insisting they play pool all day every Sunday, while the time might be better spent reading or performing community service. Roger thought a social life was important; Sharon was too stifled in Mitchell—staying home every day and night, fixing dinner, washing clothes (the dutiful farmer's wife), her only time away consisting of volunteer work at the local library. It was important to please your family, sure, but the idea could be taken too far. On top of that, Sharon was entirely too introverted, worrying all the time about the failure of religion and whatnot. Roger resolved to improve the situation by getting her out a little more—a nice dinner, a little dancing—that was what she needed.

Although languid and serene, life on the island could get pretty dull at times, and the impulse to dwell on the outside world was strong. They wondered what was happening beyond that line of sea and sky, they wondered what their loved ones were up to. This wistfulness found its way into their conversations. At some point, they decided arbitrarily on the day of the week and kept track carefully. They decided it was February, the month of Roger's father's birthday.

March rolled around, spring was in the air, and it was easy to lapse into reminiscence. When the sun hung low over the ocean on Saturday evenings, Roger would remember that it was about time to come on shift and would go over his routine—restocking the coolers, counting his till, fanning his bev naps, changing empty kegs. He would recite the comings and goings of his regulars. Gloria Patterson, recently widowed after an offshore accident, was already drunk, and had to be cut off early. George claimed her stool and had squatter's rights till closing. Jack and Dan the cribbage fiends, Rachel from Antoine's, Robert the old queen who slurped gin and tonics until he believed he was Tennessee Williams. Julian and Marion and Alberto, J.T., Agnes, and Malik—Sharon learned them all, and grew a little jealous; Roger preferred their company to hers, she suspected.

She retreated into her own familiar scenes. Sunday noons, when the sun stood straight overhead, she would imagine out loud leaving church, escorting her mother by the arm, thanking the pastor for an edifying sermon (knowing in her heart it wasn't so). She would visit with Aunt Sonia on the steps, telling her how good she looked in her polka-dot dress and her hair as hard as granite, trying to retain consciousness in the wake of her perfume. Then it was off to lunch at the folks'—pot roast, corn, and mashed potatoes, and all her mother's closed-door gossip about the female congregation, her father silent and hungry, sneaking scraps to the dog. Roger appreciated Sharon's sense of humor about the whole proceeding, but thought he could hardly endure the boredom of life in South Dakota.

It became routine soon enough. Roger insisted on working six shifts a week and never took a vacation. At first, Sharon would pull up a bar stool, but she'd given up drinking after the cruise boat experience and got tired of sipping cranberry and soda hour after hour. Roger's friends annoyed her (especially George) and the smoke was just too much. She was sure that Roger, who sometimes kept a cigarette lit at each end of the bar, would succumb to cancer before forty. She started staying home nights by herself.

Roger, on the other hand, hankering for promotion and enthralled with the fast pace of Bourbon Street, hated frittering away his off-hours down on the family farm. Sharon's mother drove him crazy. She pestered him about his smoking and asked him to get his hair cut. The old man was almost as bad, falling asleep on the couch every Sunday right during *60 Minutes*, snoring at Andy Rooney. Worst of all, Sharon had even invited Ted over once or twice (she said she felt sorry for him, but Roger wasn't sure). About the time he'd worked up enough nerve to beg his way out of these long hokey Sundays in favor of football and pool with George, Sharon had decided to up the ante to two days a week, Wednesday as well as Sunday, and it was more than Roger could stand.

He found excuses to sneak away—a sick bartender, a friend who needed advice over a few drinks. He stayed out later after work and Sharon didn't even notice. For her part, she started dropping Roger off at the bar and keeping the car to visit home or attend meetings of the historical society.

The red rose of romance no longer bloomed. Sharon and Roger still made love occasionally, but it was rote sex, sex by numbers, wholly conditioned behavior. Oh, there were lots of reasons. Sharon felt neglected—Roger had tried to take her out, but they had different tastes in restaurants, in bars, in movies (if Sharon had to sit through one more mindless action film she'd scream). And they could never seem to get to the bottom or the end of anything. Sharon wanted to talk more about her mother's passion for control, but the subject dropped like an egg at Roger's feet. Roger was always on the move—up in the world, out into the social scene; every now and then Sharon just had to stop and rest. Always on opposite sides of love's escalator, it seemed. Sure, they sought counseling—a man named Archer they found in the phone book—but all he could tell them was talk to each other, and they'd always done plenty of that.

For Sharon, it was an intolerable situation. She needed emotional support. She wanted to start a family, but Roger said they couldn't afford it on his salary. On and on and on, and the problems only seemed to multiply with time.

That next spring, just over a year since their future had looked so bright, Sharon decided to move out, and Roger hardly fussed. It was nice to have a woman's touch around the house, but a man wants his independence, too. Sharon packed up and moved east, a world away from Roger and her mother. New life, new adventure.

At first, Roger hardly felt her absence, so busy he was with work, so happy with his friends. He'd patched things up with Debbie, his ex-fiancée. But eventually he began to wonder, particularly on those few nights when he found himself home alone, what had become of Sharon. How was she holding up without him? Had she found somebody else?

After a few months, a letter arrived:

> *Roger,*
>
> *How are you? Don't smoke so much. I'm doing fine. Really. Fine. Don't let George waste all your time. Keep focused on your goals. This is just a letter to tell you that I am doing well, although I miss you. But I will not come home. Life is so fast paced here. I sometimes lose track of myself. Imagine, me, from Mitchell, right in the middle of it all, when it was you who craved the action. You did crave the action, Roger; that was what separated us. I am working at the public library. I am fine here. People are so hard to judge. They all seem so nice at first, but . . . it was nice with you. I knew where I stood. I'm doing fine.*
>
> *Love,*
>
> *Sharon*
>
> *P.S—Please send, C.O.D., my photo albums, which I'm afraid I forgot. They help remind me of home.*

She was doing fine, or so she said, but there were things in the letter that bothered him. Who were these "people"? Was Sharon getting herself into trouble? Roger searched everywhere, but he couldn't find any photo albums.

He began doubting himself. "Craving action," she had said. Was that really all he was about? Had he lost track of his goals? He was always forgetting to phone his dad—that was a bad sign. Who were his real friends, come to think of it, besides Sharon? Sometimes, serving drinks to a packed bar on a Friday night, or even at the movies with Debbie, he felt entirely alone.

Another letter arrived, this one from Sharon's mother (Roger never visited anymore). It read:

> *Roger,*
>
> *How are you, dear? Buddy and I are fine. Buddy works himself to death, but that's not news. I am content as always, in God's love.*
>
> *Roger, dear, I write to you out of deep concern for Sharon. I know that she is no longer your responsibility, but there was (there is?) so much love between you, that I wonder if some lingering feeling, or at least some spark of Christian generosity, might not move you to travel and see her. The tone of her letters and phone calls distresses me. She is hiding something from me, Roger, and I am afraid (please don't take this hard) it has something to do with men. Maybe more than one—I've heard several names. And there is something else. I cannot believe it myself (sweet Jesus, please, I pray it isn't true), but there is something strange about her voice, uneven in her handwriting—I suspect she's taken to drink, or worse. It seems impossible, I know, but I am very afraid. Go to her, Roger. Now.*
>
> *Love,*
> *Your mother (I like to think)*

This was alarming, yes, but Roger convinced himself not to go. There were too many things holding him home. Sharon had moved away by her own choice; if he went after her, it might make him look desperate, and he certainly wasn't. He'd recently purchased a vintage Lincoln Continental convertible, for instance, and was having the time of his life. And if there were other men . . . well, it simply wasn't any of his business. Sharon belonged to the past.

The days rolled by. Roger was promoted to bar manager and given a decent raise. He moved into a roomier place on the corner of St. Ann and Chartres. He cruised St. Charles in his Lincoln, Debbie's blonde hair whipping in the wind. He joined a krewe and was scheduled to ride in a Mardi Gras parade. Things were going great, and eventually whole weeks would pass when he scarcely thought of Sharon.

But another letter arrived, and this one was too shocking to ignore:

> *Roger,*
>
> *I have wrestled with my senses, undertaken repairs on the most elemental structures of my own mind. I don't know if you can see what that means. I met you accidentally, our involvement was predicated on circumstance alone, and in the hasty course of our affair I really feel I failed to learn very much about you. I know you have the capacity for imagination, and I will try to reach your imagination, in the same way I groped into my own.*
>
> *You couldn't find the photo albums. Neither could I. I looked and looked; I explored every possible means of their disappearance, and, failing in that effort, what*

*I finally located was myself. There are no photos of you and me. No past to fall back into, no memories to lead us ahead.*

*Roger, I want you to think back. What happened prior to my departure? I mean long before. Before the conflicts over "work" and "family." Before the time when we began to plan a future, whether here or elsewhere. Before the time when we were so happy, even (we were happy, in some bizarre way). Where did it all begin? Think.*

*No, that's too difficult. The cart before the horse. Let me ask you this instead:*

*Do you remember deciding, very deliberately, in fact, that the bamboo stand behind the westward cove was the "Bayou Pirate"? And you "went to work" there every day afterward, standing among the shoots?*

*It's no use. I can't take you back gradually.*

*We're on a desert island, Roger! There is no New Orleans, no Shreveport, no Mitchell. Not as far as we're concerned. I have crossed the island to watch you recently. You sit on a log during your "off-hours," "steering" a knotty root, "honking your horn," talking to somebody fictional (you got your Lincoln, I assume, and reconciled with Debbie. That's your business). Stop it, Sharon. Even now, you see, how difficult it is . . . never mind.*

*I intend to leave by whatever means available. Signal a ship in some way, build a raft. Return to the real world, the real Mitchell, even. I miss my mother.*

*I desperately need your assistance, but I am afraid to ask in any other way than by this letter. To be honest, Roger, you scare me. My reality seems rather tenuous; yours is so concrete. I'm afraid that you might talk me back fairly easily. I watch you sitting there on the beach, hour after hour, talking to yourself in who knows how many voices; there's quite a crowd in your head, more than enough people to win an argument with me. But think, Roger—where did you receive this letter? In a mailbox? Or in a bottle underneath the big palm tree by the edge of the lagoon?*

*Enough. I don't want to upset you. But I plan to leave soon, and I could use your help building signal fires or constructing something that will float. I am currently engaged, for instance, with the problem of how to make a sail. If you regain your senses and decide you want to join me, come right away. You know how to get here, Roger, don't you? Take the path we cleared up the hill (the one you call I-10), hang a left by the banana trees where we saw the big snake, then curve left again around the waterfall and on down the hill to the beach. You don't need a plane ticket! I would very much like you to leave with me, but I can't face you in your condition. If I leave without hearing from you, I'll send back a rescue ship. Maybe, then, I'll see you on the outside.*

*P.S. I refuse to sign my name—who else could it possibly be?*

Well, that did it. Desert island. Rafts and snakes and palm trees. It was what came of being an introverted person in a strange place by yourself. He'd have to go to her now. Still, he hesitated—let a day, a week, a few weeks pass. There was the business of explaining it to Debbie. He had to get some time off work. He had to scrape up money for a plane ticket.

But before he knew, it was spring again. The French doors were open wide on Bourbon Street, a warm breeze came from the river. The pattern of his days continued uninterrupted, and rescuing Sharon slipped further from his mind. She was far away, in another city, lost in her own life, beyond his reach. He walked the streets in his own bustling city, and yet at times something calm inside him drew his gaze to a point far away, where the world seemed to disappear in a line on the horizon, and in these moments he often thought of Sharon. Two ships passing, they had been, boats in changing tides, going in and going out—like that odd sail out there now upon the water, dot against the high blue sky, drifting out to sea.

# My Roommate Kevin Is Awesome

Totally. This is like after we moved into the dorms in the fall and kind of got to know each other pretty well and then we sort of got bored with shit like staying around the dorms all the time and going to classes, so we went to this place where this guy made us fake IDs "for amusement purposes only, not a legal form of identification," and we tried to use them at this bar downtown but the guy just laughed at us and took our IDs and we were out forty bucks. So we were walking back to the dorms and Kevin said, "College sucks, dude. This is lame. I'm totally fucking bored with this shit, there's nothing to do, nothing ever happens," and I said, "We should have pledged a fraternity," and Kevin said, "Yeah right, like they'd take us."

Then the next morning I woke up in the sleeping room where there's bunk beds and you have to like share the room with the two guys who live on the other side and they both study all the time and are carrying 4.0 GPAs and I went into our main dorm room and there was Kevin hanging upside down in the air. He was just hanging there like on one of those gravity-boot machines that were like the hip thing back in the day, only he was just hanging upside down there in the air with nothing attached to him. I said, "Kevin, how are you doing that?" and he said he didn't know and I told him his face was pretty red and he should probably turn over and he said he didn't know how. I thought that was pretty funny so I laughed for a minute but then he really did look like he was about to pop a blood vessel or something so I said, "Why don't you try bending your knees like on a swing, you know, get some locomotion happening?" So he did that, and it was just like he was on one of those flying trapeze things, he looked like he was in the circus, but finally when he got going good enough he tried to swing himself around but he only got halfway and busted his ass on the floor. So he didn't want to try it again for a while but after a while he did, and pretty soon he got better and better and started doing flips and he would hold his legs tight against his chest like a ball and spin really fast. I thought it was pretty cool, so I went and knocked on some other guys' doors around the hall and they came and watched and pretty soon started calling their friends and everything and by that afternoon we had like this humongous crowd of people in the room watching Kevin spin around in the air. There were even these frat guys who kept saying it was a trick and so I told them to try it themselves and they all did and just kept falling over on the floor and everyone laughed at them, even the girls, and one of them actually hurt himself pretty bad. It was definitely a very entertaining day, and that night Kevin even got with this little hottie Kristin who was a junior and I swear had only hooked up with maybe three other guys the whole time she'd been in college from what I heard.

Kevin went to her apartment and didn't come home until about 4:00 a.m., but then he shook me awake in my bunk really early because he wanted me to watch him do a swan dive, but when he jumped up nothing happened and he came down and cracked his knees on the tile floor. So he was yelling in pain and the two dudes we shared the room with, who were like totally gay, woke up and started complaining. I got out of there and went in our room in my underwear. Only when I got in our room there was this very grizzle-haired old black guy with sunglasses sitting on our couch and it scared the shit out of me. He didn't even act like he noticed me, though, like he was practically frozen there with his hands on his knees, and I put on some sweats and a T-shirt and by that time he was starting to look pretty familiar. I slipped back real quiet into the sleeping room where Kevin was kind of hobbling around. "Kevin," I said, "Ray Charles is in our dorm room."

"Who?" he said.

"Ray fucking *Charles*," I said.

"Who's he?" Kevin said. "Is he an RA?" And he looked kind of worried for a second.

And I told him no, Ray Charles was like this really kick-ass musician from way back in the day who might even supposed to be dead now because they made a movie about him and who my Uncle Doug was always trying to get me to listen to when I was little because he said my dad had really bad taste and would listen to like Bob Seger.

So we went out in the room and there was Ray Charles sitting on our couch. "Told you so," I said.

Ray Charles seemed to kind of hear me then, like his hands moved and he sort of turned his head in my direction, and Kevin went over to him and stuck his hand out for him to shake. Only nothing happened, and I tapped Kevin on the arm and kind of made this motion like, "Check out the sunglasses," and then I put my hands out in front of me and shut my eyes and groped around the air to say to Kevin, like, "He's blind."

So Kevin nodded and he went up next to Ray Charles and said, "Mr. Charles, I'm pleased to make your acquaintance. I'm Kevin. Can I shake your hand?" And Ray Charles seemed sort of startled but he put his hand out and they shook.

Then we asked him if we could get him anything and he said a glass of water so Kevin got him one. Then we asked him if he was feeling OK, and he said yes, but he was a little confused about where he was and what was happening, and he had things he was supposed to do today. So we went ahead and explained to him how Kevin was like flying around in the air yesterday but how he couldn't do it today so maybe it was only like a one-day thing, and Ray Charles kind of smiled and waved his head around and said OK, then, he would just hang out with us "cats" that day. So he did, and it was awesome. We had the whole big crowd over again and lots of people got his autograph and there were even some grad students who came by that actually really liked his music and asked him questions about being dead and stuff, but it got to be sort of a hassle because they wanted to bring this one professor of theirs by to "verify the phenomenon," and we had to tell them like, "No fucking professors, no way." And then they were cool. We got Ray Charles to do a piano performance in the student lounge down the hall where they have a piano and a whole huge crowd was there and people seemed to like the music and even Ray Charles seemed to have a good time. And that night we drove him to the store and he bought us beer. And me and Kevin by now were like the coolest guys in the whole university.

Next morning we woke up and Ray Charles wasn't there but in his place was this huge spread of real homemade breakfast foods, like right there on our desks. Waffles and bacon and ham and all kinds of fruit and French toast and blueberry pancakes and these drinks in tall glasses that we didn't know what they were but they definitely had alcohol in them and when we called Kristin and her friend Megan to come over Megan said it was mimosas. And the best part was as soon as you ate or drank any of the stuff it would all just reappear or there would be different good stuff in its place. By about noon we were already pretty drunk and a bunch of people had come by again and there were these really excellent sandwiches like you'd get from a catering service or something and still lots of fruit and lemon meringue pie for dessert and beer. So we had this big party. The only uncool part was when the two guys who shared our sleeping room from next door complained to the RA about the noise and how there were so many people around all hours of the day and night, but Gordon, the RA, was a pretty cool dude and he just came and told us to keep the noise down and then when he saw how this totally awesome thing was happening with all the food and the drinks he stayed around and got drunk with us and the douche bags from next door had to go to the library to study.

Around seven o'clock there was suddenly "beef Wellington" according to Gordon and these really dusty bottles of wine that Gordon said were probably worth like a thousand dollars each and they tasted OK if you guzzled them fast and then "authentic Cuban cigars." Then later when the party was getting really huge a keg of Heineken appeared and these incredibly excellent margaritas started blending themselves right there on the desk and then to top it all off, when most people were leaving because they had to go to class the next day, a huge baggie of killer weed that like totally fried your brain on one hit but you could still maintain and hold a conversation. Then we went to bed.

I was the first one up in the morning and when I went into our room to see what the day's events had in store there was nothing there, just our regular dorm room, except that all the empties were magically cleaned up and put in the recycling bin. But that was it. I was like freaked out because you could already hear a whole bunch of people out in the hall waiting for us to wake up and unlock the door and like initiate the entertainment. I went in the sleeping room and woke Kevin up and told him, but when he came out with me there was suddenly this gigantic blue and yellow butterfly like perched on the back of his chair. So I figured out then it only happened when Kevin woke up, not me. I was kind of disappointed, but then I thought, you know, how Kevin was an awesome dude and my roommate and my best friend.

The butterfly wasn't quite as exciting as the other days. I mean it just sat there kind of spreading out its wings and making these loud sucking noises like it was hungry but we didn't know what to feed it. But still, it was a huge butterfly with about a five-foot wingspan so it was pretty impressive, and tons of people came by to see it and like marvel at its amazing, vibrant colors.

That night Kevin and I were talking and I said, "Dude, this is all about you," and he said, "I don't know what I *did*, man. What did I do?" And we couldn't come up with much of an explanation except that Kevin said maybe he had like reached this utter peak of boredom, like he had become more monumentally bored than any other person in the history of the world and this had all happened as a result. Then we went to bed.

The next day was extremely cool. I heard this sound like firecrackers going off and I got out of bed and Kevin was already in the room sitting in a chair and there was like this huge battle going on with all these soldiers that were about one inch tall, and they were spread out in formations across the floor and up on the couch and everywhere. They had machine guns and tanks and hand grenades and everything. And they really died, too, like they would bleed when they got shot or exploded and scream out in agony and everything. Mostly it was guys who hung out that day, because the girls got really upset and cried when the little guys died or got wounded and moaned in pain and shit. It was an incredibly awesome battle, though, and you could actually pick the little guys up in your hand and they would totally freak out like they didn't know what was happening to them and would try to shoot your hand. It was hilarious.

This one guy Alex squished one of the soldiers between his fingers and the guy's head popped off and that was pretty gross so we didn't do it anymore. By nighttime the room was totally filled with smoke so we had to open the window, and then the battle stopped and Kevin and I went to bed and you could hear the little guys going around to pick up the dead and wounded and little people like crying and moaning and there were little torchlights you could see under the crack of the door. Like they say, war is hell.

We were worried about losing our supply of females after that day, but the next day we got all of them back because our shower turned into a Jacuzzi and Kevin's iPod became this awesome stereo and we had a big-screen plasma TV with like a million channels in HD, including porno. And that night there was an unlimited supply of beer and tequila shooters and we had the biggest party ever. The guys next door went home for the weekend because they couldn't stand to be around us anymore, so Kristin and Megan stayed the night and Kevin and I both got laid, but I don't remember it too well.

This had all started on a Sunday and so now it was Saturday, the seventh day, one full week. When I woke up the girls were still sleeping but Kevin was already out of bed. I found him in our room talking to an old dude in a dark brown suit who was sitting on our couch with one leg crossed over the other and a briefcase next to him. When I first saw him I thought it was like the president of the university, but whoever it was I knew by the look on Kevin's face that the shit had hit the fan. He looked really scared and his voice was like all queasy when he started talking to me. "Rock," he said, which is what everybody calls me since I busted my head open on one in a diving acci-

dent when I was fourteen, "this is the Avenging Angel of the
Everlasting Lord, Almighty God," and I could tell by his tone of
voice that I shouldn't crack a joke or anything.

Kevin said, "We're kind of in trouble here, Rock," and I said,
"Why? We didn't do anything wrong," and the Avenging Angel
of the Everlasting Lord, Almighty God said *au contraire.*

I knew this guy wasn't like part of the regularly scheduled
entertainment or anything but he was still a pretty interesting
guy once you got to know him. He'd already talked to Kevin but
he went ahead and told me now about how God in his infinite
wisdom had created the universe according to an established
set of principles that he, this Avenging Angel dude, I mean,
called the eternal verities, and how human beings during their
comparatively short historical span on this particular planet,
Earth, had solved a fair number of the essential mysteries God
had intended to remain undeciphered, but how they had done
this through disciplined scientific inquiry and extensive experi-
mentation, and how although God was not exactly thrilled with
this unforeseen development He admired humanity's spunk
and ingenuity and was willing to tolerate it, at least for the time
being. But what Kevin and I were doing was "out of the box."
We weren't scientists or philosophers and we hadn't devoted
our lives to scientific discovery or metaphysical speculation. We
hadn't, according to him, even studied for our History of Western Civ midterms, although that wasn't totally true, because
we did at least go over the quizzes. But then this Avenger dude
went on to say that while God had not sent him to smite us in
His righteous anger, He could certainly do so if He chose, and
in case we needed examples of the consequences of such smit-
ing we had only to review our Old Testament, and he asked us

if we had one and we said no and so he unsnapped his briefcase and took a Bible out and gave it to us (and it was a really
good one, too, black leather with like this gold tint to the pages
and a little bookmark that was soft like silk). He said we would
see that God could definitely "smack our fannies."

Then he asked us if we had any questions. I looked at Kevin
and he didn't seem like he was going to ask anything, so I went
ahead and said, well yeah, how did all of this happen anyway?
And it turned out we were right more or less, that Kevin's mon-
umental boredom had created a sort of vortex that dislodged
objects in the space-time continuum according to his (sometimes subconscious) whims, or some shit like that, blah blah,
and Kevin said, "I told you so."

And then the Avenging Angel of the Everlasting Lord,
Almighty God left. And needless to say, the party was over.

Although after a while, when Kevin and I would look at all
these stories in the Bible like the guy told us to, and especially
if we'd had a couple of bong hits, they started to seem like what
my high school English teacher wrote in the margins of this
fiction story I once had to write for class "implausible," like
you just couldn't believe this shit really happened to anyone.
So we told Gordon our RA about the whole thing and asked
him what he thought and he said how did we actually know
this was the Avenging Angel, etc., anyway? After all, according
to what we'd told him, Gordon I mean, this guy hadn't disappeared or like combusted in a holy flame or anything, he had
just walked right out the door to our room and me and Kevin
stood at the window and watched him get into a Nissan Max-
ima in the parking lot and drive away, which was true. But all

we could say was that if he'd been there like Kevin and me he would definitely know something was up with this dude.

So Kevin quit fucking with the eternal verities. Sometimes we still get pretty bored, though, but what we do now is sort of make secret plans for how we might start up the whole thing again, because it was definitely pretty cool and like got us a lot of attention. If we can get off of academic probation from when we missed a whole week of classes last semester while all of this stuff was going on and got like practically invisible GPAs as a result, we're going to try to talk our parents into letting us rent an apartment next year, and we're thinking that maybe a change of address will get God and the angel guy off our backs for a while. We talk a lot about what shit we could do next, and I think we've decided the first thing will be to like make Mariah Carey and Janet Jackson appear, because we both admitted to each other once that we had a thing for older babes.

In the meantime, things are OK. One good thing is that even though we aren't dating Kristin and Megan anymore, per se, they still think we're decent guys and come over to see us every once in a while if we ask them to, and we taught them how to play backgammon on this awesome board Kevin's parents gave him for Christmas before they found out about his grades. So that's pretty cool. And no matter what, I can always go outside and look up at the night sky and like cherish the memory of how my awesome roommate Kevin like tore a fucking hole in the fabric of the universe, right through the dark and empty space between the moon and all the stars.

# The Cyclist

Notes for an Aborted Story Called "The Cyclist" That
Turned Out to Be Too Much Like "The Swimmer"

G uy's getting older, still hanging around the old town. Has
new, younger girl protégé he's interested in (Lauren).
They're at his apartment or office, maybe he keeps an apartment, anyway he can't bring himself to actually make a pass
at her—he's older, it's inappropriate, etc.—but there is some
physical contact and he can't tell how she feels about it. They
go to a bar/restaurant and he knows a lot of the people in there
and so many of them are divorced/remarried, etc., lots of past
history. He's supposed to be meeting a friend who's moved to
another city at (where?) the library (?) and he excuses himself
to go meet him. He meets the guy (John?) and they have a couple of laughs and they're going someplace when he sees an ex-
girlfriend (Laura) maybe talking on a cell phone to her mother
outside the library (?) and there's a lot of past history here and
he tries to ignore her as he goes in until she calls after him in a
very soft appealing voice and he lingers to try to talk to her. But

he only gets little snippets of conversation w/ her—she keeps holding her hand over the mouthpiece to talk to him while still listening to her mother—and he finally has to leave to go after his friend feeling nostalgic and regretful and a little angry and bitter and maybe more than half in love again, maybe more half in love than he is w/ the new girl. Suddenly, as he begins to search for friend, he finds his wife, who's arrived there (library?) on some errand (or is the guy married?). She looks very pretty and happy and he's half in love w/ her. They look for John together, first in the library (?), then figuring that maybe he slipped into the bar across the street, or whatever. After a while he kind of gives up and the wife (?) leaves and then the guy remembers that his friend's next appointment was across town somewhere, so, still feeling very muddled and confused and *as if the past and present are overlapping* in the persons of this new girl (Lauren), his old flame (Laura), and his wife (Laurel? Lara?) and he can't seem to figure out which one he's most attracted to or which time in his life he's most fond of, but he gets in his old truck to go look for friend, all the time preoccupied w/ thoughts of these three women (who by now are beginning to look a lot like past, present, and future personified (or maybe not too much, and not in that order)), but as he's driving he gets less and less steady. Harder and harder to drive the truck, finds himself swerving around the road veering into opposite lanes, and he starts wondering if he's drunk maybe from the drinks w/ Lauren, but at any rate it's becoming obvious and he's getting afraid of the cops so he sees this old bicycle leaning against a stop sign at an intersection (delete "at an intersection") and he pulls the truck over and gets on the bike, but that's hard too and he wobbles along the road w/ cars honking, etc., until he finally sees the lights flashing and hears the sirens and he knows he's caught. Is this a third-person or a first-person story? It should *not* seem at all like the dream you had, other than the action of the story, which progressively leads it in that direction. Mood is *wistful*, then ominous and unnerving. Is this too much like "The Swimmer"?

The Cyclist

It's not too much like "The Swimmer." What's different about this guy—call him Patrick—is that he's not disillusioned and he hasn't wasted his life on a trivial round of cocktail parties and empty associations, he isn't slowly awakening to his own dissatisfactions, too late, and trying to manufacture some hopeless heroic endeavor that will take him through the vapid days of his past and end in nothing but existential aloneness.

This guy's problem is just the opposite—life's too full, too ripe with possibilities, all of which he's acutely aware of and yearning for. For instance, when they're at the window of his apartment, he and his beautiful protégé, talking about her music (Patrick is no loser, he's a former keyboard player for a rock band that had a Top 40 hit and a number of critically acclaimed albums—he quit when he saw the band was going downhill, and returned to his hometown to open a music school), and they brush against each other, her breast against the back of his arm and his arm moving involuntarily, bumping against her breast further (she smiles shyly—"Ouch! Watch it!" she says) and resting for a second on her shoulder, he knows immediately exactly what her breast would feel like if he were to release it from the red tank top and the white bra, the strap of which he's already studied with interest, and as he knows this he also knows and is reminded of what it would be like if he went home to his wife, who's older than the protégé but still an extremely fine-looking woman, and slipped into bed with her, how the familiarity of sex with her would be just as appealing in its own way as the unfamiliarity and newness of sex with the protégé, and at the same time he's looking out the window, and out there in the street is a guy trying to negotiate a delivery truck around a tight turn, he can see the guy's hands busy on the steering wheel and the gearshift, his eyes gauging the tightness of the turn and the traffic in the rearview mirror, and he wants to be the one driving the truck, wonders if he could coax the truck to make that turn, and then he knows, too, that there's a woman in someplace like Ecuador who would be just right for him, and a landscape there fit for dreaming. And more than that, even, he knows that in another life there might be time to write all this down or turn it into a song. He wants to be a thousand places doing a thousand things and he wants the time to turn back just one hour a thousand times. Or he'd like to travel back or go ahead a hundred or a thousand years. He wants to know the name of that tree and that flower. He wants to understand exactly why and how the wind blows and how one would go about designing the structure of that unusual building across the street. What's the topography of the Aleutian Islands, anyway? This question is capable of plaguing him.

So he goes about his days with his heart and head full.

At the restaurant he takes Lauren, the protégé, to, he sips his beer wisely, trying to maintain the proper pose in relation to her. He wants to slide his foot under the table and bring it into contact with the soft flesh of her smooth calf—nothing more than that, not now. He knows too many people here. In the next booth sits Happy Chubb, a friend from high school, and his third wife, Lisa, and her little daughter from her first marriage. Patrick and his wife don't have any children, but he thinks all the time that he'd like to. It's her job that keeps them from it. She's a Web designer and catalog-layout coordinator for a company that sells seed packets and fancy gardening tools, and she makes a lot more money than Patrick does. Her job is fascinating enough, but even more fascinating right now to Patrick is the job of Happy Chubb, who works for the Forest Service, and right in the middle of something Lauren is saying he thinks of Happy Chubb out in the woods planting trees, shaking the excess dirt off the little seedlings, probably, digging out a little hole in the dark earth with some implement, maybe something as simple as a spade, and putting the roots of the seedling into the hole carefully but quickly, the movement so practiced most likely that he thinks of something else—maybe of Patrick (who knows?) and the wild days of their youth, and how that very Patrick went on to write songs that he, Happy, now listens to on his stereo, even though the songs are getting old and he's maybe a little tired of them, and all of this is in proximity to a cool stream winding through the forest. What a job, what a life.

"Do you like going out in the woods?" he asks Lauren, and she looks a little perturbed—he obviously hasn't been listening.

"Too many bugs," she says, and he nods.

What if he could take her back to the apartment right now, he thinks (it's a *studio*, though, not an apartment, even though it has a little bed in it for the nights when he stays there late, it's a studio where he gives lessons on the piano and the guitar and even occasionally the drums, and records little pieces of music all by himself, and where he has three or four thousand albums and CDs, he's into vinyl but you can't get everything on vinyl these days, and he wants it all, everything decent and semi-inspired and semi-honest whether pop or jazz or country or classical or what have you, he loves it all and sometimes finds himself staring out the window with tears in his eyes as he listens, it happened just the other day with "Dear Prudence" of all things, that simple, wonderful little closing chord progression, wondering what made the man think of that, at what moment in his life, maybe staring out a window in the same way he, Patrick, was doing now, and how would it be to have been that man, with the world just lying down for you and still that music running through your head? He'd written good songs himself, very good songs, he knows, and yet you could never be John Lennon, you couldn't reproduce that time, that heady atmosphere, that had made the Beatles what they were, and he was more than a little sorry he had missed it, had been too young by far, and even if he had written some songs that were just as good as the songs John Lennon wrote, no one would ever say so, because he hadn't been in the right time and place), what if he could take her to the studio right now and lie down with her on the little bed, the portable fan blowing over them (how did the fan work, exactly, you turned it on and the blades whirred around, but why did it blow the air in only one direction, because of the shape of the blades, of course, and how had someone figured that out, and when, and who?), and he could take off those white shorts she wore and run his hands over her body and examine her, to what extent she shaved or didn't, for instance, and what a pleasure it would be to hear her gasp or sigh or cry out, wouldn't it? And yet at the same time how good it was not to have fucked around during his marriage, he had a long track record of not doing anything a man might be expected to do and he found that interesting, and one indiscretion would mean he had to start all over again as far as the being faithful department went.

"You're a beautiful girl," he tells Lauren, "and very talented. I'll see you next week." And off he goes, remembering his appointment with John.

John is a musician also, a former bandmate who lives in New York now and writes for a variety of popular Web sites. He could imagine having John's job, too. They meet outside another restaurant (not the library at all), and an improbable sequence of events is set in motion. First, parked in the parking lot, wondering why it is that his air conditioner won't work when the motor isn't running and whether he could fix it, given the proper tools and reference materials, he thinks about how he and Lauren could have sex and then go on from there, how he could divorce his wife and manage Lauren's budding career, how he could write songs for her and produce them, be the man behind the scenes, and they could move to New York (long before she gave up her career to have children, this would be) and live in SoHo or the East Village or what the hell Central Park West, or maybe L.A. would be better, the dry hills and the canyons and the beaches and the limousines, or even Nashville. He meets John but barely pays attention to him, thinking more about how John lives in New York and how they could meet up from time to time there.

But as they get ready to enter the restaurant there's Laura, the ex-girlfriend. It's as if he's back in a different life, looking at Laura, her hand with a little silver ring on the index finger holding the cell phone, the rather dark hair on her forearm (this had always bothered him), the high, childlike sound of her voice (which had always bothered him, too), a car's red brake lights to his left, backing into a parking space with a squeak of the wheels, and in a little downtown park just past the restaurant's entrance a crow strutting under the long branches of an oak tree, the crow cawing once, twice, and then making tiny muttering sounds, like a disgruntled old man (he's never heard that noise from a crow before—do they do it all the time? He's always been interested in birds); all of these competing sensations and observations he experiences as if from a former point in his life, like a man who stands across the street from a house he used to live in and sees a hand suddenly switch on a lamp in a window and imagines that it's his own hand and that he's there in that room he knows so well, though he'll never be inside it again (this analogy occurs to him, and at the same time it occurs to him that, if he were actually seeing a hand switch on a lamp in a house he used to live in, he might imagine that it was like seeing an old girlfriend whom one would never live with again).

He can see John inside the restaurant, already talking to the hostess, motioning out the window to him on the sidewalk, telling the hostess, "There are two of us."

But he feels like a wheel spinning fast, how at a certain point it appears to be going backward. There's Laura, and all the feelings he used to have for her and had just ten minutes ago for Lauren have spun up inside him from a place he'd absolutely forgotten, didn't know he had in him anymore (how did the mind store those feelings, how could they exist there in a place you weren't aware of? An old book falls off a shelf, falls open to a certain page where the spine is weak, it's a page you've read many times before), and it didn't seem possible that he wouldn't go to her now, put his arms around her shoulders, whisper endearments, didn't seem possible that he wouldn't arrive an hour from now at the little apartment they'd shared on First Street, home from his shift at the convenience store, and that she wouldn't be in bed napping, and that he wouldn't lie down there with her under the cool sheets in the afternoon light, and that they wouldn't turn to each other in that familiar way that always led to sex and long conversations afterward, glancing out the window at the maple tree. She had been with him back before it all started, when the band promised not to amount to anything, and it seems to him now that that was a perfect time, a time before anything was certain in life and it could all be enjoyed with a sense of anticipation.

His feet move scut-scut-scut, scraping over the sidewalk, and she sees him now, he's passed in front of her rather than behind her, it was his choice, he could easily have gone around behind, and she smiles at him exactly in that way she used to smile at him when they met unexpectedly in public and he would be thinking of something else, maybe of another girl he'd dated way back in high school, or thinking of another of the thousand things he'd never done but was always on the verge of telling himself to go do, thinking of gears and wheels and pulleys and how things kept on turning inside things, and how the earth kept spinning around and how he couldn't even see it, couldn't find one place to look at on the seemingly fixed earth where that constant motion was evident, and he tries to figure it out again now as his feet go scut-scut slowly, is he walking against the grain of the earth's rotation or with it, but there isn't time, not time to think it through, she's smiling at him and she's held up her finger to him to say, "Just one minute, I have something I want to talk to you about," and his heart is thrilled, she's as pretty and as nice as he's ever seen her, as if the ugly sessions of crying and breaking things had never occurred.

He stands waiting on the sidewalk. He listens to her talk to her mother (it's her mother, no doubt about it, the same voice she used to use when talking to her mother, not the one she used in talking to him or the one she used with her friends or the one she used with people from her office, and he wants, he thinks, to study voices, not singing voices (those he knows), but all the voices people use to express different meanings and feelings and the nature of relationships). She holds her hand over the phone—"How are *you*?" she says softly, her eyes lively, a coy smile forming the perfect center to her heart-shaped face.

"I seem to be in the middle of a lot of things," he says, but she has the finger held up again, isn't listening to him. "Uh-huh, uh-huh," she says, "you have to *quit* that, Mother, just *quit* it," and where she's sitting on the bench, her leg shows a little sign of agitation, swaying back and forth steadily, quickly, exactly the way he remembers seeing it now a hundred or a thousand times. She puts her hand over the phone again, "Just one second," she says, but there's friction in his feet, he can't hold onto this place on the ground any longer, and the scut-scut of his feet begins to pull him away, and she pouts at him (pouts!) for just one second, and then there's the intimate smile and her hand waves, just the fingers flapping, like a tiny bird's wings ("bye-bye!"), as if they'll be seeing each other back at the apartment this afternoon after all these years and this chance meeting hasn't meant anything.

His heart is sore as he walks through the restaurant, but he's revived again by the sight of (lo and behold) his wife, Lara, who's finishing up lunch, wiping her mouth with a white napkin, staring at a page in a catalog. It's as if he's spun out of a dark passageway into the full light of a sunny afternoon, and for a moment he feels that there can be nothing better than this life he lives right now.

But the feeling goes away. He sits down next to her (not across from her, because he feels he wants to be close to her at this moment, close to the life he shares with her and close to the hope that they'll have children soon to share it with), but she greets him indifferently, almost as if he's been there all the time—his appearance here is nothing special. Still, her eyes are pretty flitting across the pages of the catalog (it's work-related, of course), and her voice is mellow and easy and the swell of her thigh right as it goes up under her skirt is something to see. You could spend a life, *one* life, with this woman, he thinks.

He's forgotten all about John, isn't thinking wistfully at the moment of the music they played together onstage and in studios and hotel rooms and apartments or the time they rented a beach house in the Outer Banks and spent a week getting stoned and looking at the arc of stars in the autumn sky, and when his wife settles up the bill and asks about his meeting, he's startled to realize that John has disappeared. John is nowhere.

Maybe they missed each other somehow; he'll check at the bar across the street, and his wife will walk him out and say good-bye until that evening, when he'll be waiting for her in the living room, ensconced in front of the computer, reading up on automotive repair or the Aleutian Islands or the customary behavior of birds. On the way out, there's a guy nearly asleep on a bar stool, and at that sight he does grow wistful, remembering how, back in the old days, that was always one choice for how to spend an afternoon.

Laura is gone, not out there on the sidewalk any longer, and though he was afraid she'd be around still and there would be an awkward, sheepish moment with his wife, he's now sorry she's gone, and he's sorry, too, he realizes, that, this meeting with John having gone awry, he didn't spend the remainder of the afternoon with Lauren.

Now his wife gives him a peck on the cheek and says a few words and turns to go, and at the sight of her calf tightening midstep a thought turns in his head, and like tumblers aligning to open a lock there are these three women, one walking away down the street, one perched on a bench with a phone to her ear, one standing at the window of a studio, and each of these women is in the presence of *him*, a multiplicity of self, and each of these selves capable of its own multiplicity, capable of imagining itself on and on ad infinitum, and yet all of these selves contained, *confined*, within the one self, him, Patrick, who can only be one place, one time, one thought, one phrase spoken to one companion, always merely exactly who he *is*.

And in this strange moment when he is reminded of mitosis and mirrors and the rippling of water upon the entrance of a stone, there comes to his mind a song, his own song, he

knows, a melody laying claim to him, and yet unlike any of the
other songs he has ever had approach him in this way, something new, in a new vein, and his feet want to scut-scut to the
studio, try to make something of this music he hears, the long
slide of a guitar down a scale, eerie and almost baleful, and
a piano that feels like dead petals falling in a place as wide
and empty as he has always imagined heaven to be, or how he
remembers Wyoming. But he has to find John, seemingly.

He checks the bar across the street, the lot where the truck is
parked. There is no John anywhere, and though the song continues to occupy some space somewhere in Patrick's head (it's
been driven to a darkened corner by the jukebox in the bar),
he feels obligated to find this friend of his, this old and still
occasionally valued friend, with whom he was once a rock star
(although even as a rock star Patrick remained slightly circum-
spect, only dipping one foot into the pool, so to speak, always
poised partly poolside, thinking of opting for law school, often
visiting sites of local interest in the cities they toured instead
of doing drugs and hanging out with groupies at the hotel, as
if he were never convinced that there wasn't supposed to be
something more *to* the whole thing, some other aspect of the
experience that he stood in danger of missing), and so he hops
in the truck and begins to drive across town to a destination
that he dimly remembers in connection with John's plans.

The afternoon has come and gone, twilight has passed in a
heartbeat. At this point the story becomes strange. We know
what happens, how this man, Patrick, who is by now clearly
differentiated from the central character of the John Cheever
story "The Swimmer," the recent reference to pools notwith-
standing, becomes confused, perhaps begins to hallucinate,

wonders if he has by some unusual process become drunk during the course of the afternoon, and we can even imagine how he might see the ground, the pavement, the numerous trees and stop signs whirling past him in such a way that they remind him of the curvature of the earth, that he might begin to believe he is not getting anywhere at all, and that as he pushes the accelerator further and further toward the floorboard, he is in fact only diminishing his chances, merely speeding up the trees and the stop signs while in no way effecting the forward motion that will take him beyond the earth's opposition. The laws of centrifugal and centripetal force, friction and gravity and tides, he can't understand it all, and yet (my God!) out the windshield an explosion of stars.

He can't drive any longer, and there's the bike, then, propped against a stop sign, unnoticed by all of humanity but him. He'll hop on it, we know. He'll pedal in the dark (it's an old-fashioned bike with no gears and no reflectors) and he'll try to stay clear of all the cars, the drivers of which don't seem to have the same problems with physical laws that he has, and believe it or not all three of the women will be forgotten now, he will have only that sad song in his head, and, though the bike presents locomotion problems of its own, which he attributes to his rustiness and his bewildered state, it is much more peaceful than the truck and the fight against stasis and/or retrograde, and the sad song has time to take shape again, and as he listens it occurs to him that this is the very song of multiplicity and inversion, that to play it properly would take a hundred hands on strings and keys playing backward, like a thousand records spun all at once by hand in opposition to the spinning turntable.

He hears the sirens, he knows they're coming for him, and he stops, hops off the bike and begins to walk (I picture him now dragging the bike through some field, away from the road, down through a ditch, across railroad tracks, into some field where the night sky is whole and uninterrupted and the long dead grass of late summer whispers against his heels, and he stops, stands completely still, holding the handlebars to keep himself from spinning, because looking down at the ground he is dizzy, the spot underneath his feet turns and turns, around *him*, the hub of the ground's rotation, and he clamps down with his feet in the blind night here and now, another beginning, another movement, another song.)

# The Culvert

It was late in the winter, the time of year in that northern place when the snow lay in a hard, dirty crust pocked here and there by frozen footprints. We lived in a mining town, and the smokestacks belched soot high into the sky, and the soot filtered down to the snow, so that the snow was almost black when it had been on the ground for long. Then came a chinook wind, and with it a hard rain. The mercury in the thermometers, stuck below freezing for a month's time, rose steadily, and with it the waters of Pine Creek rose.

That area is desolate. The surrounding hills caught fire half a century ago, and with the steady outpour from the smokestacks almost nothing grew there afterward. Twisted scrub pine and tangled thornbushes and here and there by Pine Creek a stand of poplars or cottonwoods. The soil is hard and dry and rust-colored. On the day when the chinook came and then the rain, Pine Creek was swollen with brownish water cold as ice.

The creek rose and rose, and the men of our town were called to help sandbag against a flood. For a long cloud-swollen night I stood in a line passing the heavy, rain-soaked bags hand to hand. I am not a miner, not used to hard work, and soon my mind and back and arms were numb and I passed the bags to the next man no more than a foot off the ground. I had not thought to wear gloves, and the burlap rubbed my hands raw, and I could not tell whether the moisture on my hands was blood or rain. There was a kind of desperate goodwill along the line, those who were fit for the work exhorting those who weren't: *You can do it. That's right. Just keep' em coming.*

But the water rose faster than our mountain of sandbags, and soon it came over the top in rivulets and then in an icy stream. We were told, by someone who assumed authority, to go home and take care of our families.

Our house was one of the most vulnerable, just across a narrow street fifty yards from the creek, but there was a slope that began at our front yard, and I hoped it would protect us. As it turned out, there was little time before the water came. I found Natalie asleep with our six-year-old son, Alex, in the upstairs bedroom. If the water rose that high we could climb from the sundeck onto the roof. Our power had been out for hours already, and I rushed in the dark down the split-level stairway to my ten-year-old son's room. I expected to find Michael awake, scared and excited by the storm, but he made no sound when I came through the doorway. His small basement window cast almost no light, and I had trouble making out the shape of his bed across the room. I stumbled over toys and game pieces and reached my hand out for his shoulder only to find the rumpled covers thrown back, the empty pillow. I called his name, then proceeded to search the basement—the closets, the furnace room, behind the chairs near the fireplace. I searched the garage—under the shelving, behind the lawnmower, in the car. Upstairs again, I asked Natalie, but she had thought he was in bed sleeping. We lit candles. Frantically, we carried them with us from room to room, but found no sign. I returned from yet another look in the basement to find Natalie hunched over on the living room floor, her arms stretched out before her in an almost penitent attitude, making no sound, staring into the carpet.

I woke Alex and brought him out to her, made sure that she acknowledged he was there, that her eyes were alive again and focused on him, that she knew he was her responsibility, that there was a task at hand. Then I lurched back down the staircase and out the front door into the yard. There was no more snow, all two feet of it melted magically. I ran to the backyard, thinking Michael might have retreated there, but there was no response to my call. So I headed back toward the creek, shouting my son's name as I went. I stepped carefully down the slope until I was in the water. It bit at my ankles, swelling steadily and moving fast, even though I was only partway down the slope. The rain swept down, hissing as it met the rising stream, and the stream itself spoke in a steady sigh, and the wind blew my words away. I got as close as I could to the creek, or where the creek had been contained before. The sandbags were immersed already, invisible beneath the water, the water waist deep where I stood now, just across what had been our street. Despite myself I began to grow afraid, more afraid for my own life than I was for Michael, more afraid of the stream pulling greedily at me than I was of this absence that I couldn't, even then, get my mind around. Surely Michael must be in the basement. Surely Michael was somewhere in the house. The water pushed at me steadily and my legs shook from cold and weakness. I began to retreat, struggling for my balance, shoved along downstream; and as I fought my way back toward the strip of dry ground that lay before my house I found that I was talking in my head about Michael, as if I were explaining to some stranger what a fine boy my son had been, but at the same time believing that nothing had really happened, that when I walked back in our door I would see him standing there with Natalie and Alex, that everything would be explained, that even while the house flooded we would laugh hysterically with relief.

But Michael wasn't home. I spent an hour scurrying around the neighborhoods behind our house, knocking on every familiar door. Natalie had recovered hope, was sure that Michael had gotten scared and run to some friend's house in the opposite direction of the creek. But no one had seen him. The neighbors came to look with me until the water rose to their own front doors. Again I struggled home, this time arriving in the backyard. Before I reached the steps to the sundeck, I looked up to see Natalie behind the sliding glass doors, and the look on her face almost sent me back out into the water again. But now we were all in danger, the water flowing fast around our house, our house like a ship plowing through waves.

I spent the rest of that night on our roof, shouting my son's name into the rain until I could no longer shout or even speak, while below me my wife and youngest child huddled tight and cried together, and below them the water poured in torrents through broken windows, flooding high above Michael's empty bed.

By daybreak the rain had stopped and the water had become a slowly ebbing tide. I renewed my search. I was found eventually, standing nearly frozen in the stream, by two policemen in a rowboat. They took me home and forced me into bed, and there were missing person reports and widespread alerts and, in the days that followed, stories on the local and regional news. And still Michael did not come home.

When the basement was pumped clear, we were afraid that we would find his body there after all. But it was empty save for the muck brought in by the flood. I went into my son's room and tried to straighten things. Picking through the mud, I found the toys and game pieces and put them back in their soggy boxes and stored them in the closet. I placed the bookshelves back upright against the wall, filled the shelves with the ruined books. I made the room as ready as I could for his homecoming.

Because we went on as if he were alive. For long hours during the night Natalie and I would number the ways we should blame ourselves. I should have known to evacuate the house instead of going to help sandbag. And yet there had never been a flash flood before—who would have believed it? Natalie shouldn't have fallen asleep, shouldn't have left Michael in his downstairs room. And yet the danger had seemed so remote, and Michael had been so proud that he wasn't afraid. We should have known somehow that he would try to leave the house. And yet who could have imagined him doing such a thing? We should never have moved to that awful town to begin with.

Always these discussions would end with an elaborately constructed scenario that left Michael alive, and if not well, at least capable of being rescued. He had wandered from the house and been kidnapped. The kidnapper was neither a murderer nor a child molester. The kidnapper was a gentle but misguided soul who wanted desperately to have a child of his or her own, and was treating Michael kindly. Soon the kidnapper's better nature would assert itself, and the police would be informed by means of an anonymous phone call that Michael Dwyer, the child who had been on the news, had been dropped off in front of a service station or a grocery store. We would work ourselves carefully into a state of half belief, which meant, really, I feel certain now, that each of us would arrive at the conviction that the *other* believed, and that if the other believed, there might be some real chance, even though we didn't believe ourselves.

And that was enough to get us started in the morning. It was enough to make us talk to Alex about the time when his brother would come home. It was enough to keep us from going crazy when we talked to the police or the reporters or the volunteer workers who came to repair our basement for free. It was enough to keep Natalie going around the house, taking Alex to school and cooking dinner and cleaning. It was enough to keep me going to my job at the real estate office, in a building absurdly shaped like the dome of a miner's helmet, where I never, not once, told my bosses and my coworkers that I hated them for allowing me to work there, where I never told my clients that their concerns about cracks that ran along the ceiling or lack of counter space in the kitchen or laundry rooms that were in uninsulated additions were ugly and narrow and selfish.

But really our lives were intolerably empty. Alex continued to play around the house, although rather listlessly now, without all the noise and the fighting that we'd always found so aggravating before, and without any of the laughter. At times I tried to play with him, but he told me that I didn't *really* know how to play, that the games weren't real games like they had been when Michael was there, and in the end he preferred to play alone. I would stand at the door to his room watching while he engaged, wordlessly, in a pale imitation of those games, wildly imaginative, he had let Michael conduct. I knew their substance, vaguely—there were plastic soldiers and knights and monsters, and cities made of stacked books, and mountains made out of blankets and pillows. But I had never paid enough attention, never really listened to the games, and now the games were gone.

Natalie and I wandered through the house absorbed in our own thoughts, never sharing them until that desperate time when we retreated to our bedroom at night, after we made sure that Alex was fast asleep between us. Worst for me were recollections of my thoughts during the flood. Your son is not there, at a time when you desperately need him to be there. But this has happened before, you say to yourself. There have been other times when he wasn't there, and at these times you have felt yourself at the edge of panic, and you have calmed yourself with the reminder that in each of these cases things have turned out all right. That time when you arrived home to find that he wasn't in the car seat, and you felt sick momentarily— it turned out, upon a second's reflection, that you hadn't taken him in the car to begin with. There he was in the window of the house, waving at you, and you were almost overcome with tears. And so you shouldn't panic now, not *now*, because this is just another one of those occasions. All will be well in a minute. You should not run immediately from the house into the storm flailing your arms like a madman, screeching at the top of your lungs. You should take a deep breath, stop to consider.

You should search for a logical explanation. When you find the water rising around you, consider it foolish to dive into the stream, foolish to risk sacrificing your own life, because after all when you return home he will be there waiting for you. And yet I *should* have run like a madman from the house at the very first; maybe Michael wasn't too far away then to hear me. I should have dived into the stream, no matter how hopeless. Better that—better my own death—than the guilt over not having done anything.

When spring came, I made a habit of walking at night by the creek. I left the house armed with a flashlight, and I was drawn always to a church at the end of our street. Behind the church was a wooden bridge that spanned the water in an arc, and behind the bridge an old rundown shed. I walked the banks there stubbornly, over and over, each night shining the flashlight in the same places and never finding anything. At all times I cast a suspicious eye on the shed, at a leaning woodpile covered with moss that ran alongside it. Soon I began to examine the woodpile in earnest, shining the light behind it, between the cracks in the stacked wood, lifting the rotten pieces. One night, finally, I kicked in the door of the shed, but found in it only a wheelbarrow, bags of cement, old boxes, empty coffee cans. I gave up walking.

More and more, I blamed my wife for what had happened. Why had she left him in his room downstairs? How could she have fallen asleep? I distanced myself from her, and the house grew silent. Even Alex had almost stopped speaking. The three of us sat on the couch one evening, trying to empty ourselves into the noise of the TV. During a commercial, I went quietly downstairs into my son's room. The ruined carpet had been

stripped and replaced, and I stood barefoot on this new carpet that no one ever walked across, staring at my son's bookshelves. So many books—so many for a ten-year-old to have
found an interest in. I folded my arms tight across my chest
and closed my eyes and tried hard to remember what Michael
had looked like stretched out on the bed, his eyes ticking over
the words, his hand held lightly at the corner of a page, his lips
moving slightly. What were his favorites? *The Hobbit*. A book
called *Men of Iron*, about knights and castles, a book I'd loved
myself as a child. I'd given it to him for Christmas one year.
I scanned the shelves but couldn't find it. Maybe it had been
washed up under the bed or into the closet, and my wife had
found it later and thrown it away. But *The Hobbit* was gone
as well. Some others—*Tom Sawyer*, at least one of the *Harry
Potter* books, *The Giver*, maybe more titles I couldn't name off-
hand. Could he have taken these books with him that night?
I tried to picture him with an armload of books, opening our
front door and walking out into the storm. Couldn't someone
have seen him? Wouldn't he have aroused someone's suspicion? What could he have been thinking? And as I left his
room, I stopped suddenly and put my hand to the door frame.
The week before, I had looked for a ream of paper I'd brought
home from the office. I knew where I'd stored it—in my bottom desk drawer—but it wasn't there. I had looked all over,
and finally decided that the memory I had of bringing it home
with me wasn't real.

That night, I faded in and out of sleep, and at one time I felt
Michael so close to me, right there beside the bed, that I held
my hand out to reach him. I almost felt him breathing in my
sleep—as if it were his sleep, or as if I were him.

As the weeks passed, it became clear that Michael would never return, that he was dead, but I harbored my doubts, my secrets. By summer Natalie and Alex seemed to have moved on to some degree. I would come home from work to find them laughing in the kitchen, and at the sight of me they would stop, as if I were freezing them in their guilt. I was a mere ghost there, just a reminder of the family we used to be, but I would not give up Michael to join them. Every small object that could not be found around the house served as proof of Michael's presence there. When I wanted the last apple from the refrigerator and found it gone, it was because Michael had taken it. The open spaces on his bookshelf seemed to grow wider, and I noticed more missing titles. Maybe Natalie had her own secrets, maybe she pirated the books and stuffed them in drawers in the bedroom, to feel she had something of Michael's close by. But I preferred to think that wasn't the case. Often I was awakened by noises at night, shuffling sounds like footsteps, the creak of doors that seemed more ajar than I'd left them, and a noise that I could call nothing more definite than the weight and volume of a body in a room. *It's the cat*, Natalie would tell me. But I sat wide-eyed in the dark, my heart hammering into my throat.

I was constantly on the verge of some discovery. My senses became more acute. I could feel the slightest movements of the air, could feel a breeze so soft it did not lift the curtains at our open window. I could hear the wind in the treetops, the noises in our neighbors' yards and bedrooms, the groans of our roof beams. I lay awake for long hours in the dark, watching the shifting shadows of tree limbs on our bedroom wall, unaware of Natalie curled up next to me. And then one night as I lay there that way, almost lost in a dream with my eyes wide open—a dream of Michael in his room, surrounded by hundreds of toy soldiers formed in battle lines—I distinctly heard the click of our front door closing. Entranced by the shadows, by the intensity of my waking dream, I continued to lie there, hearing that click but not understanding it yet. Then, as suddenly as the dream was broken, I was up and dressed in jeans and a T-shirt, forgetting the flashlight, moving quietly down the stairs and out of our house.

The wind blew warm as I stood in our yard, the grass cool and comforting to my bare feet. It was a magical wide night with a million stars. But there was no sign of Michael, unless the twitching in my fingers at the feel of the wind, the smell of earth and grass and creek water assailing my nostrils could be taken as signs. I was tugged from my spot, as always, in the direction of the church and the little bridge and the shed on the other side. But I moved past the brick church and felt the thump of my feet on the splintery wooden bridge, and I paid scarcely any attention to the shed and the dim shape of the woodpile. These were not it, I felt certain. What drew my attention was the open field that went on past them, the field I moved across like a shadow.

At the opposite edge of the field was a winding road, I knew, and I could see it in my head very clearly before I reached it in the dark. I stood there before this road, which contained absolutely nothing, no vehicles of any sort, no other men out wandering under the stars. I looked up and down the road, peering into blackness, and I could find nothing, and I turned to look back through the distance in the direction of my house, and there was nothing. And yet I felt myself nearly vibrate with Michael's presence, and I would not leave that spot. Soon I became aware of the tiniest noise of water, almost a trickling beneath my skin. There was nothing else but a low hum, either the air sifting other noises far distant or the sound of my own blood. Maybe the trickling was inside me as well, but it was persistent, and I did not move, I took great care to silence everything inside of me. I don't know whether I slept there on my feet, if I entered the world of dreams, but it was as if my head contained another picture of the night and all the stars and the weeds and the road before me, and in this picture was a tiny stream bending away to the west, and I saw that it issued from a rusty culvert in the road bank, and when I had lost this picture, when I had awakened, the night's edges were softened with purple light, and there were the culvert and the little stream right in front of me.

I could barely squeeze my way in, so small was the opening. On the night when Michael disappeared, it occurred to me, the culvert must surely have been filled with water. And yet I knew that he'd gone in. I struggled for a long time, moving myself forward with my hands and my elbows and my knees, my shirt front and pants sopping wet. The darkness sealed me in; there appeared to be no opening to the culvert other than the one through which I came.

Then I reached a point at which there was nothing but open space before me. A hole, nothing else. Balancing myself at its edge, I reached as far as I could with my hand, but I touched only air. My choice, it seemed, was to turn back or drop down. I had no room to maneuver there in the culvert, I would simply have to fall headfirst into whatever lay below. And, once down the hole, there might be no way to return. Strangely, the thin stream of water still trickled over my hands, as if the water were being pumped up from below, as if it climbed on its own from some point deep in the earth.

Again, lying there on my belly in the absolute dark, no sound but the running water and my breathing, I felt a current pass through me, like a memory or a dream taking physical form, a sense that Michael was right there with me. I shouted his name into the hole, and my voice disappeared. There was no echo and no answer. I was reminded of standing waist deep in the flood, calling my son's name, not daring to go under. Slowly I pulled myself ahead with my hands until I fell.

My falling was outside time and space. There was no duration, no displacement. I was myself, and that was all I knew. Then I was on my feet, immersed in light, a brightness so entire that only gradually did I become aware of standing in a sort of hallway. The difference between the light and the space I occupied could only be described as an iciness—a sheen and a texture and a coldness to the surfaces. I could make out, dimly, white walls, a white ceiling that I could touch when I raised my arm, even a white floor. And across this white floor ran a thin, curling stream of clear water. I walked on.

And after some time that I could not call short or long, the hallway opened into a blinding white room, and I found my son's body resting there. He lay on the floor, twisted up awkwardly in a corner. His clothes were ragged and muddy, his face was turned away from me. His white shoes were ruined, the sole torn loose from one and a gash in the leather of the other, and above one shoe his pants leg rode up to reveal that he wore no socks, and his bony ankle and thin calf were white as pearl. It was that sight somehow—the shoes, the ankle, the thin unmuscled calf—that made me cry, and when I reached him it was to that thin leg that my hand went. I couldn't tell whether the coldness I felt was in his skin or in my fingers.

But his eyes opened wide at my voice and my touch, and he was awake then, sitting up, smiling at me—the Michael I'd always known, the Michael who had never left me. "Hey, Dad," he said, and then I took him in my arms, and it felt as if we were melting, as if we couldn't hold each other solidly enough.

I had not seen the room. It simply appeared there to my sight. In the corner where Michael sat were the books—dozens of books from home, more than he ever could have carried away on the night of the flood. Next to the books were colored markers, tape, and two stacks of paper, one blank, one covered with his neat handwriting.

The rest of the room was covered with colorful paper. On the floor were crudely drawn—but beautiful, dazzling—roads and forests and castles and cities and oceans, and tiny stick figures populating these landscapes, wandering here and there, gathered in clusters that may have been battles or celebrations. The walls were covered, too. Along one ran an elaborate, life-sized sketch of Michael's own bed at home—he had even attempted to reproduce the pillow and blankets. He had reconstructed his room entirely, even down to the small window through which the water had poured that night. But here the window contained stars, a half-moon, the silver light of clouds, the dark shape of the gangly pine tree whose shadow I watched at nighttime. And there was the shadow, too, drawn in black above the bed. There were the bookshelves, the desk, the closet doors, the posters on the walls drawn to the best of my son's abilities.

And in the middle of all of this, there at the center of the floor, ran a quiet stream, flowing past the mountains and the forests and the meadows and all the people. As I stood looking, Michael bent down to the stream, and when he put his finger to its source a jet of water spurted upward, and the water gathered strength, overflowing its banks and flowing faster out into the white hallway.

"This is where I live, Dad," Michael said.

I was crying, softly, without wanting him to see or hear, and I reached out and held my son's hand the best I could—it was really just a feeling in my cold fingers—and I did not say, *You live at home with us, Michael,* or *Michael, you come with me.* "I like it very much," I said. "Show me."

And he did. He explained every feature of the vast terrain, the world he'd created, or re-created. "What are these?" I asked him, pointing to the papers.

"Adventures," he said. "I don't need toys anymore."

We smiled at each other, and his smile looked the same as it always had. "May I?" I asked with feigned politeness, as if I were asking to see a particularly good test score from school.

"Sure."

I skimmed through the stack. The adventures involved a family named Mom and Dad and Alex, and the hero was a boy named Michael. The family sailed on pirate ships and traveled to other planets and fought demons and explored musty castles. Accompanying them on their journeys was a ten-year-old girl named Gabrielle who was "fond of Michael but not Alex" and "as pretty as something from a dream." The adventures were thorough and meticulously detailed, and I felt that I lived in them, too, that the world of my son's imagination was more real than the house and the wife and the other son, the ones whom I'd left behind.

And yet I did try once, even knowing that it was hopeless, for him and for me. "Let's go home now, Michael," I said. "You can take all of these things with you."

"I don't want to go home," he said. He looked at the floor, watching it as if the stick figures were actually moving.

"Weren't you happy there, Michael?" I asked, my voice breaking when I tried to say his name.

"I was happy," he said. "But I was sad sometimes too."

I looked into his face—so pale—and his eyes that shined like a far-off fire. "Don't you miss us?" I asked him.

"I'm with you sometimes," he said. "I come there. I watch you while you're sleeping."

I held him close again, and if I could have held him tightly enough, gotten him firmly in my arms, I might have tried to take him with me. But there was something in him that couldn't be held or moved, and something in me that couldn't do the moving or the holding.

"I'm sleepy," he said, and he lay down in the corner again, in the position in which I'd found him. "Stay here with me," he said. And then he was fast asleep.

And in a rush as I stretched out beside him I let go of all that was not in that room. I grew very tired and peaceful, and the last thought I knew before I slept was that it was better here in this world with Michael, and that no one alive out there in that other world could blame me.

## ACKNOWLEDGMENTS

First, as always, thank you to Angela, London, and Nathan. Thank you to all the folks who have made an effort to spread the word about my work during the past year or two—I greatly appreciate your help. Special thanks along those lines to Steve Almond, who has gone the extra mile for me a million times over the years, and to Donald Ray Pollock, who, even though he didn't know me from Adam, talked about *The Dart League King* to anyone who would listen. Thanks to every single one of the folks at Tin House—I can't imagine any other publisher with whom the whole experience would be so enjoyable, friendly, and relaxed. Big, huge thanks to my agent, Renee Zuckerbrot. Thanks to Jodee Stanley (*9th Letter*), Brigid Hughes (*A Public Space*), Stephen Donadio (*New England Review*), Nicola Mason (*Cincinnati Review*), and all the other editors who had a hand in editing and publishing stories in this collection. Thanks, for various reasons, some of which have to do with my fiction and some not so much, to Mom and Dad, all my wonderful colleagues in the Clemson University English Department, Bernice Lewis, Conor Linehan, the Corontzes family, and Nick's Tavern. Thanks to all my old friends. Thanks to all my new friends. Thanks to all my students, current and former, many of whom are now friends. Thanks to Sandpoint, Idaho. Thanks to my mother-in-law (Daisy, you're the best!). Thanks to all the folks I usually thank but haven't thanked this time—my hope is that it goes without saying. Special shout-out to my nephew Will "I Promise You the Cubs Are Going All the Way This Year" Carter—see, Will? I told you I'd get you in here. And thanks, above all, in this day and age, to readers of fiction everywhere.